Janelle stepped forward, fists clenched at her sides. "Did you bring it?" Her voice was low and edged like a blade.

"That was the job," Killian replied as she opened the trunk. The other women moved closer, clustering around their leader. It was a warm night with a bit of a breeze, and Killian could smell the mingling of their perfumes, shampoos, and sweat.

There, curled up and bound on a sheet of plastic, was a man. Light shone on his bald head, highlighting the sweat on his cheeks and brow. He was gagged, but that didn't stop him from making noise when his eyes adjusted to the light. He reared up at them, muffled curses punctuating the night.

Two of the women stepped back, but not Janelle. She held her ground. Killian gave her a look of respect before slapping the man into silence. She only had to hit him twice.

"Is that him?" Narissa asked, wide-eyed.

Killian nodded. "Vonte McKeithen of Bridgeport. Drug dealer and pimp. He's the man who trafficked your daughters." She locked gazes with Janelle. "And killed yours."

By Kate Kessler

Dead Ringer

KILLIAN DELANEY NOVELS

Seven Crows
Call of Vultures

AUDREY HARTE NOVELS

It Takes One
Two Can Play
Three Strikes
Four of a Kind
Zero Hour (novella)

CALL
OF
VULTURES

KATE
KESSLER

REDHOOK

Copyright © 2020 by Kathryn Smith
Excerpt from *It Takes One* copyright © 2016 by Kathryn Smith

Cover design by Lisa Marie Pompilio
Cover images by Arcangel and Shutterstock
Cover copyright © 2020 by Hachette Book Group, Inc.
Author photograph by Kathryn Smith

Redhook Books/Orbit
Hachette Book Group
1290 Avenue of the Americas
New York, NY 10104
hachettebookgroup.com

First Edition: December 2020

Redhook is an imprint of Orbit, a division of Hachette Book Group.
The Redhook name and logo are trademarks of Hachette Book Group, Inc.

The Hachette Speakers Bureau provides a wide range of authors for speaking events. To find out more, go to www.hachettespeakersbureau.com or call (866) 376-6591.

Library of Congress Cataloging-in-Publication Data
Names: Kessler, Kate, author.
Title: Call of vultures / Kate Kessler.
Description: First Edition. | New York, NY : Redhook, 2020. | Series: Killian Delaney novels
Identifiers: LCCN 2020013083 | ISBN 9780316454261 (trade paperback) | ISBN 9780316454278
Subjects: GSAFD: Suspense fiction.
Classification: LCC PR9199.4.K4725 C35 2020 | DDC 813/.6—dc23
LC record available at https://lccn.loc.gov/2020013083

ISBNs: 978-0-316-45426-1 (trade paperback), 978-0-316-45428-5 (ebook)

Printed in the United States of America

LSC-C

10 9 8 7 6 5 4 3 2 1 2020

For Steve, my #1 fan.
And for B.E. for having the patience of a saint.

ONE

It would be a great place to get rid of a body.

The address she'd been given was for a nursery and gardening supply operation in Middlebury. Killian Delaney surveyed the dark property as she drove down the narrow lane between the store and greenhouse. There were some serious potholes that needed attention, but she wasn't driving her own car, so she didn't care if she hit them. In fact, she made a point of hitting every damn one, regardless of how the car jerked and bounced, and grinned with her teeth clenched every time the ass end bottomed out.

It was after two in the morning and rural enough that it wasn't just dark—it was black. She had the headlights on low to illuminate the rough dirt road. And then, as she crested a small hill, she caught sight of a faint light at the bottom, coming from an old barn. Her contact had given her good directions.

The car coasted to the bottom of the hill. Killian killed the headlights and gave the brakes a gentle tap, rolling to a stop in the weak light coming from the barn door. Four women stood in that space, backlit. She didn't have to see their faces to recognize them. Janelle was the tallest, built like a bloody Amazon.

Narissa was a little shorter, with an abundance of soft, full curves. Then came Maya, who was a bucket of chicken—all boob and thigh—followed by Vishna, who was five foot nothing if she was lucky, and about as big around as Killian's leg. These women didn't have a lot in common and they hadn't been friends all that long, but Killian liked—and respected— each of them.

She put the car in park and opened the door to get out.

It was quiet there. Eerily quiet. Stars shone in the beyond-black sky. Connecticut was like that. You could be in the middle of a city and then fifteen minutes later be in the middle of nowhere.

"Ladies," Killian greeted, making eye contact with each of them.

Janelle stepped forward, fists clenched at her sides. "Did you bring it?" Her voice was low and edged like a blade.

"That was the job," Killian replied as she opened the trunk. The other women moved closer, clustering around their leader. It was a warm night with a bit of a breeze, and Killian could smell the mingling of their perfumes, shampoos, and sweat.

There, curled up and bound on a sheet of plastic, was a man. Light shone on his bald head, highlighting the sweat on his cheeks and brow. He was gagged, but that didn't stop him from making noise when his eyes adjusted to the light. He reared up at them, muffled curses punctuating the night.

Two of the women stepped back, but not Janelle. She held her ground. Killian gave her a look of respect before slapping the man into silence. She only had to hit him twice.

"Is that him?" Narissa asked, wide-eyed.

Killian nodded. "Vonte McKeithen of Bridgeport. Drug dealer and pimp. He's the man who trafficked your daughters." She locked gazes with Janelle. "And killed yours." She'd seen the photos when she took the case—three young women still alive, but broken, and a fourth brutally ended.

Janelle swallowed, the whites of her eyes bright. She offered Killian an envelope, fat and sealed.

Killian hesitated. "I don't want your money."

The tall woman's eyes narrowed. "We don't want your pity."

Understood. She took the envelope and shoved it in the waistband of her jeans. "He's all yours."

"I've been waiting so long for this, I don't know what to do," Narissa commented. The other women nodded in agreement.

"Whatever you want," Killian told them. "No one's going to miss this sorry sack of shit. At least not for long." She pulled on the pimp's arm, easing him out of the trunk. He whipped and coiled his body like a snake, swinging his head at her fast and hard. Killian easily sidestepped the attack and punched him in the jaw in retaliation. His feet were bound and the blow knocked him off balance. He fell hard against the edge of the car.

None of the women moved to help him. Vishna, the pixie of the group, sneered at the man, who was easily a foot taller and probably close to a hundred pounds heavier than her. "My baby still has nightmares about you," she told him, her voice raw. "There isn't enough pain in this world to make up for what you did to her."

Her words seemed to stir something in her companions. Any uncertainty or hesitation they might have had seemed to evaporate under the heat of Vishna's rage. Hate—it was contagious. Janelle gripped the pimp's chin in her long hand and forced him to meet her gaze.

"You destroyed the only thing in this world that I truly loved. We're gonna destroy you now." Then, to Killian: "Thank you."

Killian nodded. She hoped this brought the women some kind of peace, but she knew it wouldn't. Nothing they did to this douchebag would change the damage he'd already done. It wouldn't bring back innocence, or life. It might give them a little justice, though, and that was why she'd taken the job in the first place. She knew firsthand that revenge had little healing power. But a little was better than nothing. Better than feeling powerless.

She closed the trunk and handed Janelle a syringe she'd taken from her jacket. "He'll tell you whatever you want to know if you give him this." She'd no sooner handed the needle over than the pimp bolted. Where the hell did he think he was going, hopping like a scared jackrabbit with his arms tied behind his back?

Maya picked up a rock from the damp ground and threw it—hard. Killian's brows rose in admiration when she heard the thud and saw the pimp drop to his knees. Nice shot.

"If you need anything else, you have my number," she told them, rounding the driver's side of the car. They wouldn't use it; she knew that. Sometime in the next day or two, Vonte McKeithen would cease to exist. Maybe traces of him would show up in fertilizer or soil, but nothing that anyone would ever find. The cops certainly weren't going to waste their time looking for a missing pimp. The only people who would miss him would be a few messed-up girls and his mama, and the girls would eventually get over him.

The last thing she saw in her rearview, as she left the scene, was them dragging him into the barn by his feet. The sad part was that his death wouldn't change anything. There were two others waiting to take his place. They'd fight over who got his territory, and then his drugs and his girls would be under new ownership and it would be business as usual until another mother decided to take matters into her own hands.

Killian hoped she got the call when that happened.

It was almost four by the time Killian pulled into her parking spot behind the condo. She had to pick up her own car along the way—the other dropped off at the "cleaners" so all traces of Vonte McKeithen could be eliminated. She also stopped at an all-night Chinese place for something to eat. Kidnapping pimps and wrestling them into a trunk always gave her an appetite.

She'd taken on several traffickers since accepting Maxine Hollander's job offer with the Initiative—a secretive network of gray-work specialists—and it gave her a real sense of satisfaction to do so. Killian had first learned of the Initiative through her boyfriend, Dash Clark. Then she found out Maxine had been watching her for a while—even when she'd been in prison for assault.

Taking the job had been the best thing she'd ever done. She got to hit people on a regular basis and get paid for it, and since they were all terrible people, she got to feel good about it, too. The only hard part was keeping it secret from her parole officer.

Her paychecks came every two weeks, deposited directly into her account. On paper she worked as a security consultant with New Amsterdam Security Inc.—a global company with their closest headquarters in New York. It made most of her income legal, and any off-the-books funds were deposited in an offshore account. It had made it possible for her to leave her shit-box apartment and rent a nice condo. She owned new furniture for the first time in her life. She was also able to help her sister save money for her nieces' education.

She didn't feel like a fuckup anymore. Sure, if she was ever caught she'd get sent back to prison in a heartbeat, but that was a chance she was willing to take. Tracking down "bad guys" was something...No, that wasn't it. *Violence* was something she was good at, and violence was pretty much the only thing the people she was sent after understood.

Her condo was on the first floor of an old Victorian house in a suburban neighborhood in New Britain. Nothing too fancy, because she wouldn't be comfortable, and it would look odd. It was still the nicest place she'd ever lived in. Hardwood floors and trim along the ceiling. It had been freshly painted right before she moved in. No roaches and no neighbors blasting music at two A.M.

Killian unlocked the door and stepped inside. Before her fingers flicked the light switch, she became aware that she was not alone. In one swift movement, she dropped the bag of takeout to the floor, pulled the .38 from the waistband of her jeans, and aimed it at the intruder.

Light filled the space, illuminating the shocked face of her niece—her biological daughter—Shannon.

The reality of what might have happened hit like a brick to the solar plexus. Killian dropped her arm, muscles twitching and trembling. "What the fuck, kid? We talked about this."

Wide-eyed and clutching a pillow—as if it would have done any good—Shannon stared at her. "I texted you."

Killian frowned as she punched the combination on the safe in the closet. "When?"

"I don't know. A few minutes ago. When I got here and you weren't home."

"I didn't get it." She put the gun in the safe and locked it. "You should have called." It was a struggle to keep her voice calm.

"I thought you might be at Dash's. If I didn't hear from you I was just going to crash."

Picking up the bag of takeout, Killian set it on the coffee table. "Lucky for you I got enough for two. You hungry?"

The girl nodded. Inside, Killian sighed. "What happened?"

"Mom and I had a fight."

She tossed her jacket on a chair and pushed up her sleeves. "Over?"

"Dallas."

The flavor of the month. The girl had terrible taste in guys. Killian didn't have to wonder too hard to figure out where she got that. She opened the bag and began setting containers on the table along with napkins and plastic utensils.

"You're going to have to give me more than that."

"She doesn't want me to see him anymore. She says he's a bad influence."

Killian dug a piece of barbecue pork out of the container with her fingers and shoved it in her mouth. "Is he?"

"Don't you have plates?"

"You got something against containers? Answer the question."

"No, he's not. He's a good guy. He's just gotten into trouble." Shannon dug a wonton out of a bag and took a bite. "She doesn't understand that sometimes good people mess up."

"What did he do?"

"He got into a fight. Hurt a guy pretty bad."

"For doing what?"

"I don't know."

"News flash, good people don't hurt other people without good reason."

"You hurt people all the time and you're a good person."

"Sweetie, I am not a good person. Does Meg know you're here?"

Shannon shook her head. "I'm not talking to her."

Sighing, Killian stood and took the container of meat with her to the kitchen. She loved her kitchen, not that she spent much time in it. It had an old-fashioned vibe to it that she found comforting. Standing in front of the sink, she pulled out her phone and dialed her sister's number.

Megan answered on the second ring. "Is she with you?"

"Yup."

A frustrated sigh came through loud and clear. "I knew it. She has to stop pitting us against each other like this."

"There's no pitting. I'm on your side. Always." It was the agreement she and her sister had made a few months back, after Killian rescued Shannon from an asshole who wanted to use the kid to get revenge on her. That's when Shannon found out the truth about where she came from and that Killian had been the one to actually give birth to her when Killian was a teenager. Back then Killian had decided that Megan would be a better mother than her, and her opinion on that hadn't changed.

"At least I know she's safe."

Guilt stuck hard in Killian's heart. Ever since Shannon had been taken, Megan had become extra vigilant, worrying if Shannon was even five minutes late for curfew. Shannon, of course, felt like her mother should trust her more. The problem was, Shannon couldn't be trusted.

"You want me to bring her home?"

"No. She'll want to fight and I'm exhausted. I'm going to go to bed. Do you mind bringing her over in the morning?"

"Not at all. It'll give me and her a chance to talk. I'll see you in the morning. Love you."

"Love you, too."

Killian hung up and grabbed two sodas from the fridge before returning to the living room. She handed one of the sodas to Shannon. "Your mother was worried."

Shannon snorted. Her father had been of black and Puerto

Rican heritage. Mix that with Killian's Irish and Iranian background and you got an incredibly beautiful girl who had just enough sense of her allure to be stupid about it.

"She knew I'd come here. She just wants me to feel guilty."

"You can't run away every time you don't like what she says." Killian picked up the container of beef and broccoli. She'd left the pork in the kitchen, shit. "And you can't keep using me to piss her off."

The kid had the nerve to look affronted. "I'm not using you."

It was Killian's turn to snort. "You've got to up your lying game, kid. It's shit." She dug through the carton for a choice piece of beef. "You use me to get to her and you use her to get to me and it's got to stop. She's your mother. Her word's law."

"*You're* my mother."

"Not in the way that counts. All I did was push you out. She's been there for all the important stuff."

"She didn't save me from traffickers."

"I was the reason they took you in the first place. If you're going to be mad about that, you'd best be mad at me." Killian sighed at the hurt look on the girl's face. "Look, I love you as much as I'm capable of loving anybody—maybe more. But Megan? She loves you in ways I'm not capable of. She's a better person than me. She's better than most—and that's why she's your mother and I'm your aunt and not the other way around."

"But—"

Oh, for crying out loud. "Say I'd kept you. How much would you resent me for spending more than half your life in prison? How embarrassed would you have been when your friends found out about me? The only reason you don't feel those things now is because I'm not the person you counted on to be there for you."

Tears slipped down Shannon's smooth cheeks. "You didn't want me then and you don't want me now. I get it."

"Fuck." Killian reached over and grabbed the girl's hand in a grip that was probably a little too tight. "What I want—what I've always wanted—is for you to have the best life possible. That's a life I knew I couldn't give you. I pulled a gun on you, for Christ's sake."

To her surprise, Shannon laughed. "Fucking psycho."

Killian grinned and moved her hand up to cup the girl's face. "Listen to me. You're the best thing I've ever done. And the best thing I ever could have done for you was let my sister raise you. This doesn't have to be a soap opera unless you make it one."

Shannon nodded. "Okay."

"I'm going to grab a shower. Don't eat all the wontons before I get back."

A few minutes later, Killian stood beneath a pounding spray of water, thinking about that day more than sixteen years ago when she'd made the most difficult and painful decision of her life. She'd made the right one; she knew that with all her heart.

But that didn't stop her from crying over it.

Shannon was still asleep in the guest room when Killian woke a few hours later. It wasn't a surprise; the kid was like a cat. She'd sleep all day if you let her. Killian quietly dressed in her running gear and left the apartment.

Spring in Connecticut was a strange thing. It started off wet and messy and then quickly jumped into hot and oppressive, which meant humidity levels that could feel like an anvil to the chest. That morning it was blessedly cool, but the sun had already begun its ascent into the sky and it wouldn't be long before cool gave way to hot. All the weather apps were calling for record highs that Memorial Day weekend.

She jogged to a nearby park where there was a playground and did her usual routine of crunches and pull-ups on the various equipment. Hanging from the monkey bars, she repeatedly tucked her knees up to her chest until her shoulders burned and her abs protested.

Killian dropped to the ground to find a young woman with a toddler watching her.

"Hi," she said, rolling her shoulders.

"You make me want to run home and join a gym," the woman replied with a slight smile. "I thought chasing him was all the exercise I needed, but seeing you I'm pretty sure I'm wrong."

Laughing, Killian shook her arms at her sides. "I'm sure he keeps you on your toes."

It was obvious from the way the woman looked at the kid that she was enraptured. "He sure does." The toddler bolted toward the swings, giving his mother no choice but to follow. "Have a nice day," she called as she gave chase.

Killian watched them go, waiting to see if she got that pang she'd heard other women talk about, but nothing happened. She might have doubts or regrets when it came to Shannon, but there was one simple fact Killian couldn't ignore—she had never wanted to be a mother. In fact, the thought of being responsible for another person like that made her uneasy.

When Rank Cirello kidnapped Shannon last fall to force Killian to come after him, he'd pushed the right buttons. Killian had been more scared than she would admit, and she beat the snot out of every last person who stood in her way when she set out to bring the girl home. But when she brought Shannon home, it was to Megan's house, not hers.

She really did love the kid as much as she was able. It just wasn't what Shannon deserved.

Turning away, Killian limbered up for her run home and set out for her apartment. It was several degrees warmer than it had been when she'd left, the sun inching closer to noon.

There was a shiny silver Jaguar she didn't recognize parked on the street in front of her building when she approached. It was a little flashy for that neighborhood, the kind of car that attracted attention. Her friend Story, who was a professional driver, would never be caught dead in one for that reason.

She walked into the apartment greeted by the smell of bacon and eggs and coffee. Shannon might be difficult sometimes, but the girl was one hell of a cook. Killian toed off her sneakers and padded into the kitchen, stomach grumbling.

"Smells good," she said, then stopped in her tracks.

Raven Madera sat at the table with Shannon, drinking a cup of coffee. Dressed in a red jumpsuit and heels that screamed *money*, she looked more like she was ready to hang out in the VIP section than pay a social call. She raised a sharply arched brow at the sight of Killian. "Too bad you don't," she quipped.

Killian might have rolled her eyes if she trusted her old cell-mate enough to take her gaze off her for that long.

"What are you doing here?"

Shannon got up from the table and poured a cup of coffee, which she then handed to Killian. "Raven needs your help. Sit down. I'll get your breakfast while she tells you about it."

Killian's gaze narrowed. "Figured telling her would increase the chances of me saying yes, huh?" Shannon had witnessed firsthand the kind of violence of which Killian was capable; there was no point hiding what she did for a living from her.

Raven smiled coyly, her full lips the color of ripe cherries. "Something like that."

"You could have called."

"This is the kind of conversation I like to have face-to-face."

"It's a conversation you should have with someone else," Killian told her. "I'm not interested in whatever you're selling."

"Killy," she admonished softly. Killian scowled. How many times had she heard that husky voice whisper her name in the dark? Raven had been her cellmate, her friend, and her lover for several years. It had all been a setup—Raven had been planted there by Maxine—and Killian hadn't found a way to forgive her for it just yet.

"Please, sit," Raven tried again. "I'm here because I need your help and you're the only person who can do what needs to be done."

Those were the last words she expected to hear from a woman Killian had once seen beat the snot out of three inmates and a guard. Against her better judgment, she pulled a chair out from the table and sat down across from Raven. Shannon set a plate in front of her before joining them.

She was ravenous and not even a snake at her table could stop her from digging in. "What kind of help?" she asked, cutting into a fried egg with her fork.

"The personal kind."

"Does Maxine know you're here?"

"Of course." The other woman sighed, shifting her long body. She was beautiful in an intimidating kind of way—dark skin, high cheekbones, eyes that were almost black, and glossy natural curls. Her father was Puerto Rican and her mother was from Ghana. They divorced when Raven was five—if she'd been telling the truth—but they made three beautiful babies first. "I wouldn't be here if she didn't."

Raven didn't take a shit without Maxine knowing about it. Still… "I find it hard to trust you."

"I lied to you about why I was in prison. I never lied to you about anything else. *Never.*"

They were inching into uncomfortable territory. Killian backed down because she didn't want to go there. What happened on the inside stayed on the inside. It wasn't part of this world. Plus, Shannon was watching the two of them with far too much interest.

"What do you want, Rave?"

The other woman reached into the large purse on the floor beside her and withdrew a folder, which she then offered to Killian. "It's a job offer."

Killian hesitated. "I thought you said it was personal."

Raven's gaze was direct and unflinching. "It's both."

"I was hoping to take a vacation after this one." She and Dash had talked about maybe driving up to Boston for a few days.

"Please."

There was something in Raven's voice that made her hesitate. Sighing, she took the folder and opened it. "Fill me in."

"The photo on the left is of Dylan and Lyria Woodward. Their mother is—"

"Ilyana Woodward," Killian interrupted, shooting her a sharp glance. "I don't live under a rock, you know."

Raven smiled slightly. "I wouldn't have thought you'd care about Hollywood and celebrity."

"I don't, but I've seen a few of her movies. Everyone has." She flipped through the pages in the file. "Incarnyx? What the fuck is that?"

"You haven't heard of them?"

"I wouldn't have asked if I had." She flipped through more pages. "It looks like a self-help group?"

"That's how they sell themselves. They popped up a few years ago in LA, referring to themselves as 'facilitators of self-empowerment.'"

Killian grimaced. "So, basically they started preying on people with fragile egos and impostor syndrome."

Raven nodded. "Exactly. And at first they seemed to help a lot of people. Their supporter list read like a collection of Oscar and Grammy nominees."

There was an awful lot of material in the file, all of which

Killian intended to read, but before that, she needed to know the whole story. "Bottom line me here, girl."

"Ilyana and I have been dating for six months."

Killian's eyebrow twitched, but she kept her expression neutral. She wasn't jealous, but she was surprised. "Since when do you like delicate white girls?" Killian didn't include herself in that category. She certainly wasn't delicate, and her skin and features reflected enough of her mother's Persian ancestry to never be mistaken for all white.

"Since I met her." The reply came with a slight smile. "Killy, Ilyana believed these people were legit, and she started going to their retreats. She took her oldest daughter, Dylan, with her. But then Ilyana started to get a weird vibe from Shasis and Magnus, the leaders of the group."

Killian couldn't stifle her snort. "I know what Magnus means, but Sha-see?"

"She says she took it from a couple of different words that mean *queen*."

Shannon snorted, reminding Killian of her presence—and that she ought to be careful what she said.

"Right. So, let me just give you a hand here—they're fucked-up, right? Like, we're talking full-on cult?"

Raven nodded. "Yeah. Ilyana thinks it's a sex thing, but this guy, this Magnus, he's got serious charisma. The people that follow him are convinced he's the real deal."

"That'll get him laid on the regular."

"Nothing's gone public yet, but Ilyana's talked to a couple of other actresses who just got out. Magnus and Shasis are like the

Jay and Bey of the Kool-Aid crowd. Magnus likes slipping his dick into anything wet and willing."

Killian studied a photo of the couple. They were a good-looking pair—they practically glowed. Sexy, too. He was blond and chiseled; she was dark and vibrant. There was something familiar about her profile.

"Oh, fuck me," she growled.

"Recognized her, huh?"

She couldn't believe it. "You could have led with the fact that she's Tara fucking Washington."

"Who's Tara Washington?" Shannon asked, looking from Raven to Killian.

Killian's attention stayed on Raven. "Someone we used to know."

"Was she in prison with you?"

"Yeah," Raven told the girl when Killian merely shook her head. "She was. You see now why I need your help."

Tara had done a lot of things to get her ass tossed in prison, not least of which was pimping. In Killian's books a pimp was the only thing worse than a snitch. If she had her claws into some young girls, there could be only one reason—she planned to turn them out.

"Feds onto them yet?" she asked.

Raven nodded. "You know it. And it's only a matter of time before the FBI raids their New York compound."

"So, what do you want me to do? Go in and get the girl?"

"Girls. Lyria's there, too."

Killian sat back and closed the folder. "Your woman knows

how dangerous that is, right? I mean, I figure she knows it's illegal, but there needs to be deprogramming and shit if the girls have drank the Kool-Aid."

"Dylan is in deeper than Lyria, but both of them know something's not right. Lyria wants to come home, but they've got collateral on her—pictures and video. And regardless, Ilyana says she won't leave without her sister."

"Of course they've got leverage. What's a cult without its control?" Sighing, Killian met her former cellmate's gaze. There was more going on than Raven had shared. "What do they have on the other one? Dylan, or whatever?"

"Same—video and photos. Plus, I think she really believes in what Magnus is selling."

That was trouble. "If she's in love with him, then he's working her. What's the FBI got on her?" When Raven blinked, Killian smiled. "That's the real reason you came to me and not the cops, right? I'm supposed to get her out before the FBI can arrest her?"

Sighing, the other woman took a drink of coffee. "She's been used in recruitment videos and literature. She's even been soliciting other celebrity kids on social media. Ilyana's afraid of criminal charges if Dylan's there when Magnus and Shasis are arrested. The kid's loyal to them. Even chose them over her own family."

"That's gotta be some sweet pipe he's laying if she's turned her back on her own."

"I hear he and Shasis are a package deal, so maybe she got one of those magic coochies."

Killian chuckled. They used to joke about some of the women inside having sexual power over others and blamed it on having voodoo between their legs. "Maybe. This is going to be a shit show either way, Rave. If the kid doesn't want to leave, I'm looking at kidnapping, regardless of what this group has done to her. People who have been programmed don't respond well to that." Neither did pimps, but she didn't give a fuck about them. These were girls who had been taken advantage of.

"If anyone can make her see the reality of her situation and get out of there before the FBI raids the place, it's you."

Killian made a scoffing noise. "So, I'm damage control?"

"There are rumors of cartel connections. Ilyana doesn't want her girls getting killed, or trafficked. You're the only chance two young women have of getting out of a horrible situation before it all goes to hell. "

And that was really all she needed to hear. Raven knew it as much as she did. "You've got people ready to help them when they come home?"

"Ilyana has already secured help from one of the top deprogrammers in the country. All you have to do is destroy what they have on the girls and bring Dylan and Lyria home."

"How much time do I have?"

"I don't know. Maybe a couple of weeks."

"Jesus Christ. I have to get in and out of a paranoid cult in fourteen fucking days?" She tossed the folder on the table. "How am I supposed to do that?"

"They're having a retreat this weekend." Raven dropped another file on top of the first. "You're already registered. An ex-con looking to change her life and make something of herself. They'll love you. You've got two and a half days to convince them you're Incarnyx material."

Killian's jaw tightened. "Already registered? That's pretty fuckin' brazen, even for you."

"I went on the assumption that you'd actually be game to save two girls who have been exploited and abused."

"Don't start singing that fucking song again." That was Killian's weakness and she knew it.

"Please, Kill." Warm, strong fingers seized hers as Raven leaned across the table. "I was always there when you needed me, and now I need you. Please."

"Shit," Killian muttered. She never turned her back on a debt. Never. "Fine. I'll do it."

Raven's relief was palpable. "Thank you." She squeezed Killian's hand again before letting go. "Thank you so much."

"Yeah, yeah." Killian curled those same fingers into a fist. "You're welcome, but I want payment up front." She wasn't surprised when Raven handed her a fat envelope. Shannon's eyebrows rose, but she stayed silent.

Raven rose to her feet. "I've taken enough of your morning. I'll be in touch before the weekend—make sure everything's a go."

Killian walked her to the door. "I don't want to come home and find you here again. You want to talk to me, you call."

There was a flicker of something in her gaze—hurt, maybe. Or maybe she was constipated. Whatever, Killian didn't care. "Right. I'll call you, then."

Killian locked the door behind her when she was gone and headed back to the kitchen and her breakfast, which was no doubt cold at this point.

Shannon leaned back in her chair and smirked at her as she sat down. "So, you and her, huh?"

Killian piled her bacon and remaining egg between two pieces of toast and made a sandwich. "Go get your shit together. I'm taking you home."

TWO

"**S**on of a bitch."

Dash Clark, Killian's boyfriend, looked up from his phone at her outburst. His green eyes narrowed. "What's up?"

Killian slouched back in her chair. "This registration form Raven filled out for Incarnyx. She made me sound like a douche. 'My years incarcerated have left me feeling awkward in social situations. I'm afraid people will judge me personally and professionally based on my past.'" She grimaced.

"I think she just wrote what she thought would appeal to them."

"I never would have written that, regardless. I don't feel fucking awkward in social situations."

"I took you to a party last weekend and you fidgeted and scratched all the way through it."

"I'm not used to wearing a dress."

"It was a romper."

"Same thing."

"No, it's not. I know this because you told me it wasn't the same thing when you bought it. You said that you could still kick someone in the head without flashing them in a romper."

Killian's gaze narrowed. "Whose side are you on, Clark?"

He smiled slightly. "Is this really about the form?"

She tensed. It was a good thing he was so pretty; otherwise she'd bust his condescending mouth. "What else would it be about?"

Dash met her gaze directly and held it. "You two were together for a while. Are you jealous that she's with this actress?"

Jealous? "For real?" Didn't he know that *gay for the stay* was a legit thing?

He merely arched a brow, which made her want to throw her cup at him. Then make him swallow the pieces.

"Prison's its own world," she reminded him. "You do things inside that you don't do on the out."

"That doesn't make it less real."

"You don't know fuck all about it," she retorted. He'd never been arrested as an adult. "Maybe you're the one that's jealous."

"I know what it means when you get defensive." His tone stayed low and even, as he subtly reminded her that he'd known her since she was a kid. "And this isn't about me, it's about you, but for the record, I'm not above a little insecurity, either."

He made it impossible for her to maintain anger sometimes. It used to be so easy for her to get ahold of some rage and hang on to it. Sighing, Killian leaned back in her chair. "I'm not jealous. I just feel stupid. She played me and I never saw it."

His green-gold eyes glittered. "So, it's about ego."

She could argue... "Yeah. Okay."

"Look, maybe it did start off as just a job, but it couldn't have all been a lie; otherwise you would have seen through it. And how she came into your life doesn't change the fact that she had your back. She could have gone to anyone in the network for help and they would have said yes because of her connection to Maxine, but she came to you because she trusts you."

"You can shut up now." She tossed the registration form on the table.

Dash smiled. "Sure. Still think she made you sound like a douche?"

"Yes," she replied hotly. "I know it's to make me sound susceptible to what they're selling, but it creeps me out. I never got sucked into religion or gangs on the inside. Not that any of them wanted me."

He was still smiling. "You were too badass."

Okay, that made her laugh. "Too much of a pain in the ass." And a little too notorious. The bounty Rank put on her head made her a target, and no one who's trying to keep their head down wants to associate with a target—unless they're crazy. Killian did have a couple of allies on the inside, but not many. Raven had been one of them, though she'd done it for a paycheck. Nothing Dash could say would erase that fact.

"Okay, so what's the plan?" he asked, setting his phone on the coffee table. For almost ten years Killian hadn't owned a cell phone. She'd gotten one immediately after getting out of prison because Megan insisted she needed one. The dependence society had on the device made her shake her head. Even Dash, who was by no means a social-media butterfly, spent a lot of time staring at his phone screen, as he conducted a lot of his business through it.

"I attend the seminar this weekend and hopefully get an invitation to join them for a longer session at their campus in upstate New York. That's apparently where the Woodward girls are."

Dash lifted his coffee cup and took a drink. "They use their workshops as a screening process? Smart."

"Allows them to focus on the ones that really seem susceptible to their BS, I guess. I just really hate having to pretend to be one of them."

He patted her knee. "Think of how good it will feel to fuck them over."

There was that. "You sure you don't mind watering the plants for me?"

"I told you I didn't. Doesn't Shannon normally house-sit for you?"

"Yeah, well…" She sighed. "I don't want to be put between her and her mother right now. There's already tension."

Frowning, Dash leaned his elbow on the back of the couch. "Between you and Megan?"

"And between me and Shannon. She wants me to be her mother, but if I was any good at that, I wouldn't have given her up."

"I suppose it's difficult to find a way to articulate that without making the kid feel like she wasn't wanted."

"She wasn't," Killian admitted. She would only ever admit that to him. "I love her, Dash. I really do. I'd die for her, but when I found out about her I didn't want her. You know that." He'd been her best friend at the time, and her boyfriend Jason had been in lockup. Jason never even knew Killian had been pregnant, or if he had, he never let on.

Which wouldn't be a surprise given that he'd had two children Killian didn't know about with another woman Killian also knew nothing about.

He nodded. "I was going to take you to your abortion appointment."

"And then fucking Meg—barely twenty-one—begs me to let her raise her. She wanted a baby so bad. I don't know what the fuck she was thinking."

"Maybe she knew that guy she'd been dating wasn't worth it."

Killian shrugged. "She'd already met Cam by then." Cam and Megan eventually got married and had a daughter of their own, Willow, but Cam hadn't known where Shannon came from originally. He and Shannon found out the truth around the same time. It turned out that Cam had his suspicions, but he didn't really care. He'd helped raise Shannon and loved her like his own. As far as he was concerned, she belonged to him and Megan in all the ways that mattered.

And that was what Killian wanted.

"Anyway, Meg and Cam and the girls are all the family I have. I don't want to lose that because they think I'm trying to take Shannon away."

"Come on, they'd never think that."

"Maybe not, but all I'd have to do right now is say the word and Shannon would move in with me. It's bad enough that she runs to me whenever she's pissed at them."

"Have you talked to her about this?"

"You know I have. I'm not sure she's listening. So I have to put some distance between us—as much as I fucking hate it."

He closed the distance between them and put his arm around her shoulders, pulling her against his chest. He kissed her forehead. "I'm sorry."

Killian leaned into him. "Thanks. It'll be fine, but I'm almost looking forward to getting involved with a cult this weekend so I don't have to deal with it. How crazy is that?"

Dash's arm tightened around her. "Sounds about right where family's concerned."

Late Friday morning, as Killian was putting her bags in the trunk of her cherry-red '66 Impala—tricked out by Dash, of course—her phone rang. It was Donna, her parole officer. Only another two months to go before she was finally in the free and clear.

"Hey, Donna," she said, closing the trunk. "What's up?"

"You tell me," came the strangely clipped reply. "Why did I get a phone call from the parole board concerning you?"

Killian's stomach twisted slightly. She'd go back inside if she really had to, but she'd prefer to avoid it if possible. "No idea. What did they say?"

"They were pretty tight-lipped. They asked a lot about your employment and recent activities. They wanted to know how much trust I had in you."

She dug the car keys out of her pocket. "What did you say?"

"I told them I had no reason to distrust you."

Killian chuckled. "Nice way to put it. I hate to tell you,

Donna, that I can't help you. I have no idea why they'd be checking in."

"I can't help you, Killian, if you're not honest with me."

"I am being honest. I have no idea why they'd want to talk to you about me." *Except that I've been working for this secret group that likes to skirt the gray areas of the law . . .*

"You'd tell me if you were in trouble?"

She opened the driver's door and climbed in. "I'd ask for your help if I needed it." Donna wasn't the only one who knew how to turn words around.

"Are you going somewhere?" Donna asked.

"Actually, I'm going to a retreat," Killian replied with forced enthusiasm. "One of those self-improvement things."

Silence.

"Seriously?"

Killian grinned as she slid the key into the ignition. "Seriously. I'll bring the receipt to our next meeting. You can put it in my file if anyone calls again."

"I really don't want to get blindsided by something, Killian. I really don't like it when I invest in someone and they fuck me over."

"I respect that. I promise that I am not trying to fuck you over. You've been good to me and I appreciate it."

"Thanks." When Killian didn't respond, she added, "Enjoy your weekend. I'll see you Tuesday."

"You bet." Killian hung up and sighed. Heat from parole was the last thing she needed, but it was probably just some noob with a hard-on for putting ex-cons back in jail sniffing around.

The cover the Initiative made for her was strong enough to withstand all kinds of scrutiny—she wasn't their only employee of criminal background. They had to look legit. She'd put a text in to Maxine and let her take care of it if there was anything to take care of.

She plugged the address into her phone before fastening her seat belt and starting the car's engine. A few minutes later, she set the phone in the holder on the dash and set out. Traffic looked good, but it was still going to take her almost two hours to get to the retreat site.

She headed west on I-84 into New York State. Her route took her along 684 and eventually the Saw Mill River Parkway—a much more scenic drive, though it could be a real bitch if there were any slowdowns or accidents. She took that into Mount Kisco and finally stopped at the Holiday Inn she'd booked to drop off her belongings and get ready for the retreat.

Killian wasn't much of a makeup person, but she needed to play the part of someone who was uncomfortable in her own skin. She wore her dark hair down, brushing it and smoothing it until it was sleek and shiny. Then she put on some concealer, mascara, and lip gloss. She traded her T-shirt for a blouse that covered most of her tattoos and her boots for a pair of flats she'd picked up on sale at Macy's.

No weapons, but that was okay. She'd learned a long time ago that just about anything could become a weapon in the right hands, and even she would admit that her hands were pretty damn capable. So were her feet, and her knees and her elbows...

She sprayed her hair and checked her watch. Registration for the retreat opened in ten minutes, and it would take her fifteen to get there, so she had to get going if she wanted to look enthusiastic, but not *too* much so.

Killian threw her phone, lip gloss, a pen, a nail file, and some gum into a small cross-body bag and slung it over her head. Then she made her way to the lobby and out into the sunshine. She hoped they had air-conditioning.

The Incarnyx public headquarters was located in a semi-industrial area between Bedford Hills and Mount Kisco. The building was red brick with white trim—nothing too fancy, but not shabby, either. It shared space with a weight-loss company, a walk-in clinic, and a fitness center for women.

There was a small coffee shop just around the corner. Killian got some much-needed caffeine and then joined a couple entering the Incarnyx building. They smiled at her. She forced herself to smile back. She probably looked like a psycho. She felt like one—and the mascara on her left eye was making it itch. She had to force herself not to rub it and smear makeup all over her face.

Inside, the building looked almost like a spa. The walls were painted in a soft cream, filled with serene paintings and inspirational quotes about finding your power and being your most "authentic" self. The carpet was a dark sage, and all the furnishings were a warm-honey shade of wood. There were two selections of water—cucumber and lemon—along with an organic herbal tea.

The place gave her the creeps. Like, any minute some guys

in lab coats would come grab her and drag her out back, where they'd scoop out part of her brain and send her off to cult land. Or maybe they'd reprogram her into becoming some sort of perfect woman.

No, the brain scooping was more likely to work.

Killian naturally fell into place in line in front of the reception desk. The woman sitting there was young—probably in her midtwenties—with long, straight blond hair and bright green eyes. She was ballerina thin, her breastbone delicately visible beneath her pale skin. She'd shatter with one punch. So far, so good. If everyone in the joint was built like her, there wouldn't be anything to worry about.

"Hi there!" she chirped when Killian stepped in front of the counter. "Welcome to Incarnyx. Our goal is to help you become the person you were meant to be."

Killian tried not to grimace. "Fabulous." She gave her name and the girl checked her in via computer. Then she gave her forms to fill out on a clipboard, and a tote bag full of everything she would need for the weekend. It was a nice bag, she'd give them that.

The forms were all about what she hoped to gain from the retreat, what she thought her problem areas were, and what she needed to work on. There was also a section for strengths and things she liked about herself.

Was the fact that she knew how to kill someone with a chopstick a strength? Probably not one she ought to share in this venue. She scratched in "loyalty" instead.

Jesus, this was tedious, trying to dissect herself for their exploitation. How did she make herself sound like she could be easily manipulated without making herself seem weak? Fuck it, she'd just be fairly honest and let the cards fall where they would. Ilyana Woodward could buy her daughters' freedom. Why hadn't she suggested that to Raven? These people would probably hand both girls over for enough coin.

She filled out the forms as quickly as possible, with answers that were close enough to the truth that she'd remember them. Once that was done, she and others who were finished were grouped together and escorted into another room by a redhead who was as waifish as the blonde.

"My name is Heather, and I want you to think of me as your concierge," she said. "Anything you need, I'll take care of for you. These lockers are where you will store your coats and personal belongings, including cell phones. All you have to do is enter a four-digit PIN when prompted and the door will open or lock immediately."

"We can't have our phones?" a young woman asked, an expression of panic on her face.

Heather smiled gently. "We don't want you to be distracted during the seminars, but don't worry. There are scheduled breaks throughout the day, so you'll be able to check your messages in case of an emergency."

The woman didn't look comforted. Killian mentally shook her head. Maybe she didn't share the phone addiction because she hadn't yet figured out how to seriously maim a person with one.

"Bring your tote bag with you," Heather continued. "It has

your retreat binder in it. In the binder you'll find paper to take notes, as well as all the important handouts and information you'll need for each pod of this weekend's retreat. There's also a couple of pens, a highlighter, information about Incarnyx, a calendar of all our scheduled events, and a white bracelet that we ask you to wear for the entirety of the retreat. Think of it as a symbol of the beginning of your journey to becoming your best self."

A bracelet? Killian found it near the bottom of the tote. It was just one of those white rubber things that a lot of charities used for fundraising. Given the price of their programs, she thought they could do better. Then again, at least it wasn't a sash or a pin—or worse, a hat.

After they put their things in the lockers, they were escorted into another room where they were given name tags and left to mingle while the remaining participants checked in.

Name tag pinned in place, Killian headed straight for the food table. There wasn't any alcohol, so she couldn't make herself numb. Instead, she piled a plate with cheese and vegetables and stuffed her face in a corner, hoping no one would try talking to her.

She got her wish.

Half an hour later, the place was packed. Another young woman—this one a brunette—came into the room with a microphone.

"Welcome to Incarnyx!" she greeted them, her voice bouncing off the walls. Enthusiastic applause followed. Killian didn't clap.

"My name is Darcy, and in a few minutes I'm going to take

you all into the seminar room so we can get started. If you need to go to the restroom or get a drink, please do it now."

Christ, yes, she needed a drink. Killian sighed.

The seminar room was like a small auditorium—like a college lecture hall, she supposed, not that she'd ever been in one. She wanted to take a seat in the back, as far away as she could get, but that wasn't part of her "cover," so she made herself sit a few rows from the front instead. Sitting like that, with her back exposed to the rest of the hall . . . it made her twitch.

Once everyone was seated, the lights brightened a little over the podium in front. Two women walked out onto the raised dais. One was an Asian woman with shoulder-length black hair, wearing a red blouse and a black skirt. The other was a young woman with fine blond hair wearing a peach-colored dress.

It was Lyria Woodward. Killian's gaze narrowed. The girl was almost painfully thin—her cheeks were hollow and the cords of her neck stood out under her skin. She looked like a paper doll that would tear if you handled her the wrong way.

Raven had said that the younger sister wasn't as into Incarnyx as Dylan was, and that the organization had resorted to blackmail to keep her in line. Were they starving her as well, as some kind of punishment or control?

The older woman introduced herself as Mina, a "phoenix" within the group, meaning she had gone through all the training and had been reborn into the person she was meant to be. Lyria was introduced only as a "starling," whatever that meant. It was Mina who was going to talk to them for the next two hours before they got a break.

Killian sat up a little straighter in her seat. She took out her notebook and made like she was the most keen of students. She made a point-form list of what Mina said—all pretty canned self-help slop—but her attention was focused almost exclusively on Lyria. She might look like she was broken, but there was a defiance in her eyes. Killian saw it in the split second when their gazes met. Killian smiled. Lyria blinked and looked away. Then back again. A small smile curved her lips.

That was the moment Killian knew she was going to do the job, regardless of parole or Raven or anything else. Someone was trying to break this kid, but they hadn't succeeded. She was going to make sure they never did.

After the presentation, there was a getting-to-know-each-other reception in the conference hall. Killian waited for a few minutes, then approached Lyria Woodward.

"Hi," she said with a smile. "I enjoyed listening to you talk."

The girl looked surprised. "You did? I thought I messed it up."

"Not at all. You came across as very sincere."

Lyria glanced away. "Great."

Yeah, so the kid knew this whole thing was full of shit. "I was surprised to learn we have a mutual friend."

The young woman lifted her curious gaze. "Who's that?"

"Raven Madera." She let that just hang there for a second between them.

Blue eyes widened. "You're..." The girl swallowed and glanced over her shoulder. "...friends with her and my mom?"

Still smiling, Killian nodded. "I am. Don't look so surprised or someone's going to ask you what we're talking about. Look like you've got me on a hook and are reeling me in."

Instantly, her expression changed. Obviously, the acting gene ran in the family. "Why are you here?"

"Raven asked me to help get you out of here. You and Dylan."

"She did?" The girl actually seemed surprised. "Okay."

"Do you know where they keep the information they have on your family?"

"I can find out."

"Good. Where's your sister?"

"She's not here. Look, you need to know—shit. Here comes Mina."

Killian didn't even look. She brightened her smile. "I found it really interesting when you talked about how you began to see yourself as you wanted to be after just three Incarnyx classes."

"Lyria is one of our most prized disciples," Mina interjected, joining them. "She's gone from defiant resistance to embracing the program wholeheartedly." She smiled proudly.

A good jab in the throat would fix that smile. "And it was all because of the principles of Magnus's teachings?" Enthusiasm left a bitter taste on Killian's tongue.

"Not just Magnus," Mina corrected. "Shasis as well, along with writings of other great thinkers and spiritual leaders. That's the beauty of Incarnyx—it draws its teachings from not just one source, but many. Our program is number one in the US and Canada for actualizing one's true self."

Well, if the Canadians were falling for it, it had to be real. "How fascinating. This is the first I've heard of it, to be honest."

"And what are your impressions thus far?"

That you're con artists and probably pimps. "Well, you certainly seem committed to changing the way people see themselves."

"We *are*." The woman touched her arm. "Forgive me. I'm Mina Lee, and you are?"

"Killian Delaney."

Something shifted in Mina's gaze. Recognition. Slowly, she barely turned her head in Lyria's direction. "Lyria, honey, would you mind making certain we have enough refreshment for our guests while I talk to Killian, please?"

It was a dismissal, of course. Lyria cast a nervous glance in Killian's direction before hurrying off to do what she was told.

"She's become so much more obedient," Mina commented, her gaze never leaving Killian's face. "I don't mean to be rude, but I hoped our paths would cross after reading your registration form."

"Oh? Why?"

"Because of your rather interesting past." She paused, touching Killian's arm once again. "Or is it too painful for you to discuss?"

Jesus, she needed a drink. "Not at all. I wouldn't have mentioned it if it were."

"Oh, good. I find it interesting that you said on your form that you feel prison formed you into a darker version of yourself and that you were sometimes afraid that version might be who you are meant to be."

The only things prison had changed about her were that she was better at sensing when a shiv was coming her way and that she didn't mind getting fingered by a chick when the itch was there. "Prison's not a place for vulnerability," she allowed. "I sometimes feel like I don't have that anymore—that it's affected my ability to empathize with others."

"What are you truly hoping to achieve this weekend, Killian?" Mina asked softly, taking a step closer, as though they were discussing something intimate and not a load of crap.

Killian shifted toward her, lowering her head as though about to whisper a secret. "I would like to catch a glimpse of who I am meant to be and start to figure out how to embrace being her." She laughed softly. "I want to feel like I belong in the world. Obviously, I know it won't all happen in just a couple of days." *Always make them think you're willing to give them more money.*

Mina's dark eyes brightened. "No, it won't, but making these first few crucial steps will be so rewarding for you, trust me."

Not any further than I can throw you, bitch. No, not even that far.

"You know," Mina was saying, "there's another seminar after this one. I think you might benefit from it. There's a beginner's track and one that's a bit more advanced that might suit you quite well. We'll see how the weekend progresses, but if you flourish as I think you might, I'll put in a word with my teammates."

"Oh, that's so nice of you. Thank you." *Flourish? Did she honestly look like the type of person who might grow in this sort of environment?*

Mina patted her arm. "Don't thank me yet. Now, if you'll excuse me, I should mingle. We wouldn't want you to look like teacher's pet this early in the experience." She laughed and Killian forced herself to laugh with her. She hoped she looked delighted, because the expression on her face felt like it might just as easily be demented.

Alone once again, Killian rolled her shoulders to ease the tension there. She had a bit of a headache and was hungry, but there was nothing to eat except snack food. Hopefully this thing would soon be over. It was kind of like being in the prison yard, waiting for someone to jump her.

"Excuse me."

Killian turned to find a black-haired woman a little younger and a little smaller than herself standing there with a hesitant smile on her face.

"Are you Killian Delaney?"

A frown tugged at Killian's eyebrows. Not another Incarnyx recruiter? "I am. Have we met?"

The woman held out her hand. Killian took it. "No. I'm Maryl Blake. I was a huge MMA fan in high school. I've seen you fight. You were awesome."

For a brief time Killian had entertained the idea of being a professional fighter, but then life happened, and then prison happened, and that was the end of that. Funny, how she still ended up getting paid to do violence, just not in front of a crowd.

She smiled at the younger woman. "Thanks. That's nice to hear."

"I can't believe you're here. I mean…why would you need a self-help class?" Maryl held up her hand. "I'm sorry. That's none of my business."

"No, it's okay. I'm here because I thought Incarnyx might have something to offer me. Same reason you're here, right?"

Maryl hesitated. "Yeah, sure. My fiancé bought me the weekend for my birthday. He thinks the program will help me."

"Does he?" Killian kept her tone light.

"Yeah. I think he's right. Just listening to Mina and Lyria makes me want to be a better person."

Killian willed herself not to cringe. "They were inspirational."

A second of awkward silence fell between them. Maryl smiled. "Well, it was awesome meeting you. Would it be okay if I said hello to you tomorrow?"

"Of course. I'll appreciate a friendly face."

The younger woman's smile brightened. "Great. I'll see you tomorrow."

Killian watched her walk away. What was it about her that attracted people who were abused by others?

"Everyone, may I have your attention, please?" Mina called out. All eyes turned toward where she stood at the front of the room, Lyria by her side. God, the girl looked exhausted.

"I want to thank you all for joining us today, and tell you how much all of us at Incarnyx look forward to taking these first steps of self-discovery with you. A reminder that we start tomorrow morning at nine o'clock, so please plan to be here a few minutes early. We'll have coffee, tea, and a continental breakfast, and we'll provide lunch as well, during which we'll have a very special guest speaker. So, go have yourselves a lovely rest of the evening, and we'll see you in the morning!"

Everyone else applauded, so Killian did, too. Lyria shot her a quick glance, but it was pointed enough for Killian to know that they'd have to continue their conversation the next day. The girl had started to tell her something, but what?

Killian followed the crowd out of the room—much like a herd of sheep, she realized—and collected her belongings from the locker where she'd left them. She had a text from Dash on her phone, just checking in. She'd call him when she reached the hotel.

On the way to her car, she caught sight of Maryl in the parking lot. She was with a guy who had ahold of her by the arm. Maryl had to hurry to keep up with his longer stride. He had to be the fiancé, the asshole who wanted that sweet thing to be a "better person." He was the one who needed the attitude adjustment. Christ, he practically tossed Maryl into the car like she was luggage instead of a person.

Killian hated bullies. But she loved smacking them around.

She unlocked the door to the Impala with the hint of a smile. It just might make the weekend worthwhile if she got to knock Maryl's fiancé on his ass before the end of it. She'd consider it a bonus.

THREE

W ell," Joe began as he closed the truck door. "How did that go?"

Maryl rubbed her arm where he'd grabbed her. Tossing her around like a bag of flour was part of the deal, but it still hurt. "Good, I think. I told her I was an MMA fan and recognized her from her fighting days. I think she bought it."

"She doesn't look that tough."

She snorted. "Seriously? Did you watch the videos of her fighting?"

He started the engine and put the truck in reverse. "No. I've been spending most of my time surveilling our power couple." He twisted his torso to look out the back window. The truck began to move backward. "Explain to me why she is a person of interest again?"

Maryl sighed. Joe was a great partner who always had her back, but he really wasn't one for doing any kind of homework unless he had to. He let her do it. "She's friendly with Ilyana Woodward's girlfriend. She's got a criminal record and she was visited by Woodward's girlfriend just a few days ago. Also, a third party paid the registration fee for her to be here this weekend. Doesn't that seem a little too coincidental to you?"

"Yeah, but what's her objective? Did Woodward hire her to protect her daughters, or to get revenge on her ex? Or is it something else?"

"I don't even have a guess, but when someone like her suddenly shows up in the middle of one of our operations, it's worth looking into."

"True. Hopefully she won't be trouble."

"Oh, she's going to be trouble regardless. I just hope neither one of us has to go up against her."

Joe smirked. "Seriously?"

Maryl rolled her eyes. "You're the one she thinks is abusive. I wouldn't be so cocky if I were you. Maybe she doesn't like bullies."

He shrugged. "I'm not too worried. What was she locked up for anyway?"

"How have you not gotten yourself or someone else killed yet? She beat a man to the brink of death with her bare hands and an assortment of other weapons."

Joe cast her a narrow glance out of the corner of his eye. "You shitting me?"

Maryl shook her head. Now he was paying attention. Good. "Remember Rank Cirello?"

"Crime boss who offed himself a few months back? Yeah, no one cried for that guy. He looked like Dr. Frankenstein put him together."

"Yeah, Delaney did that."

"Fuck off." His expression was comical. "That was her?"

Maryl laughed. "You know, you really should read the files we're given. You'd know all of this if you had done the homework you were supposed to do."

Joe grinned. "No reason for me to have to do it when you've done it. Shit. I guess she's tougher than she looks."

"I guess so. Anyway, I think I can get close to her without making her suspicious."

"Careful. If she did time she might have developed a preference for taco." He waggled his eyebrows suggestively.

"Jesus. If I made a joke like that to you, you'd be all indignant for your asshole." Maryl shook her head with a smile. "Pull into a drive-through. I'm starving."

The first fast-food place they found was a Wendy's, so Joe pulled into the line. "So, what if Delaney proves to be trouble rather than an asset? What's the plan?"

"We remove her from play," Maryl replied resolutely. "Bringing down Incarnyx could make both of our careers. I'm not about to let some bitch get in the way of that, no matter how much respect I have for her skills."

Joe turned to look at her with an arched brow. "All right. What do you want to eat? I'm guessing *not* taco salad?"

"Oh, for fuck's sake," Maryl muttered as he laughed at his own joke. "I really hope Delaney decides to beat your ass."

"Beat mine. Eat yours."

"That's it." She opened the passenger door and climbed out. Angrily, she stomped toward the restaurant door. She could hear him laughing all the way across the parking lot.

*   *   *

Killian slept until two A.M. Then she got up and dressed and quietly left her hotel room. The place was deserted except for the front desk clerk, who looked at her strangely but smiled in return when she smiled at him.

Outside, it was quiet. A nice, surprisingly cool night for mid-May. She unlocked the Impala and slid behind the wheel. Before starting the engine, she consulted the map she'd purchased before making the drive to New York State. GPS and mapping apps left digital fingerprints, and Killian would prefer to leave as little evidence of her activities while in New York as possible. After checking the address, she started the car and began driving. The Impala's engine rumbled in the quiet night. It wouldn't be a problem until she reached the right neighborhood.

Many of the Incarnyx "family" who worked at the school lived in the area, on a communal property where Magnus and Shasis also stayed when in town. There was a larger campus upstate where the "magic" took place. Her assumption was that the classes offered at the school were a screening process that not only made money, but then pointed a finger at those who would pay even more money to give themselves completely over to Magnus's influence.

There were a lot of big-ass homes in Bedford Hills. A lot of people with a lot of money and a lot of landscaping bills. The Incarnyx mansion sat way back from the road, down a long, gated drive. The entire property was fenced off on one side by a high wall of evergreens that led to thicker forestation in the back. The other side had some trees and a fence that led to the neighboring property—which was the disciple house. It was blocked off on the other side in a similar fashion. The entire property had to be at least ten acres, with several outbuildings as well, and a large pool plus a tennis court.

Shit. What did the upstate property look like?

She pulled off onto a side road and parked. Then she made her way toward the property on foot.

Headlights came around a corner as she neared the estate. Killian ducked behind a shrub just seconds before a private security van drove by. Pulling out her phone, she went into the camera function—no flash—and started snapping photos. Thankfully, the streetlights provided all the light she needed. The woman on the passenger side paid particular attention to the Incarnyx house. Were they on the payroll, or were they undercover FBI doing surveillance? Should be easy enough to find out—she had the license plate on her phone now, and the name of the security company.

She slipped out from behind the bushes and turned her attention to the house where Lyria and the other "disciples" lived while in town working at the school.

At first she'd thought it was a separate property, but now that she got a good look at it, she could tell it was a smaller version of the larger mansion. It had to be a guesthouse or something. A guesthouse that could hold a lot more guests than she could ever imagine inviting over. How many people lived there? A dozen? How many other houses did the group own in the area? God, there could be easily a hundred Incarnyx fangirls and boys in town.

What was it about this program that sucked them in? It certainly wasn't the crap Killian had heard them spewing earlier that night. There had to be something more going on within those walls, something darker and more seductive.

Raven was delusional. There was no way she was going to find out anything from a weekend's worth of training. No one was going to invite her into their inner circle after just a few days.

She'd trusted Raven almost immediately—as much as she trusted anyone in prison—but mostly because the other woman had come to her aid when she was getting her ass kicked. She fought beside her, proved herself an ally, then manipulated her way into Killian's head and body. Not that it had turned out badly at all. She probably wouldn't have survived prison if not for Raven.

That didn't mean she liked being fooled. Manipulated.

But there was no point in thinking about that. It would only make her angry. She turned her attention to the main house. A large silver SUV was parked out front, and she could see a guardhouse at the foot of the drive. Up near the house a guy in dark clothing stepped out of the shadows. Of course they had private security. She'd be more surprised if they didn't. Maybe the people in the van were on the Incarnyx payroll, but she doubted it. It was just a feeling, but she trusted her instincts.

Not wanting to be caught by the van or the men in black on their next sweep, Killian quickly made her way back to her car. She'd only wanted to check the place out and get an idea of what she was up against. Money and power—that's what she was up against. People who had both and wanted more. The kind of people you never showed your hand or your back to.

Back at the hotel, she stripped out of her clothes and climbed into the king-size bed. Lying in the dark, she closed her eyes and let her mind go. Some people counted sheep to go to sleep. Others indulged in fantasies. Killian practiced her kicks and punches on a faceless opponent, and she always went for the places that would do the most damage.

She was asleep within minutes.

The next morning, Killian got up early and went for a run on the treadmill in the hotel gym. Normally, she preferred the outside, but she was in a strange place, and staying put made her situation easier to control. She finished her cardio, did some strength training, and then ate breakfast before returning to her room to shower and get ready.

She didn't hide her tattoos as much as she had the night before. Mina had seemed to like the fact that she was an ex-con, so maybe playing it up a bit more was a better tactic. Nothing too blatant; she put on a camisole with a sheer blouse over the top so some of her ink showed through. She paired that with cropped jeans and flats. She left her hair down and put on a little makeup once again. Then, for shits and giggles, she took a selfie and sent it to Dash. She was just heading out the door when he replied:

Sexy soccer mom. Swiping right.

Then he sent a shot of him and his fur-kid, Hank, out for a walk. She smiled at the sight of their faces before tucking her phone away and gathering up her bag for the retreat.

She arrived fifteen minutes early—plenty of time to grab a coffee before starting. Not from the urn set up on a table, but from the same place as yesterday. She didn't trust cult coffee. Seriously, if she ran a cult there'd be mind-altering drugs in everything.

They were splitting the group between two of the classrooms that morning. Killian just happened to end up in the same room as Maryl, so she sat down across from her at the table near the front of the room, even though she wanted to sit in a corner with her back to the wall. She told herself there wasn't much risk of danger but made sure she could see all exits regardless.

"Good morning," the other woman said.

"Hey," Killian replied. She took a mechanical pencil and the Incarnyx-sanctioned notebook from the tote bag and placed them on the table in front of her. Maryl had already doodled on the cover of hers.

"Nice bruise. Your fiancé give you that?"

Maryl touched the side of her mouth. "I—"

"Fell?" Killian suggested, looking her in the eye. "Ran into a door? Slipped? Punched yourself?" She kept her voice toneless—no judgment, no mockery. Just words.

"I thought I covered it," Maryl said quietly.

"You did, for the most part." Killian took a sip of her coffee. It was pretty good. "But you're the one who needs to be a better person, huh?"

Gripping the sides of her chair, the young woman both slouched and leaned forward. "I must seem like such a cliché to you."

"Him, maybe, but you? Nah." She curved her lips into a slight smile.

Maryl's eyes were bright and wet, but she didn't cry. "Thank you for not lecturing me, or giving me the whole 'there are people who can help' spiel."

Killian shrugged. "That stuff only works if you want it. If you get to that point, you let me know."

She was saved from having to be understanding by the arrival of other people at their table. It wasn't that Killian was without empathy; it was just that she honestly didn't get it. The last guy who hit her ended up, well, dead. Not by her hand, but she'd left him pretty broken at that point.

She didn't understand not fighting back. She'd tried to fight against her stepfather as a child, but he'd been bigger and stronger. She hadn't known how to fight him. As soon as she learned to fight, she found herself. She'd started fighting back and she hadn't stopped. She never let anyone hurt her again, at least not physically, and she never hurt anyone who hadn't deserved it.

She couldn't imagine Maryl deserving it.

The two other women at their table were named Belle and Lou. They were strangers to each other as well. Lou's wife had been put in the other group.

"It's weird," she told them, cradling her coffee cup. "I thought we'd go through this experience together."

"Maybe they think you'll share more with strangers," Maryl suggested.

Killian said nothing, just turned her head to face the front of the room, where Mina now stood, smiling and perfect like a mannequin. There was no point in telling them that cults like to divide and conquer.

"Good morning," Mina said, voice filling the room.

Everyone fell quiet. Killian had known bigger, tougher women who couldn't command respect with such ease.

"I want to welcome you all to your first official day in Incarnyx. This morning we're going to isolate the root of your inhibitions and fears and free you from them." She made it sound as though it was going to be just that simple. Killian wished her luck.

Through the door of the classroom, four women and one man entered, lining up across the back of the room like they were the last defense against a run for the exit.

Killian eyed them warily. They were well dressed, perfectly groomed.

"These are your pilots," Mina informed them. "They will help you get to where you want to go."

She couldn't help it; Killian rolled her eyes. Maryl saw it and giggled, earning them narrow glances from the other women at the table. It wasn't even ten A.M. and already she wanted to stab someone with her pencil.

There was a "pilot" for each group. Killian's table was flying with a woman named Natalie who was probably in her early thirties. If she was older than Killian it wasn't by much. She was a redhead who wore her hair in a sleek bob. She had freckles and bright blue eyes and skin that was so fair it was almost pure white. Her pantsuit was a light cinnamon color and her heels matched.

She sat down in the empty chair to Killian's right. She smelled like cloves and oranges.

"Good morning, everyone," she began with a bright smile. Perfect teeth, of course. "I'd like to start by getting to know each of you a little bit. Why don't we go around the table and you can each tell me what you hope to get out of this weekend. Let's start with you." She read the name tag. "Killian."

Of course she'd want to start with her. Killian cleared her throat. "I want to walk away from my past and build a better future for myself."

Natalie smiled again. "That's a lot to ask from one weekend, but we'll give it a go."

The others at the table chuckled. Killian forced herself to smile. If only someone would slap her or throw a kick her way. She'd know how to deal with that. This passive-aggressive ridicule chafed.

Maryl said she wanted to work on becoming a better person. Lou wanted to find her confidence, and Belle murmured that she had been painfully shy her entire life and would like to get beyond it. For each of them, Natalie had a cute little response.

"We believe that the invisible bonds that hold each of us back as humans begin in childhood," Natalie explained. "This is a safe environment for each of you. Whatever you say stays here, in this room. I want you to think about your worst childhood memory—a moment that changed everything. What was it? Belle, we'll begin with you."

"When my father walked out," she replied without hesitation. "There were six of us and Mom had to work three jobs."

"I'm so sorry that happened to you," Natalie told her. "Lou?"

"My best friend died of cancer when I was eight."

"I'm so sorry. Maryl?"

"Seeing my father beat my mother so badly she couldn't get out of bed for two days."

"Jesus," Killian whispered. She reached over and squeezed the other woman's arm.

"That must have been terrible," Natalie said in that dispassionate tone. "Killian?"

Might as well go for it. "The first time my stepfather raped me."

They all stared at her.

Natalie opened her mouth, but Killian stopped her. "I know, you're sorry. Thanks, but it was a long time ago."

"Maybe so," the redhead agreed, "but it's obvious it still hurts you very much. Do you know why?"

"Because home should be safe and he made it unsafe."

"Yes, and you've never let go of that. You've never let go of him. I bet you've spent your entire life trying to be safe again."

If there was one thing Killian hated—more than bullies— it was someone thinking they could get inside her head after knowing her five fucking minutes.

"I was in prison," she told the "pilot." "That's not exactly the place to be if you're looking for safe."

"You were in prison?" This was from Belle—wide-eyed. "For what?"

"I tried to beat a man to death," she replied honestly. "I failed."

"I imagine prison is a good place for someone who thinks

they don't deserve to be safe," Natalie interjected, regaining control of the conversation.

Killian arched a brow. "Why would I think I don't deserve to be safe?"

"Because maybe there's a part of you that thinks you did something to make him hurt you. You blame yourself for what he did."

She sucked in a breath. Under the table her fingers clenched into fists. "I blame him."

Natalie smiled that little smug smile. "Good. But there is something in your past of which you are ashamed, Killian. It's what won't allow you to have the life you want."

"Shame's a useless emotion."

"What about regrets?"

Oh, she had a fuck-ton of those. "I regret not actually killing the guy I went to jail for assaulting. Does that count?"

Natalie's smile wavered a little. "Of course! It's a...a start."

For the first time since setting foot in the place the day before, Killian smiled a genuine smile. "Yay me." At least she was going to get to have a little fun.

Focus moved on to Maryl, then Lou, then Belle. Each of the other women became visibly emotional when they talked about their childhoods and pasts. Maryl and Belle both cried and talked openly about how their experiences shaped their lives. And all three of them went on and on about shame and regret. To the point that Killian shifted uncomfortably in her seat.

She wasn't a sociopath—she knew that—but there was definitely something wrong with her. Something that made her so different from these women. It wasn't like she'd never cried or felt bad; it was just that it had been a long time since she'd cried or felt bad *for herself.* She didn't get sad. She got angry, and she was really good at putting most other emotions in a box and dealing with them later when they weren't in her way. It made her a good fighter. Made her good at her job.

Did it make her a lousy person, though? She looked at Belle, dabbing at her eyes with a tissue Natalie had conjured seemingly out of nowhere. Lou rubbed her shoulder and Maryl said something encouraging to her.

All Killian could do was sit there and watch. Awkwardly at that.

"Excuse me," she said, standing. When Natalie gave her a questioning gaze, she added, "Restroom." Then she left the room as fast as she could without breaking into a run.

She found the restroom just down the hall and ducked into a stall. The air smelled like lemons. It would undoubtedly smell like lemons and shit at some point before the day was over, but for now, Killian focused on that clean, tart smell.

She used the toilet and washed her hands. Her knuckles were scarred and probably bigger than they ought to be. The pinky on her left hand bowed outward a little from having been set wrong after being broken on a chick's jaw. On the back of her right hand there was a faded tattoo of the Om symbol. Supreme consciousness, the ultimate reality. She smiled—it was exactly the reminder she needed.

Killian knew who she was. If nothing else, prison gave a girl plenty of time to reflect and delve into her deepest self. She'd made her peace a long time ago, and damn all these frigging crying women for making her doubt herself even for a second.

After drying her hands, she headed back to the classroom, centered and ready to face Natalie and her smile. They spent another hour going around talking about painful things from their pasts and the damage done, and then Mina was back at the podium.

"Everyone, we're going to take a break now to listen to our special guest speaker. Will you all please join us in the lecture hall?"

Mina and the pilots led both classrooms into the hall where they'd been the night before. Already seated to one side were a couple dozen men and women ranging from their twenties to their fifties. Each was attractive and well dressed, Killian noticed. At least they weren't all white. That would just be creepy, like a bunch of Barbie and Ken dolls.

Mina and the pilots sat on the other side, while the students were directed to fill the middle section. Somehow, Killian ended up sitting next to Maryl in the front row. It was not a comfortable place for her to be.

Once everyone was seated and settled, Mina went up to the podium and spoke into the microphone. "Everyone, we have such a special treat for you today. This is not the sort of thing that usually happens in a first-time orientation, so I want you all to be aware just how fortunate we are to have with us today our own divine goddess, our sister, mother, and friend, Shasis." She began to applaud and both groups on the sides applauded as well. A few of them even shouted out their praise like they were at a revival.

Killian clapped—only because it would look odd if she didn't. All eyes were on the raised platform as a woman of average height walked out. She wore a white jumpsuit and heels that had to be at least four inches high. Her hair was long and sleek and obviously had come from the head of some woman in Brazil. It was a good weave—the kind that will cost you at least a grand at the salon. Her dark skin glowed under the lights and her lip gloss glistened. Shasis, aka Tara Washington, cleaned up good. She looked like a woman in control. In reality, she was just a sparkly pimp pretending she was all about empowerment rather than exploitation.

And then Shasis looked right at Killian and smiled. So, Tara remembered her, too. Good. Killian couldn't help but grin back. *Now* things were going to get interesting.

FOUR

In school the worst thing you could be was a tattletale. In prison, it wasn't any different. Everyone hated a snitch, which Killian thought was funny because everyone was also out to save their own ass. To her, while being a snitch might be a little cowardly—and playing Russian roulette with your life—there was something worse. *Much* worse.

The pimp.

Anyone who made their money selling the body/soul/pride/dreams of another person was the bottom of the barrel, especially when the person wasn't given a choice.

She couldn't remember if Tara had coerced her girls into the life, but she did know that she'd started out as a bottom bitch (or top girl, depending on whom you talked to) for some New York "gangsta" before killing him and taking over his business. That was the story, at least. She'd done the world a favor by killing her own pimp, but then she'd stepped into his shiny shoes. Maybe she'd been better to the girls. Maybe she'd given them a choice.

Maybe Killian didn't really have anger issues. Maybe she was just misunderstood.

There wasn't any *maybe*. Tara had even been pimping from prison, running her business from inside with ruthless authority. She was bad fucking news. She'd taken on a hate for Killian because Killian challenged her title as baddest bitch, because while Tara had actually killed her pimp, she'd done it with a gun. She took Killian's physicality as a personal affront.

And there she was standing on a stage, shining like a diamond coated in baby oil.

There was no denying Tara recognized her. Every inmate who went through that prison while Killian was in it knew who she was. It wasn't just that she was pseudo-famous for what she'd done to Rank Cirello, but there'd been a bounty on her head because of it. More than two dozen people had tried to kill her during the nine years she was locked up. A couple almost succeeded.

There'd been rumors that one such attempt had been orchestrated by Tara, but she'd never found out for certain—no snitching, right? But honestly, inside, a rumor was as good as truth. People had a hard time keeping their mouths shut. Knowledge was currency. Power.

Killian had no choice but to sit there and listen to the woman spout some drivel about believing in yourself and finding your inner power. She sold a good game, but whoremongers rarely changed their spots.

Shasis talked about her own humble beginnings, growing up in poverty with a single mom. Talked about being abused and shamed for most of her life. She even talked about being in "the life" and "the system," though she glossed over it like it was nothing more substantial than a wrong turn—just enough to be the victim. Then she started talking about finding her inner strength and making the decision that she didn't have to be held low anymore, that she could rise above and become something different. Something better.

"A few years ago I met this amazing man—my Magnus—and together we built Incarnyx so we could help others realize their full potential and find the personal happiness we've found. Within in a year, we'd helped thousands of people and had schools across the country. Now we have campuses in the US, Canada, and Mexico. And we are currently looking into expanding into Europe. We've helped hundreds of thousands of people, many of whom are now sharing what they learned as our pilots and navigators."

This was met with applause. Sounded like a pyramid scheme.

Killian arched a brow. "Navigators?" she whispered to Maryl.

"That's what they call the instructors—like Mina."

How had she missed that? And what was up with all the flying references?

Shasis wrapped up by assuring them all that they would leave the retreat well into their journey of self-discovery.

"There are also a few spots left in our next module that begins this week. Those spots will be made available to those of you who have made the most progress, and who show the most enthusiasm for continuing your amazing journey."

And those who can pay, Killian added silently, gritting her teeth.

They broke for lunch when Shasis left the podium. Killian debated going after her, but she had security, and while she might be able to take one or two of them, that wasn't what she was there for.

She went to her locker and got her phone, then made for her car, dialing Raven as she walked.

Her former cellie picked up almost immediately. "Killy?"

"I just saw Dirty T." It was a stupid nickname, but appropriate. "She's running a good game. Everyone around her treats her like she's Oprah giving out advice rather than cars."

Raven was silent for a moment. Killian unlocked the Impala and got in.

"Is she running girls out of the business?" Raven asked as the driver's door closed. Her voice was low, making Killian wonder if maybe she hadn't told Ilyana what Shasis really was.

"No idea, but I wouldn't be surprised. And no, I don't know if either of the sisters is involved. I haven't seen Lyria yet today, and I haven't seen Dylan at all."

"This is not going to be good for Ilyana if one or both of her girls is involved in a prostitution ring."

"It's trafficking when they're not given a choice, and yeah, fucking think of their mother right now instead of them, Rave. That's awesome."

"Hey, she told those girls she thought the group was bad news. They paid their dues with her fucking credit card, and it's her name the press is going to rag on."

"You're right, that's so much worse than being raped a couple times a night." Killian scowled. "You're tripping."

"Bottom line's still the same, you got to get what Magnus has on them and get those girls out of there."

Right, Magnus. "Could be that she's his top."

"Doesn't matter. You're not there to take them down, Killy. The feds are going to do that."

Killian didn't respond. She knew the job. Didn't mean she liked it. She looked out the window at people standing outside smoking. Lunch was going to be served in half an hour, but meanwhile everyone was getting their fix—either nicotine or caffeine or their phones. Her gaze narrowed when a familiar truck pulled into the parking lot. "Hey, can you do me a favor?"

"What?" Raven's tone was wary.

"Run a check on these plates." She rhymed off the numbers. "New York State. I wanna know everything you can find out about the asshole driving 'em."

"Has this got to do with Dylan and Lyria?"

"It might," she lied, easily, guiltlessly. Just because Raven was paying her didn't mean she was calling the shots. "Oh, and check out this security company—Secural Solutions. They did a drive-by of the compound when I was there last night. Send me everything you find via the secure server." One of the first things she'd been given upon joining the Initiative was a login for the server, followed by a flash drive that generated IPs and a bunch of other stuff she only partially understood.

"I wouldn't send it any other way." And then: "So how did Tara look?"

"What?"

"How did she look? Good?"

Killian laughed. "You are not seriously asking me that."

"Get your head out of your pants. I asked because there could be a chance this Magnus is pimping her, too."

"I doubt it. She talked about them starting Incarnyx together. More than likely they're partners in every sense of the word. They probably do all the breaking in together, too. If I remember correctly, Tara didn't care if it was sausage or taco, she just liked to eat."

Raven made a scoffing sound, but Killian could hear the chuckle in it. "You can be so crude, you know that?"

"You used to like it." Shit. Shouldn't have said that. She leaned her head back against the seat and closed her eyes.

"I did," Raven replied softly. Then: "You going to be okay up there, or do you want me to send backup?"

Killian could hug her for not making it more awkward. "Nah, I'm good. I've got someone I can call if I think I need it."

"Dash." There was something in her tone, but Killian didn't bother trying to analyze it. She didn't care what Raven thought of her boyfriend.

"Actually, I was thinking Story. This crowd's mostly women. Not sure what that says about us as a gender."

"It says we spend a lot of time being put down and trying to pull ourselves back up."

"And then other women like Shasis take advantage of it," she remarked absently as she watched Maryl's man get out of the truck. He was a built fucker, but that just meant he'd fall all the harder when she took him down.

"Dirty T's not a woman. She's a fucking shark."

"True." She cracked her neck. "Once I get those girls home, she's fair game, right?"

"I don't care what you do to her once Ilyana's daughters are safe. She's all yours. Just don't get yourself picked up by the FBI."

"I'm not stupid, Rave."

"No, just impulsive. Sometimes there's not much of a difference. Okay, I gotta go. I'll email you later. Be careful, Killy."

"I will." She hung up and checked for messages. There was a text from Dash asking how everything was going—like any other concerned or caring boyfriend, but really he just wanted to make sure she was still conscious and alive. In their line of work—especially hers—it was a very real concern. She sent him a quick reply so he wouldn't worry and promised to call later. He'd know something had happened if she didn't check in again by midnight and would come looking for her.

Nothing from Megan or Shannon, but then she hadn't expected to hear from them. Hopefully her not being around for the next few days would allow the two of them to work out their drama and tighten up their relationship again. The two of them—and little Willow—were all the blood she had who really mattered, and she really didn't want to be a point of contention between them.

Killian sighed. Sitting in her car at least made her feel a little more grounded again. Seeing Tara had been a shock, but she was almost over it now. She got out of the car and locked it again before heading back toward the main building.

Maryl's fiancé stood by his truck, leaning his back against the driver's door, long legs stretched out in front of him.

"You waiting for Maryl?" she asked.

He lifted his chin, like her question offended him. "Yeah."

Killian stopped in front of him, hands in her pockets. "That bruise on her face is pretty nasty. What did she walk into again? Your fist?"

He straightened, face flushing. He was a tall son of a bitch. "Are you insinuating I hit her?"

"Pretty much, yeah." She shrugged. "You did, didn't you?"

"What are you, a fucking cop?"

She tilted her head. "Do I look like a cop to you, moron? Look, just don't hit her again, okay? Go join a gym or something."

"How 'bout you just mind your fucking business?"

"How 'bout if you hit her again, I break your face?" Killian countered with a grin. "You have a good day, asshat." She left him standing there as she crossed the driveway. She met Maryl on the way out.

"He's waiting for you."

"Yeah." Maryl adjusted her purse strap on her shoulder. "He just wants to see how the morning went."

Killian shook her head. "Right. Hey, you don't have to put up with that shit from him."

The other woman glanced at the man waiting for her, then shook her head. "You're nice, but what can you do about it?"

Killian smiled. "So many painful things." Then she patted Maryl on the shoulder and went inside.

The rest of the day was tedious to say the least. If one more woman in the class dissolved into tears, Killian was going to flip a table. Hey, she was all for epiphanies, but witnessing so freaking many got a little...irritating.

"I think you might have a dissociative disorder," Lou said to her after Killian told them about her former boyfriend, Jason, bleeding to death in her arms after being shot. She recounted the story with eyes—and tone—dry as dust.

Killian shrugged. "It was a long time ago. I guess I did all my crying then." Besides, crying was only useful if it manipulated someone into doing what you wanted, or cleansed your soul. She didn't need either at the moment, or the headache that often came with it.

"When was the last time you cried?" the older woman pushed. "Everyone else in this room has cried at least once today, but you've been stoic as a deaf judge."

Caught between a frown and a smile, Killian shook her head. "I love your analogies, Lou. Seriously, you ought to write them down."

"Stop deflecting," Belle jumped in. "You said shame's useless, so if you're not ashamed to answer, what is it?"

"Jesus, you're confrontational," Killian responded. "Okay, I cried a week ago." It was a lie, of course, but she wasn't going to tell them about Shannon—no fucking way.

"What happened?" That was from Maryl, who still had a balled-up tissue in her fist.

Killian sighed. "I watched *Coco* with my youngest niece and wept like an idiot." Dash had teased her for it. She hadn't really cared. The tears were good. The movie was good. And they hadn't made her feel vulnerable because neither Dash nor Willow was any sort of threat.

Maryl chuckled. "Oh, I cried at that, too!"

"Mm," Lou agreed. "*Up* was even worse for me."

"Oh, I won't watch it," Belle informed them. "Uh-uh."

Lou asked Belle about another family movie and the two of them launched into a discussion. They were supposed to be talking about significant relationships they'd had in the past, but Killian didn't mind the diversion.

"Hey," Maryl said, leaning closer, voice low. "Did you say something to Joe in the parking lot earlier?"

"Joe?"

The younger woman arched a brow. Playing innocent had never been Killian's forte. "My fiancé?"

"I said hi to him, why?" Lying, on the other hand...

"He just asked who you were."

"Well, you can tell him all about my sordid past if you like. Then we can compare dick size."

Maryl laughed. "You're so strange. Hey, you want to have dinner tonight?"

Her reply was fast and resolute. "Not with Joe, I don't."

"He'll be at his mother's. I mean with me." She smiled hesitantly. "Do you like wings?"

"I'm breathing, aren't I?"

"There's a great place not far from here. You game?"

She wasn't getting paid to socialize, but she had to eat, regardless, so why not? "Sure. Thanks."

Maryl gave Killian her cell number and the name of the restaurant. "Meet me there at seven."

From there they went back to group work. Natalie joined them again for more tear-inducing memory reliving. By the end of the day Killian had a headache from clenching her jaw against all the emotion bombarding her. It really started to annoy her, all the crying and vulnerability. Sometimes "sharing" was just another term for "pissing contest," and tragedy wasn't a competition as far as she was concerned.

She wanted to hit something.

She'd half expected Shasis—Dirty T—to show up at any moment, but nothing happened. Was it possible the pimp hadn't recognized her after all? That was almost offensive. Killian prided herself on her notoriety in prison. *Everyone* had known who she was.

No, Shasis would know who she was. You never forgot a bounty you tried to collect.

And where the hell was Lyria? They were supposed to talk, but the girl hadn't shown her face all day. Still no sign of Dylan, either. This whole thing was turning into a long weekend from hell that wasn't going to yield anything more than TMJ and having to buy some Excedrin.

They finished the day with a video of the man himself— Magnus. He sat on the beach, the breeze ruffling his sun-kissed hair. His eyes were so blue, Killian thought they had to be digitally altered—likewise his startlingly white teeth. He spoke with a low, Southern drawl, the origin of which she couldn't place.

Half the women in the room sighed at the sight of him. Yeah, he was good-looking, but she'd never really been attracted to that model-perfect aesthetic. Dash was the exception to that rule, and only because he didn't wear it like a badge of entitlement.

"I just want to welcome you all the Incarnyx family," Magnus crooned, grinning in 4K. "Shasis and I are so very honored that you've chosen to take your journey with us. This module you've begun is just the beginning of your personal transformation. The first stop on a road trip of awakening, if you will." His slightly self-deprecating tone kept the remark from being too corny and made it strangely endearing as well.

He was good, Killian realized. Compelling, even. Every set of eyes in the room was glued to that screen. Most of the women even smiled when he did. Laughed on cue. Maryl was one of the few who didn't, but even she looked borderline enraptured.

Unease slithered down Killian's spine, like a slug leaving a trail of cold slime. Charisma was a powerful thing when used for the right reasons. It was even more powerful when used as a weapon. It made for a successful pimp. A powerful CEO. A ruthless dictator. Charles Manson had been a short, scrawny ex-con with barely any education and a full screw loose. But he'd had charisma. He knew how to get inside someone's head. That's what made him dangerous. He didn't have to lift a finger when he could talk someone else into doing it for him—and making them *want* to do it.

Killian didn't like it. She didn't trust it. But more important, she was afraid to fall for it.

After class, she returned to the hotel to freshen up and clean off the mental scum Incarnyx left on her brain. She also wanted to unwind and check her email before meeting Maryl. Sitting at the desk with a beer she'd brought with her, Killian logged in to the Initiative VPN on her laptop. Eight months ago she'd thought virtual private networks were only good for hiding porn or watching Netflix in other countries; now she wondered what kind of crazy things people used them to hide.

She logged in to the secure email server and found a message waiting for her from Raven. In it were two zip files. One was titled "Dirty T" and the other was simply called "Private."

Killian opened the "Dirty T" one first. It was mostly a history of arrests and incarceration that started when Tara/Shasis was still a teenager and ended just a couple of years ago. Mug shots and newspaper articles about her getting arrested for trafficking minors were included. She managed not to do too much time by turning the tables on the men who worked with her, throwing them under the bus and testifying against them for lighter sentences.

All that double-crossing explained why she disappeared, or decided to stop being herself. From what Killian could glean from the information Raven had included about the identity of Shasis, Tara had adopted it shortly after her last stint inside.

It was no wonder it hadn't come up on the first investigation. On paper, Shasis (born Naomi Johnson) had lived a quiet life in middle-class Connecticut. She'd done well in school and college. She had a degree in psychology. It was an entire fabrication, of course. The real Naomi Johnson had died as a kid, but with some really good professional aid, Shasis had been turned into a real person, probably with the help of her criminal connections who were able to craft a new identity just as believable as the feds'. You'd only see the holes if you dug deep, and no one really dug that deep when doing a background check. She had a believable history, no criminal record, and college transcripts to back it all up. All of it had been pieced together from various real people and tied together with a neat little bow. On paper, Naomi "Shasis" Johnson wasn't only a real person, but a good one.

As for the psych degree, well, Killian supposed someone could fake that if they read enough textbooks and had a decent understanding of people. And really, any good pimp understood their victims and knew how to manipulate them.

There was background on Magnus as well. Aka Deacon Ford, he'd been born in Tennessee and moved to New York in his late teens to study acting, but eventually dropped out. No criminal record, but he had a long list of failed businesses, many of which were pyramid schemes. He also seemed to have an overly inflated ego. He liked to brag about his own intelligence in interviews and was borderline obsessive about his appearance. His vanity would be the key to getting to him.

Oh, this was interesting. He'd been treated for drug and sex addiction. Was that how he and Shasis had gotten together? If she'd been making money on her back, he could have been a client. Or she could have been providing him girls. Maybe they'd decided to pool their resources and experience.

"A match made in bodily fluids and ego," Killian remarked

out loud. Then she saw a photograph that made her raise a brow. A photo of Magnus with a South American businessman whom some people suspected of being a cartel leader. Apparently Rafael Abelino Vargas was a big fan of self-actualization. Right.

She clicked on the second file. There wasn't much in there— a few photographs and a couple of text transcripts. It was enough, of course. One of the photos was of Dylan Woodward having sex doggy style and looking really into it. The guy's face was turned, but she assumed it was Magnus, even though there wasn't any proof to back that up. Nothing saying when the photo was taken, either, or by whom. Had it been sent to Ilyana as a warning or demand for payment? She asked that very question in her email to Raven.

There was a brief exchange between a blocked number and Ilyana. Obviously the message had originated with Magnus, Shasis, or an employee of Incarnyx. They went back and forth with vague threats, but it ended with the photos of the girls and a note that said, *Your girls have found such enlightenment with us. It would be a shame if you stopped funding that, don't you think?*

This was followed by another exchange between Lyria and her mother. The girl told Ilyana she wanted to come home but couldn't because she didn't want to leave her sister.

And the third exchange looked to be a photo of a phone screen. It was someone named "Bae" and Dylan texting one another. Maybe Lyria had taken the photo? Or Ilyana.

BAE: I'm obsessed with your sweet pussy. I can't wait to see you again and bury my cock inside you.

DYLAN: You can bury it wherever you want. My body is yours to devour, my lord, my master. ♥☺

There was more sex talk, but Killian just skimmed that. The takeaway from the conversation was obviously the whole "lord and master" fuckery.

Some women were attracted to overly alpha guys, just like some guys seemed drawn to crazy women. Killian understood it to an extent. She liked guys who she knew could hold their own in a fight, but she wanted an equal, not someone to control her. It was one of the things she loved most about Dash—that he knew she could look after herself and make her own decisions. He didn't always agree with those decisions, but when she fucked up he didn't lecture her—much—and tried to help her figure out how to fix things. She did the same for him. They were partners.

Maybe it was because they'd started out as friends when they were young. He'd been her best friend for a long time. Regardless, she would never, ever call him her master. And he'd be grossed out if she did.

Killian checked her watch. She'd spent more time in front of the computer than she'd planned. Her ass was starting to hurt and she only had half an hour before she needed to meet Maryl.

Now, there was a situation. How could she stay with a man who hit her? She couldn't actually believe he loved her, could she? There had been many—*many*—times when Killian enjoyed hitting people. So many times. Never once had she hit someone she loved. Never. And the people she hit always deserved it. And they were capable of defending themselves.

How was Maryl supposed to defend herself against such a big guy? Unless she'd been trained to fight like Killian, she wouldn't stand a chance. Even with that kind of training it would be hard. Lots of bigger guys had smacked her around during the course of her life. Killian had bested a few of them, but it was only because she'd found a weapon or a weak point. If you were smaller than your opponent, then you had to be faster and dirtier and more determined to survive.

Maryl didn't strike her as a dirty fighter. Didn't strike her as a fighter at all, which was probably why a douche like Joe had picked her.

Killian closed the laptop and got up. As she grabbed her belongings, she noticed she had voice mail on her phone. She dialed in. It was from Donna. Shit, now what?

"Killian? It's Donna. Look...I don't know what's going on, but now my boss is asking about your file. She wants to see it, which means the parole board has been talking to her as well. I know you told me you haven't done anything, but I don't think I need to tell you I'm concerned." There was an audible sigh. "Are you certain you don't have any idea what this might be about? I don't want you going back to prison any more than you do, and having your parole revoked won't look good for me, either. I'm changing our appointment to Monday so we can get on this ASAP. Okay, that's it. Bye."

Killian took the phone from her ear and stared at it. "Fuck," she muttered. This was a pain in the ass she didn't need.

The second voice mail was from Shannon. "Where are you? Your sister is being *such* a bitch right now. I need you to talk to her, or I swear I'm going to lose my shit. Everyone is going to the beach for Memorial Day and she says I can't go. I'm fucking going, whether she likes it or not."

Sighing, Killian deleted the message and put the phone in her bag. On second thought, maybe going back to prison would be a good thing. At least then she'd get some fucking peace and quiet.

"You okay?" Maryl asked when Killian sat down at the table a little while later. "You look stressed."

"I'm good." She wasn't going to think about parole right now. She could handle it if it happened. She'd make it through. It would only be for a few months and then she'd be released again—provided they didn't add time for a violation.

Fuck. Fuck. Fuck.

She'd known this was a possibility when she took the job, but Maxine, her boss, had assured her the Initiative would be there for her if anything like this happened. She was going to have to tell Maxine about this, as much as she didn't want to. She should have sent her a text before even crossing the state line. She really didn't want to be a liability, especially if Maxine decided she wasn't worth the cost.

Maryl slid a laminated menu in front of her. "You want a drink?"

"Yeah." Killian glanced up at the waitress who had suddenly appeared. "Rum and diet, please. A double."

The woman nodded and disappeared.

Maryl frowned. "Seriously, what's up?"

"Personal stuff. Nothing I want to talk about."

"I told you about Joe."

"It's just parole bullshit." She couldn't believe she said that much. "Just drop it, okay? I don't want to think or talk about it right now."

"Okay, sure. Sorry."

"It's fine." She looked at the other woman. "You look different."

"Yeah, I put on a little more makeup." She smiled. "I wanted to look pretty for you."

Killian grinned. "Right. Does Joe know you're out?"

"No."

"Isn't that dangerous? He'll wonder where you were, won't he?"

"He will, and I'll tell him the truth. He just won't know if it's the truth. He might get mad, but usually he gets worried I'm going to leave him and he's extra nice for a while."

Shaking her head, Killian opened the menu. "That's fucked-up, girl. No offense."

"None taken. I know it is. I've never told anyone that before."

"Not even Natalie?" Mock horror.

Maryl chuckled. "God, she's so over the top. I like Belle, though."

"She's blunt, I'll give her that."

"Do you really think shame's a useless emotion?"

"Yup." She found a seasoning of wings she wanted to try and closed the menu. "There's no value to it. That doesn't mean I don't think people should feel it. Some people deserve it, but for most of it, there's just no point."

"You're an interesting person, Killian Delaney."

"That's what the prison psychologist said, too."

"How long were you in?"

"Nine years."

Maryl's eyes widened. "Jesus."

Killian shifted in her seat. "Yeah, well, the court frowns upon trying to beat a guy to death, you know. They take it seriously."

"Yeah, but he was a bad guy, right?"

Her drink appeared in front of her. "Thanks," she said to the waitress. "Funny thing, it turns out bad people have rights, too."

"Sorry. I don't mean to be nosy."

Killian shrugged and took a sip of her drink. It was so strong and so exactly what she needed to take the edge off. "Not like it's a big secret. In some circles I'm positively famous."

Maryl lifted her beer. "The woman who took down Rank Cirello."

She went still. People laughed and talked around them, but Killian's attention was focused solely on the woman across from her. "You looked me up?"

Looking sheepish, Maryl nodded. "Yeah. Like I said, nosy."

How should she take that? Killian didn't spend a lot of time with people who were mostly good. She spent a lot of time with people whose view of the world was decidedly gray. Maryl wasn't one of those people.

"And you invited me to dinner anyway." Her tone was light, but with an edge. "I'm beginning to think maybe you're one of those people who are drawn to danger or something—first the fiancé and now me."

"I could be." There wasn't any offense in her tone. "Or maybe

I just like you despite your sordid past." She said this with dramatic flair.

And Killian liked her despite the fact that she made herself a victim. That wasn't fair of her, she knew it, but she still thought it.

The waitress returned and they ordered their food.

"So, why are you really in this workshop?" Maryl asked.

"What do you mean?"

"You tell them it's because you want to overcome your past, but you don't seem to be all that messed up from it."

Killian laughed. The rum jostled warmly in her empty stomach. "I think your idea of messed up might be a little skewed."

Maryl laughed, too. "Yeah, I guess. But I don't get it. I don't see anything wrong with you."

It was nice of her to say, and so very, very fucked-up. "That boyfriend who bled out in my arms? I spent nine years in prison for avenging his death only to find out that I was his side piece. He had another woman—kids, too. If I don't seem like a mess to you, it's because I know just how much of a mess I really am." It was probably the most honest and insightful thing she'd ever admitted to anyone other than Dash.

And she'd admitted it to a person who was practically a stranger.

Holy hell, was this self-help crap actually getting to her?

Maryl covered one of Killian's hands with her own. "Oh, honey. I'm so sorry."

Killian couldn't bring herself to tell her the rest of the story—it was just too much. Too revealing.

"I had an abortion when I was sixteen," Maryl confided.

"I'd been assaulted by a friend of my brother's. Couldn't bring myself to actually have it."

"Why would you? Did anything happen to the guy?"

Maryl shot her an amused glance. "You mean, did someone beat the snot out of him because of it? No. Nobody but my mother ever knew the truth."

"Your mother should have done something."

"My mother wasn't exactly a strong woman. Not like yours."

Right, she'd told that story, too—about her stepfather. She'd revealed more about herself over these past couple of days than she liked to admit. Not that it mattered. Really, what did any of these people care about her or her life? None of them were there to make anyone else feel better, or to get invested. They were all there trying to fix themselves.

"What do you hope to get out of this weekend?" she asked Maryl.

The other woman sighed, running her finger along her glass of beer. "I want to get the balls to stand up for myself. I want to be strong."

"You don't need a class for that. You just need to leave."

"I did that once. He found me."

"So, you go to a shelter. They can hide you."

"I'm not worried about me. I'm worried what he'll do to the people I love."

"Sounds like you're being a martyr to me."

Maryl pointed a finger at her, clicking her tongue against her teeth. "Bingo. You get the gold star. I don't want to be a martyr. I just want . . . I just want to not be afraid."

Their food came, and so conversation turned lighter as they ate. They talked about their families. Killian forgot all about Donna's voice mail for a while, packing it into the box of things to be dealt with as they happened.

An hour later they left the restaurant. It was dark out, a cool breeze drifting through the night. As they walked through the parking lot, a familiar voice shouted, "Maryl!"

"Oh shit," the other woman whispered.

It was Joe, coming at them like a Scooby-Doo villain— shoulders up, arms slightly akimbo. He even scowled.

Killian instinctively stepped closer to Maryl, putting herself between the two of them. "Take it down a notch, Joe," she advised, voice low. "You're in a public place."

"Get the fuck away from my wife," he snarled.

She didn't correct him. She didn't move, either. "What are you so mad about, buddy? We were just having dinner."

"You expect me to believe that when she's painted up like a cheap whore?"

He gave Killian a hard shove—hard enough that she fell against the side of a nearby Volvo. Then he turned his rage on Maryl.

The slap rang through the parking lot. Maryl flew back into a Volkswagen. Her head bounced off the window and she slid to the pavement.

Joe moved in.

He never saw Killian coming. One minute she was on the Volvo and the next she was on him—sort of. She kicked the back of his knee, buckling it; then as he went down she kicked him as hard as she could in the taint and balls.

He groaned, listing to the side, and that was when she delivered a solid punch to the side of his head. He crumpled to the pavement like a rag doll. Then, just for the sheer fun of it, she kicked him.

Maryl stared at her from where she sat on the ground. Her mouth was bleeding.

Killian walked over and offered her a hand up. "Let's go," she said. "You're staying with me tonight."

FIVE

They left Maryl's car in the parking lot after getting what she needed out of it. Then Killian drove to the nearest Walmart so the other woman could pick up a toothbrush, underwear, and some clothes. Killian bought a baseball bat and a bag of jerky.

"I can't believe you did that," Maryl said to her at the self-checkout.

Killian scanned their items. "I don't like bullies."

"You sure you don't mind me staying with you?"

"I'm only here 'til the end of the retreat." And then what? She was already two days in and no closer to getting information or the girls. Instead, she'd picked up a battered woman and was in shit with her parole officer. What she ought to do is head back to Connecticut and let the FBI clean up Ilyana's mess—save her kids. But she wouldn't—couldn't—just walk away and she knew it.

"I'll take you to a shelter after that, if you want, before I head back."

Maryl's gaze weighed heavy on her skin. "Why are you doing this? You don't even know me."

Killian frowned. "Why should that matter? I wouldn't stand there and let some asshole beat on a woman, or anybody for that matter."

"You're a good person."

She snorted. "Sure. The best." She swiped her card through the machine.

At the hotel, Killian asked the clerk at the desk for a second room.

"Put it on my card," she told him.

"No," Maryl interrupted. "You don't need to do that. I have a credit card."

"That the douchebag can check?" Killian arched a brow. "He doesn't know my name, does he?"

Maryl shook her head. "Not your last name, no."

"Good. Then he can't find me and he can't find you." She met the curious gaze of the clerk. "You didn't hear any of this, yeah?"

He nodded. "Deaf as a doornail." He ran her card and gave them keys. The room was just two doors down from her own. Convenient.

"Come on," she said to Maryl. "Let's get you settled."

They rode the elevator up to their floor. Killian walked Maryl to her door, pointing out her own room along the way. "If you need anything, I'm right there."

"Thanks again for helping me. I've never..." Maryl cocked her head to one side. "I've never met anyone quite like you. Should I ask why you have a baseball bat?"

Killian smiled. "It's in case I need to whack some balls."

"Oh." Maryl laughed. "Oh, that's horrible! I feel guilty for laughing."

"Don't. He didn't feel guilty for knocking you into a car earlier. And I won't feel guilty if I need this." She met her gaze. "If he finds you, you call the cops, then me."

She nodded, suddenly serious. "I will." And then, before Killian could realize what she was about, Maryl threw her arms around her and hugged her hard, the Walmart bags in her hand bouncing against Killian's back.

Killian hesitated. Hugs were weird for her, because she both loved and hated the physical connection forced upon her. She never knew if she wanted to hold on or shove the person away, so she just stayed perfectly still and gave them a countdown. The only person who could hold her for any length of time was Dash.

"I'll take you to pick up your car in the morning," Killian promised, pulling away. "Do you have any apps on your phone he could use to find you?"

Maryl shook her head. "No. He'd probably install one if he could." She slipped the key card into the lock. "Thanks again, Killian. I mean it."

She lifted the bat over her shoulder. "No problem. Have a good night."

"Good night."

In her own room, Killian set the bat just inside the entryway closet. Then she flicked all the locks into place and kicked off her boots. She called Dash but it went to voice mail, so she left him a message saying she would talk to him the next day and put her phone on silent. She turned the TV on to one of those shows about aliens in history, set the alarm to wake her up in several hours, and stretched out on the bed.

Prison had given her few gifts, but the ability to fall asleep anywhere was one of them. Her brain had also seemed to work out being able to tell the difference between ordinary noises and dangerous ones. So she could sleep through someone dropping a dish, but the turning of a doorknob woke her up.

As the show's narrator talked about the Egyptians and their relationship with beings from outer space, Killian closed her eyes and was asleep before the commercial break.

The alarm buzzed softly near her head at one A.M. She turned it off and sat up with a yawn. Time to get to work.

She put her hair up in a messy bun and pulled on her boots. Then she used the bathroom and brushed her teeth. She wiped away the mascara that had smudged beneath her eyes as well. Then she grabbed her keys, phone, and room key and quietly exited to the corridor.

She glanced at Maryl's door. The DO NOT DISTURB sign was out. Would the woman stay? Or would she run back to her abuser before morning? She'd find out in a few hours, she supposed. Though if she skipped out, she was paying Killian back for the room.

When she reached the Impala, she opened the trunk, then the secret compartment Dash had installed in the bottom of it. From there she removed her favorite knife and a set of brass knuckles. The knife went into the sheath in her right boot and the knuckles went into her jacket pocket. As usual, she was dressed entirely in black so she could sneak about with relative stealth.

This time when she drove to Magnus and Shasis's neighborhood, she parked in a different location, just in case her car had been noticed last time. Paranoia was a virtue in her line of work.

The air was fresh and damp and smelled of cut grass. Somewhere nearby, the gentle swishing of a sprinkler cut through the silence as it watered an already lush lawn.

Killian kept to the shadows as much as possible. There were probably security cameras around, but she kept her hood up so they couldn't discern her face. Most of them wouldn't be detailed enough to worry about anyway, but again, it didn't hurt to be paranoid.

A row of trees—along with the iron fence—separated the disciple house from the next sweeping property. These were big old trees, with thick limbs and wide trunks. Lower branches had been removed—presumably to render them less climbable—but Killian managed to make it to the one above her head with a little agility and upper-body strength.

She had always been good at climbing, which she believed took a lot of the same skills as grappling. Gripping one of the heavy branches, she pulled herself farther up into the embrace of the tree, until she was higher than the fence. Easing forward, she moved farther along the branch until she was over the fence; then she lowered herself as far as she could and dropped the rest of the way to the grass below.

Her left ankle protested when she hit the ground but, thankfully, didn't give out. The last thing she needed was an injury. It twinged when she began to move again but didn't kick up too much of a fuss.

Solar lights cast a soft glow along the perimeter of the house, illuminating her path for her. The house itself was quiet and dark, all the good little disciples in bed, presumably. She kept an eye out for sensors and cameras and tried to stick to the shadows as much as possible. When she reached the gate between the two houses, she found it unlocked. It didn't even creak when she swung it open.

This side of the main house was more shadowed than the rest of it. Like the disciple house, it was completely dark. The only light was around the pool out back. The water shimmered and rippled in the soft glow. A beach ball bobbed on the serene surface.

Silently, Killian made her way toward the patio. The house probably had a state-of-the-art security system, with sensors at every door and window. Maybe even motion detectors. This was going to work only if she found an open window or balcony door, which, on such a beautiful night, had good odds. Still, she'd be lucky if she made it out of there without security showing up.

The sliding door leading out to the pool was open. Even the screen was slightly ajar. Luck was on her side—that or she was about to walk right into a trap. Whatever, she'd deal with it when it happened.

As she reached for the door handle, something shifted in the air behind her. She felt the disturbance like a whisper on her skin rather than a sight or sound. *Shit.*

Slowly, she turned, her hand in her pocket, slipping into the brass knuckles.

There, on a lounger, barely distinguishable from the shadows around her in her black kimono, was Shasis. She rose to her feet with a dancer's grace and moved toward Killian. It wasn't until she was just a few feet away that Killian could see she had a glass of wine in either hand.

Shasis smiled, white teeth glinting. "I was wondering when the sweet hell you were going to show up."

Killian didn't drink the wine. Even she didn't take chances with sexual predators.

She did, however, join Shasis by the pool, sitting in one of the other lounge chairs, though on the edge so she could get up quickly, if necessary.

"How did you know I'd show up?" she asked.

The other woman leaned back against the chair, turning slightly on her hip to face Killian. It was like watching a cat stretch in the sun. "Soon as I saw you in the audience I knew who you were, and I knew you knew me. If the situation were reversed I'd be on your doorstep right now. Figured you might come round the back." She smiled.

Was that an insult or a compliment? Regardless, she'd repay either by not wasting anyone's time with niceties. "You running girls out of this setup of yours, T?"

She took a sip from her glass, regarding Killian over the rim. "First of all, I ain't—" She closed her eyes for a second, as though composing herself. "I'm not T anymore. I legally changed my name to Shasis a while ago."

"Changing the leopard's name doesn't change its spots."

Shasis laughed. "Come on, now. You know if you don't adapt you die. What about you? Still running around beating people senseless whenever you feel like it?"

Killian shrugged. "When the need arises, yeah. So, what? You're doing this so you can have an all-you-can-eat buffet of women who think you're their savior?"

The other woman inclined her head. "If I wanted a buffet, I could have stayed where I was. This isn't about sex. It's about the respectability. The money. Do you know how much people will pay to feel better about themselves?"

Killian gave her a dubious look. "Stroking egos instead of pussy?"

"Something like that." She smiled coyly. "I just give them what they want, same as always. I sell, they buy, and no one has to get screwed."

"When did you get a psych degree?"

"I took an online course, and I've read the books. A lot of the books, I should say. The big ones. You know, all those ones about loving yourself, eating, praying, and daring." She smiled. "My favorites are the ones about not giving a fuck."

Killian set her untasted wine on the small stone-topped table between them. "So basically you charge six grand to regurgitate, what? Thirty-two dollars' worth of plagiarized material?"

Laughing, Shasis crossed her incredibly long, shapely legs. "It's not that simple. I don't just regurgitate what I've learned; I apply it. It's a legit business. I take what I've learned and offer it up to others in a package they find completely accessible."

"You're telling me that all you're running here is a con? Because I heard that you're running some kind of sex cult."

An elegant hand with astoundingly curved, sharp nails waved lazily between them. "That's not me; that's the stupid-ass white boy I made the mistake of getting myself hooked up with." She grimaced, as though her own choice of words left a bad taste in her mouth.

Killian absently cracked her knuckles. "He's the pimp and you're back to being bottom bitch, huh?"

Her mockery was met with a hard look. "No. When I first came up with this idea I realized that people will listen a lot more to a good-looking white man than they will a mixed-race woman—regardless of how fine she might be. Magnus and I are partners."

Killian nodded. It was sad but true. "So he started off your front man?"

"Exactly. At first he was in it just for the money, but then a bunch of pretty little things started showing up and he let his other head start thinking for him, like they all do, eventually. You know how men are."

"Yeah, I know." She agreed, even though she couldn't imagine Dash ever being ruled by his dick rather than reason.

Shasis crossed her toned legs. "Okay, so that's my story. What's yours?"

"Well, I thought I was taking a self-help course."

"Liar." Dark eyes narrowed. "You had access to the same library I did. Why are you really here?"

She could tell the truth, but since she was pretty sure Shasis was lying to her, it would be stupid to tip her hand. "I saw you in the brochure. I wanted to see what you'd gotten yourself into—and see if I can get in on it."

At that moment, a female moan cut through the night. Killian glanced up at the windows of the house. "Friend of yours?"

"Magnus has company," Shasis replied with a roll of her eyes. "I swear to God the man's got a magic wand between his legs. Some of these women sign up for every program just to get with him. And when he's done with them, they just follow along behind him like little puppies begging for scraps. I tell him what to say, and he sells it—100 percent."

Killian was beginning to understand. "You're not selling girls; you're selling *him*."

She laughed. "I suppose so—just don't tell him that. He thinks he's the magic behind all of this, and as long as he does, I have the life I've always dreamed of living. Do you know what that's like?"

"Not really," Killian admitted. "But I understand to a point." Had that been what Maxine offered her—to an extent—when she invited her to join the Initiative? "So, you've honestly gone legit?"

"I have, yeah."

But if it was all done willingly, why was Lyria afraid to leave? Why did Shasis have blackmail material on her disciples? Or was it Magnus who kept the incriminating evidence? It didn't seem that he was smart enough to think of something like that. Shasis, on the other hand, was all about the money.

Regardless, Killian couldn't ask, because it wasn't something she should know about. And it didn't really matter because her job was to get the girls and get the blackmail material, and that was it. The feds would take care of the rest.

"It's a sweet setup," she remarked, glancing around. "It pay for all this?"

"It's a rental—leased by the company, of course. We have satellite offices in LA, Toronto, Vancouver, Mexico, and we're about to start spreading into Europe."

She was still preying on people's weaknesses, except now she was making her victims pay for the privilege. Still, what was she doing that other self-help gurus hadn't done? It was Magnus who had crossed the line. No doubt Shasis had made sure of that as well. If anyone was going to take a fall, it wasn't going to be her.

"I've even started a section that helps women unleash their sexuality."

There it was. She should have known. Once a pimp, always a pimp. "How's that working for you?"

"The first module was last week. It was all about finding your own power. The sex stuff is just part of it. I had twenty women signed up at ten thousand a head."

"You're fucking kidding me." There was no hiding her shock.

More laughter—it echoed off the water. "I am not. It was mostly a bunch of society ladies from Connecticut. Their Viagra-chewing husbands have their sugar babies and now the women want their turn."

"You ever have any trouble?"

"Sometimes. Nothing I haven't been able to handle so far. We've had a few people start some crazy rumors, and one time a husband showed up looking for his wife. Thankfully, the police showed up. Never thought I'd be happy to see the po-po." She smiled. "Isn't that a ridiculous word, *po-po*?"

Killian smiled. "Maybe you could use a little extra security."

Shasis's gaze narrowed. "Why should I trust you?"

"What point would there be in lying? You know how hard it is on the outside for women like us. People are afraid of women who do things men usually do. A man almost beats someone to death in revenge and it's fucking romantic. A woman does it and it's psycho."

"I hear you. I had a judge once tell me that I was despicable for selling my own gender. Gave the brother before me—who'd messed up one of his girls—a lighter sentence than he gave me, just because I was a woman."

"You were right to change your name," Killian praised her. "Society's harder on female ex-cons. Only job I could get was tending bar, and the boss thought that gave him the right to put his hands on me." That was a lie. Her boss at the club had been fairly respectful of her—and maybe a little afraid.

The other woman studied her. "You'd probably be good at this. I heard about your assertion that shame is... what did you call it? A 'useless emotion'?"

Killian inclined her head. "Who's got time for shame? I'm just trying to survive."

"Amen." Shasis held out her glass, so Killian clinked her own against it. "Usually we promote from within the program, but your skill set makes you hard to beat. Not many of our employees know how to take someone down."

"So," Killian pressed. "What do you think?"

Shasis thought and drank for a moment. "Tell you what—you come to the workshop this week, and if it goes well, we'll discuss bringing you in."

"I have to go back to Connecticut to see my parole officer."

Shasis made a dismissive noise. "Not like it's that far. You do what you have to do. We begin on Wednesday. Classes will be upstate at what we like to call the main campus."

It was the perfect opportunity to look for the Woodward blackmail material. And to look for Dylan and now the missing Lyria.

Dash would understand, she knew that. Probably better than she would understand were the situation reversed. You did what you had to do to get the job done. She was just…concerned, that maybe she might like it.

Whatever. She'd deal with that later.

"Okay," she agreed. "I'll stay."

Smiling like a snake, Shasis offered out her glass again. "I think this is the beginning of something spectacular, Che-che. I really do." And then she drank.

Killian didn't drink, but she pretended to. She hadn't been called that stupid name in years, but it was a nod to the fact that they'd done time together. None of this meant either of them trusted the other, and they both knew it. Shasis wanted her for something, and it wasn't because she was good with people. If she was willing to trust Killian—someone she once tried to kill—then she had to be seriously afraid of something.

But what?

*   *   *

From the bedroom window, Maryl watched as Killian finally got up and left Shasis sitting alone by the pool. Seemed both of them had clandestine plans to complete before morning. What was that all about?

"Hey, darlin'. Why don't you come back to bed?"

Maryl rolled her eyes at the overdone Southern drawl. She was willing to bet "Magnus," aka Ryan Anderson, aka Deacon Ford, was no more Southern than she was, and she'd been born in Jersey.

"I have to go," she said, turning away from the window. "I have class in the morning, remember?"

The light coming through the window was just enough to illuminate his beautiful chiseled face and finely toned physique. There was no denying he was gorgeous. Normally she'd enjoy sleeping with him—and the sex was okay—but the size of his ego diminished whatever other attributes he might possess.

Magnus grinned. "You're coming back for the week, though, right?"

"That's up to you. Did you ask Shasis if it was okay?"

He scoffed. "I don't have to ask her permission."

"But you're waiving the cost of the module. Won't she be upset that you're letting me come for free?"

"I'm not letting you come for free, baby. I'm letting you come because you make me come."

Ugh. Maryl forced a smile. "You're too good to me."

"You scratch my back and I'll scratch yours."

Picking up her underwear from the floor, she stepped into

them and slid them up over her hips. "You got mad at me for scratching your back."

"Metaphorically, darlin'. My body's a temple, can't have it damaged."

Mm. Meaning he didn't want any of his other women to know he was sleeping around. Whatever. It wasn't like she was actually interested in the asshole. Well, she was interested in him, but not in the way he thought.

She continued getting dressed. "When will I see you again?" She hated the slightly desperate tone in her voice, even though she'd put it there on purpose.

"I've got meetings and such the next few days, but I'll find you. Hey, don't look at me like that. I'm a man of my word."

"I know you are. I just miss you when I'm in class. It's not like you're there."

"Well, I'll be around plenty for this one." He pulled his phone out from under his pillow and began scrolling, the screen casting colors on his face. "Now, don't you go getting all jealous when you see me with those other girls. I'm supposed to be teaching them to love themselves, remember. I want them to see themselves as the beautiful creatures they are."

"I'll try. So long as I know I'm your special pet." The words tasted sour on her tongue. God, this guy was a bastard. She couldn't blame anyone but herself for this. It had been her idea to use sex to worm her way into Incarnyx. Seducing Magnus had seemed like an easy and quick way into the organization, and it had been just that. He wasn't a bad lay, but *God*, he could be tedious.

"You are," he said, not looking up from his screen. "You know you are."

Maryl finished getting dressed, then gathered up her purse. "You'll call me?"

"Mm-hm." Whatever was on the screen had his full attention now. Probably another woman. He was such a dog. At least this way she didn't have to kiss him goodbye.

Quietly, she opened the door and slipped out into the hall. As far as she knew it was only Magnus, Shasis, and a couple of their most trusted employees who lived in the big house. The empty rooms were for those who excelled at their courses, with a house down the street for those who didn't take to the program quite as well.

She'd been led to believe this was a sex cult, but she had yet to see it in action. Mostly it just seemed like a haven for a slut to plow the fields of as many unhappy women as he wanted. No one seemed to be coerced, and she'd found no evidence of this craziness people spoke of, which was why she was wrangling for a place at the campus upstate. That had to be where the *real* heart of Incarnyx lay. This setup was just to weed out the possibilities from the no-goes. She needed to be a possibility. She needed to get into that inner circle soon; otherwise everything she and the others had planned would go up in flames, and with it, her future.

The car she'd ordered was waiting out front when she opened the front door. As she climbed into the back seat, she knew from experience that Shasis would soon be along to set the alarm. That woman was a hawk, and the real danger to Maryl's plans.

Tara Washington had a rap sheet as long as a trip to the

DMV with no internet access. She'd been a prostitute, a pimp, a drug dealer, and a gang member—and that was the juvenile record. After that it was more of the same, along with some extortion and trafficking charges. She'd only escaped serious jail time by snitching on those she ran with. No wonder she'd bought herself a new identity and ran to a different state— though not like New York was that far from Connecticut. They were next door to each other, for Christ's sake. If she'd really been concerned about her safety, she would have gone farther away. She would have assumed an identity with a lower profile.

It took real balls for a pimp-snitch to set herself up as a self-help guru.

She pulled a pack of cigarettes out of her purse along with a lighter and held both in her hand until the driver dropped her off in front of the hotel. She'd quit two years ago but always kept a pack for emergencies.

Outside, she moved to a more private location near the outdoor pool and took a cigarette from the pack. She lit it, then dug in her purse for her phone.

In her call history, the first entry was listed as Joe. She tapped it to dial. Exhaled a long stream of smoke while she waited.

He picked up on the third ring. "'Lo?"

"Did I wake you up?" she asked in a low tone.

"Kinda. I must've dozed in front of the TV. Everything okay?"

"Yeah. I'm back at the hotel."

"How was lover boy?"

"Self-impressed." She took another drag.

"You don't have to sleep with him, you know."

"Says the man who's been giving it to that security guard of theirs for what? Two weeks now?" Exhale. He'd picked her up in a bar and only found out afterward where she worked. Leave it to Joe to literally fall into bed with the right person.

"I'm just saying."

"How are you doing anyway? Balls okay?" She smiled as she asked.

"Yeah, you laugh. That woman hits like a freight train."

"You're the one who provoked her."

"I got into character. I didn't hurt you, did I?"

"I'll have a bit of a bruise tomorrow, but that just sells the story all the better. Seriously, you okay?"

"No lasting damage—I don't think. So, what's the plan?"

"I'm in the course for upstate, but get this—guess who paid a visit to Miz Washington tonight?"

"From the tone of your voice, I'm going to guess Killian Delaney."

"Ding, ding, ding."

"What was that about?"

"No idea, but it definitely makes it look like she's involved somehow. First Woodward's woman and now this?" It was a little disappointing. She kinda liked Killian. She wanted to believe she was more than just some ex-con looking to slip back into the only life she'd ever known.

"What are you going to do?"

"Keep an eye on her. It's all I can do. Maybe she'll flip on Washington if given the chance."

"Yeah, well, be careful. I saw the photos of what Delaney did to Rank Cirello. It wasn't pretty."

"Killian won't hurt me." But it was all false bravado and they both knew it. She threw her cigarette to the ground and crushed it with her heel. "I'd better hit the hay. I just wanted to check in."

"Thanks. I'll talk to you tomorrow. Night."

Maryl hung up and deleted her call history. Then she walked around to the side door and used her room key to unlock it. She took the stairs to her room, peeking into the corridor to make sure Killian wasn't around before quickly skulking to her own room.

Inside, she sagged against the door and breathed. She grimaced at the taste of cigarette in her mouth. It always tasted so good at the time, and then made her feel like a walking ashtray after.

She thought about Killian and the baseball bat. It was for Joe, not her. Killian's record had been clean since getting out of jail. Her parole officer's reports had nothing but good things to say about her. Killian was a model parolee.

Maybe she really was there to better herself, and not to get into a criminal enterprise with an old prison buddy. Either way, Maryl would find out the truth and she'd deal with it.

She just hoped she figured out the truth about Killian before Killian figured out the truth about her.

SIX

The next morning, Killian came down for breakfast and found Maryl already eating. In the morning light, without any makeup on, Maryl didn't look as young as Killian had first thought. In fact, she was beginning to think they were closer in age after all.

"Hey," the other woman said. "I knocked on your door earlier but you didn't answer."

"I was probably in the shower. I went for a run when I got up."

"I figured with pipes like that you must work out a lot."

Killian glanced at her arms, covered by a lightweight button-up. "I do. It centers me."

Maryl grinned over the rim of her coffee cup. "Look at you using the self-help jargon."

Laughing, Killian shook her head. "I'm going to grab some food. You want anything else?"

"Could you snag me a peach yogurt?"

She returned from the breakfast setup a few minutes later, with eggs, whole-grain toast, coffee, a banana, and two peach yogurts.

"Can I ask you a question?"

Killian placed one of the yogurts by Maryl's empty plate. "Sure."

"Do you miss fighting? In the octagon, I mean."

"Sometimes. I don't think winning is a good enough reason for me to fight anymore. I can't fight just to fight, you know?"

Maryl shook her head. "No, but I think I get it. Do you ever miss prison?"

Killian swallowed the forkful of eggs she'd shoveled into her mouth. "That's two questions. I only agreed to one." She smiled. "Yeah, sometimes I miss certain aspects of it. Not that I ever care to go back, though."

The other woman watched her for a moment—just long enough that Killian frowned. "What?" she asked. "You don't believe me?"

"Oh no. I do. Sorry. I'm just trying to put myself in your situation. If this was a movie, there'd be some group or person trying to lure you back into the life with promises of easy money and no one looking down at you because you're an ex-con."

Well, that was almost a little too close to home. "There's no such thing as easy money. And there's always someone ready to look down on you, for whatever reason. I don't really worry about it."

"So you haven't been tempted?"

Killian set down her fork and braced her forearms on the table. "Are you going to ask me to rob a bank with you or something?" She kept her tone light.

"Oh no!" Maryl actually blushed a little. "I'm sorry. I'm just nosy."

It wasn't just nosiness, but Killian didn't bother to pursue it. The last thing she wanted was for an abused woman to ask her to kill her abuser, because frankly, it would be a pleasure.

"Did Joe call last night?" she asked.

Maryl opened her yogurt. "No. He's probably too angry."

"Mm." She regarded her for a second. She liked Maryl, she really did, though she had no idea why. Maybe it was because she seemed otherwise unaffected by her lover's violence. Joe beat her but hadn't broken her.

"Listen," Killian began, digging into her eggs. "I think you shouldn't spend any more money on Incarnyx."

Maryl paused, coffee cup halfway to her mouth. "What do you mean?"

"I mean, if you get an invite upstate, turn it down."

"Why would I do that?"

"Because..." How to explain it? "Because I don't think these people are good people."

The other woman smiled slightly and sipped her coffee. "You're so suspicious."

"Yeah, I am, but I still think you should stay away."

"Are you going up there to kill someone or something?"

"Jesus Christ. No." Not like she'd tell if she was. Killian sighed. Snitching went against every code she had, but she really didn't want Tara and her fuckboy getting their hands on Maryl.

"Then, what? I'm not very good with 'Because I said so.'"

Killian bit back a retort about Joe. "I know Shasis," she said in a low voice.

"Really?" She looked disappointed. "You could introduce me, you know."

"She's not someone you want to know." Killian took a drink of coffee. "This is just between us, okay?"

Frowning at her tone, Maryl leaned forward. "You're serious."

"Of course I'm serious. Shasis and I did time together."

Maryl's eyes widened. "Get out."

"Her name isn't Shasis and she's not someone qualified to tell anyone how to live their best life."

"Did you know it was her before you came here?" At Killian's nod, she continued. "Then why did you come?"

"A friend asked me for a favor."

"So you're not here to become the best version of you."

"I'm afraid I'm as good as I'm ever going to get."

"Self-deprecation doesn't become you."

"Getting the crap beat of you doesn't become you, either, but here we are." *Fuck.* "I'm sorry."

Maryl inclined her head. "That's true. Harsh, but true." She dragged a spoon through the container of yogurt in front of her. "I don't want trouble, Killian. You helped me out, but if being your friend is going to bring shit down on me, I'm going to have to walk away."

Killian shook her head. "I'm not doing anything illegal— since that seems to be your big concern. I don't want trouble, either, but I have to warn you, it tends to find me."

She smiled. "Trouble like me."

Smiling as well, Killian shrugged. "Maybe I invite it sometimes. But I understand if you want to pretend we never met."

"I'm good," Maryl replied. Then, changing the subject: "So what do you think Natalie will try to make us cry over today?"

The conversation remained fairly light for the rest of the meal, and Killian was relieved. While she'd been truthful that she'd understand if Maryl cut her loose, she was glad the other woman didn't jump at the opportunity. She didn't have many friends, and had never really wanted many, but she liked Maryl, and if the other woman did attend the upstate program, she'd do her best to make sure she didn't fall victim to whatever Shasis had planned.

After breakfast they both returned to their rooms to get what they needed for the day. They arrived at the Incarnyx compound fifteen minutes before class was to begin.

It was their last day of classes, and as it drew to an end, what concerned Killian the most wasn't the amount of crying Natalie tried to induce, but the fact that she hadn't seen Lyria since that first night.

Then, as luck—or something—would have it, Lyria entered the classroom later that afternoon, along with Mina. She had a box of envelopes under her arm. She looked better than she had that first night—rested and more alert.

Mina began. "Everyone, may I have your attention, please?" She turned that megawatt smile to the entire room, and everyone instantly quieted. "I trust you all have enjoyed your time with us and will look back upon this weekend as one of the most significant of your lives. I hope you leave here today with a better understanding of yourself and so much love for the person you are becoming." She made eye contact with each of them, as though seeking affirmation.

Killian forced a smile.

"Now, we've reached the point in the process where we at Incarnyx would like to thank each of you for putting yourselves into our capable hands and allowing us the privilege of guiding you along your journey. In these envelopes are personalized thank-you notes from Shasis and Magnus themselves. And for a few of you, there are invitations to join us this week for a very special, private retreat at the Incarnyx compound."

Hopeful murmurs rose around the room. Killian closed her eyes to keep from rolling them. Would her envelope contain an invitation as Shasis had indicated? It would be the perfect cover for her to get into the house and look for what she needed without having to pretend she was there for the program.

At Mina's nod, Lyria began handing out the envelopes alphabetically. She looked Killian in the eye and gave her the same bright smile she'd given everyone else. "Hope to see you upstate!"

Killian thanked her and took the envelope. Inside was a card. When Killian opened it, a small piece of paper fell into her lap. She picked it up but read the card first. It was a note from Shasis thanking her for choosing their program and all that BS, and also inviting her to the next module. Bitch better waive the cost if she had recruitment in mind. Or Raven would be footing the bill.

Then she looked at the paper. On it, printed in ballpoint pen, was a series of numbers. Not long enough to be a phone number, but possibly a PIN or a code? Below it was one letter, a capital *L*. *Lyria*. It had to be. Unfortunately, there was no way she was going to be able to get close enough to the girl to ask. Once the envelopes had been handed out, Mina whisked her away to the second classroom to repeat the process, so Killian couldn't talk to her.

It had to be a combination, maybe for a lock, or for the safe where Magnus kept the blackmail material he had. Given the girl's words, it had to be at the main campus.

Maryl caught her by the arm, leaning in across the table. She had a cat-who-ate-the-canary expression on her face. "I got into the next module!"

Belle and Lou cast glances in their direction. Killian forced a smile. "So did I."

Lou looked around the room. "From the look of it, I'd say we all did."

Maryl slumped back in her chair. "Really?" She glanced around at all the happy faces in the room. "You're right. So much for being *chosen*."

"Maybe they do that knowing not everyone will be able to attend," Killian suggested, and hated herself for making excuses for what was nothing more than an elaborate and terrible con. She gave the other women at the table a sharp look, daring them to argue.

"Probably," Belle agreed quickly. "I mean, it's not like everyone can afford it, right?"

"Are you going?" Lou asked.

Killian hesitated. "I don't know yet. Maybe."

"They need an answer before we leave today," she continued. "You might want to check your bank account."

"How's your bank account?" Killian asked.

Lou tossed the envelope on the table. "Too rich for my blood. I don't really feel the need to go looking for my female empowerment. I think I already found it."

Killian bit her tongue before she could suggest the woman return it for a refund. She looked at Belle instead. "What about you?"

"I think so. I've been saving up for these programs. It was my birthday gift to myself this year that I take time just for me—away from the husband and the kids, you know?"

Lou nodded. "Honestly, it's just too much to pay for the two of us when we need a new air conditioner." She smiled. "You three have fun, though."

Killian's lips pulled tight—more grimace than smile. "Yeah, thanks." It was going to be so much damn fun trying to get the Woodward information and get those girls out of this place while worrying about Belle and Maryl, too.

By the end of the day—which was a mere hour later—eight from their class, including the three from Killian's table, had signed up for the next module, which was scheduled to begin on Wednesday. Killian would drive back to Connecticut, check in with Donna the next day, have some time with Dash, and then head upstate the day after. That was, if she wasn't sent back to prison by the parole board.

Well, at least if she went back she wouldn't have that bounty over her head anymore. She had to try to remain positive, because the thought of going back inside made her want to run. Get a fake ID and head to Canada. But that wasn't the problem at hand. One thing at a time.

She accepted the invitation to the next module. Checking that box felt like signing away her soul. It was melodramatic, but true. Nothing good was going to come of this. Every instinct she had told her to walk away.

"Are you leaving?" Maryl asked, when Killian stood.

"Yeah. I have some stuff to take care of. Laundry, you know?"

The other woman laughed. "Right. I should do that, too."

"You going to be okay?" She could offer to go home with her, but... *sigh*. "Do you want me to go to the house with you?"

"No, thanks. I'll be okay. He's at work right now. I can get my things and be gone again before he comes home. I think I'll go back to the hotel."

Killian nodded. "I'll see you later, then. You've got my number if you need anything."

When she got her phone out of the locker, there was a message from Dash saying he'd be home later that evening. Did she want to get together? She replied that she did and told him to meet her at her place for dinner.

There was also a message from Shannon, wanting to know if Killian was coming to her party Memorial Day weekend. After all the upheaval and trauma of the fall, the kid had still managed to finish her sophomore year at the top of her class. It seemed schoolwork was great therapy—or distraction.

Killian hesitated. Would she be at the party? She wanted to be there. She wanted to be a lot of things for the kid.

With bells on, she typed, and hit Send. If she actually managed to avoid going back inside, she'd make sure she had at least one set of bells on her when she arrived, if for no other reason than to make Shannon laugh at her.

She didn't want to go back to prison. She didn't want to be that woman. She wanted...she wanted...

She wanted to be a damn role model. Yeah, 'cause shoving pimps in her trunk was so inspirational. No, screw that. Killian wasn't about to go all morose and "poor me." She'd taken out some really bad people since being released from prison almost a year ago.

God, almost a year of freedom. And in that time she'd gotten rid of Rank and at least half a dozen other scumbags the world wasn't going to miss. That was something to be proud of, even if it was on the shady side of the law. If jail time was the price, then she'd pay it, but she really hoped it didn't come to that. Mostly because she didn't want Shannon and her little sister, Willow, to have a jailbird auntie again. She didn't want her sister to have to face that embarrassment. Again. She didn't want to leave her apartment or Dash. She liked her life and wanted to keep it.

That was why, before she left the parking lot, she texted a code to the phone number for New Amsterdam Security, requesting a call back. The code, along with her number, would get sent directly to Maxine Hollander, her boss. Maxine ran the East Coast division of the Initiative, and she took the position very seriously. If anyone would know what was going on with the parole board—and how to get out of it—it was Maxine.

She'd packed up the Impala that morning when she left the hotel, so Killian left straight from class. Normally, it wasn't a terribly long drive back to Connecticut, but she was going to hit rush-hour traffic. She'd probably be better off just waiting it out, but patience wasn't exactly one of her dominant virtues.

And she wasn't going to run like her instinct demanded. She didn't have much in the world, but she had her reputation, and that meant she had to keep her promises.

Too bad self-destructiveness wasn't a virtue; otherwise she'd be a damn saint.

The parole office had to be the most depressing place on the planet. It reminded Killian of high school—which she'd hated with a passion. Every time she stepped through the doors she felt like she was about to be tested and fail.

The interior of the office wasn't exactly welcoming—kind of a grayish yellow ambiance with a side of quiet desperation. Most of the people sitting in the waiting room were there because they had no other choice, and the rest of them were there because they'd driven the ones that didn't have a choice. Point was, no one was there because they wanted to be.

Killian only had to sit for a few minutes before her appointment time. Donna was pretty good about keeping on schedule. As she entered the office, she had to give the woman kudos for at least trying to make the place look welcoming. Not like she could do a whole lot with it.

"Killian, good to see you," her parole officer greeted her. "Have a seat."

"Hey, Donna." Killian sat down in the chair in front of the desk. "How are you?"

"Can't complain," the small blonde replied with a smile. "And no one would listen if I did." It was what she said almost every time Killian came to see her. She wondered how many other people she said it to in the run of her day.

Nodding, Killian returned the smile. "What's this business with the board?"

"First things first—you doing okay?"

This was only partially asked out of caring. It was also Donna's habit to ask the same questions every meeting. She had a checklist she liked to follow before changing the conversation.

"Yes. Work is good. Personal life is good. I've been staying out of trouble."

"Are you sure?" That wasn't habit. In fact, it was the first time Donna had questioned her in a long time. "Honestly, you've been staying out of trouble?"

"Donna, I haven't associated with anyone with a record. I've been working and spending time with family. I have no idea why the board wants to check on me."

Gimlet blue eyes locked with hers and held. Killian had no trouble returning the stare. She had nothing to feel guilty about. "You know how parole works, right? Normally if there's been some kind of violation, it would be me who takes it to my supervisor, then to the parole board. This is the first time it's happened in the opposite order. Someone on the board contacted my boss and told them that they had reason to believe you'd violated the conditions of your parole."

"How?"

"They insinuated that you've been playing vigilante. Is that true?"

Well, shit. "No, but I wouldn't admit to it if it was." Who knew about her activities? She kept that all pretty quiet. Not even Megan knew about her job. Only a handful of people knew what she did for a living, and she didn't think any of them would play her like this.

"True." The blonde sighed. "Killian, tell me you haven't been playing me this whole time."

"Donna. I've been doing what I think is right."

"That doesn't answer my question. In fact, it just makes me nervous."

"I haven't been playing you." It was mostly true. She was always as honest as she could be whenever she talked to Donna.

"So, if I call New Amsterdam Security, they'll tell me you still work for them?"

"They will."

"And if the parole board has specific dates they need checked?"

"They can ask my work." Thank God the Initiative had the covers that it did to present a legitimate front. From an employment perspective, everything about Killian's life looked totally aboveboard. "Donna, they can't just do this because they feel like it, can they?"

"They're the parole board. If they want, they can put you back in jail, but I just can't understand why someone would go over my head to report you. That's what has me worried. Are you sure you haven't pissed off someone higher up the food chain?"

"I have no idea who that could've been if I did. Donna, do I need to be worried?"

She shook her head. "I don't know, Killian. I really don't. In the twenty years I've done this job I've never had anything like this happen. I've had to start revocation proceedings, but I've never had anyone bring them to me. We'll know more after my supervisor and I meet with them later this week. Meanwhile, don't go far, okay?"

Killian nodded. New York State wasn't that far. Not really. She could be back in a matter of hours if she needed to be.

This was ridiculous. She'd go talk to Raven. Give the money back, do something. Maxine hadn't called her back yet, which was kind of odd, but not completely out of the ordinary. She might be traveling.

"Whatever information you need to help make this go away, I'll give it," Killian promised.

"I know you will. Honestly, you've been one of my best clients. I can't imagine what this is all about, but they wouldn't call for this meeting if it wasn't important. I don't want you to worry unnecessarily, but we need to be prepared either way. I'm not sure if they'll want to talk to you or not, so make sure you have your phone with you."

"I'm working this week, but you know I'll get back to you as soon as possible."

"As soon as you can, yes." Her concerned gaze narrowed. "You're positive...?"

"Jesus, Donna!" Killian threw her hands up into the air. "I'm positive, okay?" She didn't like lying, but there was no way around it. She wasn't going to tell Donna the truth. Even if she understood, there was no way she wouldn't turn Killian in.

"I know. I'm sorry. I'm just worried. You have enemies, Killian."

Now it was Killian whose eyes narrowed. "What are you saying?"

Donna sighed. "Is it possible that someone has a vendetta against you? Someone who might want to get you sent back inside?"

Now, that list might have more names on it than Killian could even remember. Over the course of the last few months she had made enemies. Most notably, she'd not ingratiated herself with the White Reaper or Sons of Bitches motorcycle clubs, but this hardly seemed like their kind of tactic. They'd be more likely to organize a drive-by or blow up her car. And really, all she'd done was shake things up for them. Gangs like that were like Hydra. Cut off one head and two more rose from the bloody stump. No, if someone was trying to have her put back inside, it wasn't them. It was someone who wanted to remain removed from it. Someone who knew what she'd been up to since getting out of prison.

"Not that I'm aware of."

Maybe someone who was actually missing a pimp? Or maybe someone who wasn't what they appeared to be. Killian studied her parole officer, searching for any sign of duplicity. Maxine had told her that the Initiative was aware of Donna when they first offered to recruit Killian. Killian had never thought to ask exactly what that meant. Stupid of her, probably.

Donna had asked if she was playing her, but was it Killian who was getting played? It wouldn't be the first time someone had fooled her.

She'd find out soon enough.

"She specifically asked if you thought someone might be setting you up?" Dash asked Killian as he set a plate on the table in front of her.

Her mouth watered at the sight of the steak. She wouldn't kill a cow to feed herself, but damn if her hypocritical mouth didn't love the taste of one. "Yeah. I hadn't thought about it before, but it makes the most sense. I mean, I'm not exactly liked by a lot of people."

"Yeah, but who knows what you do? I mean, it's only other people involved with the Initiative. Anyone who would rat on you would be putting the entire organization at risk—not to mention their own life."

That was true. "Maxine doesn't strike me as the type to tolerate betrayal."

"She's not." He speared a bite of roasted potato with his fork. "What's your gut say?"

"It's someone with a grudge. I called Maxine but haven't heard back yet."

"She's in Europe. Tell Raven about it when you talk to her. She'll take care of it."

Killian arched a brow, pausing in the act of lifting her fork to her mouth. "You think?"

He shook his head. "Whatever happened between the two

of you, Raven would *not* risk Maxine's wrath. Trust me. Her loyalty is to Maxine, all the way."

"Why? What did Maxine do to earn it?"

"I don't know all the particulars, but Story told me Maxine saved Raven's life."

Killian nodded. "Blood debts do inspire fealty." And if she thought about it—really, honestly thought about it, she knew Raven had integrity. It was only her own wounded pride that made her think otherwise. Raven might have been paid to have her back in prison, but the rest of it had been real, or, at the very least, real enough.

She chewed her vegetables and swallowed. "I'm seeing her tomorrow. I'll talk to her then."

"What time are you heading upstate?"

"Sometime on Wednesday." She sighed. "Every instinct is telling me to not go."

"So don't go." He held up his hand. "I know. You gave your word. You sure you don't want me there for backup?"

"I'll call Story. No offense, but you're too pretty. All those women would be all over you, and Magnus might see you as a threat. I need someone who can blend."

Dash grinned. "I can't be offended when you call me pretty."

Killian chuckled. For years she'd teased him about his beautiful face, and then she saw it in her dreams when she was locked up. Taking it for granted was not something she planned to do ever again.

"I'd feel better if you had Story with you," he continued. "Not that I doubt you—you know that, right?"

He was so cute. No one else ever appreciated her ability to take care of herself like he did. What she had done to Rank was a point of pride for Dash. "I know." A slight noise made her head whip toward the living room. "What was that?"

It was the front door. Killian and Dash exchanged glances. Neither one of them had a gun on them, but there were plenty of knives and a fire extinguisher within reach...

"Hey," their visitor called out.

Killian slumped. It was Shannon. For fuck's sake, she should have never given the girl a key. She looked up as Shannon entered the kitchen. "How many times do I have to tell you to call first?"

The girl shrugged. "Would you have said yes?" She looked at Dash like he was the one intruding. "What is this, 'date night'?" Her words dripped with mockery.

The corner of Dash's mouth twitched. "Something like that. Have you eaten?"

"Did you cook it?"

He nodded.

"I'm good, then."

He barely managed to stifle a laugh. Killian didn't find the situation all that funny. "You here for a reason?"

Shannon leaned against the wall, gaze downcast. "Megan's being a bitch."

"Translation, your *mother* told you something you didn't want to hear."

The girl looked up, a hard light in her eyes. "She was being a bitch."

Killian leaned back in her chair. "But you weren't, huh?" She shook her head. "I thought we agreed you wouldn't pit us against each other."

Shannon ignored her, turning her attention to Dash. Her movements were slowed, a little heavy. Was she high? "You were friends with my father, right?"

"I was."

"But you got no problem fucking my mother?"

Dash's brows rose and a hard glint flashed in his golden-green eyes. "No," he replied quietly. "No problem at all."

It was the closest Killian had seen him come to real anger in a long time. Usually he was beyond patient with Shannon and her moods. "Apologize or leave," she said.

Shannon looked shocked when she realized Killian was talking to her. The glassy sheen in her eyes answered the question as to whether or not she was high. "You trippin'? Apologize for what? The truth?"

"Apologize for talking out your ass about stuff that's none of your fucking business."

"He was his best friend!"

"Right, and you know Jason considered me his side piece, because you've met your half siblings. He's gone. It doesn't matter anymore. You just want to pick a fight."

Dash smiled slightly. "Wonder where she gets that."

Killian sighed. "Shan, you have to stop this. You can't just show up here when you're mad at your mom. I don't like being put in the middle. You have to start talking to her about things."

"You think she understands how I feel? She doesn't know

anything about what happened. You think she knows what it's like to be raped?"

Killian didn't answer—it wasn't her truth to tell. "Have you asked her?"

"No." The look the kid gave her was slap-worthy. Then, to Dash: "Were you the one who talked her into giving me up?"

It was obvious Shannon was angry. It was obvious she was jealous of Dash. What was just becoming obvious to Killian was that Shannon was angry at her. So angry, but she didn't know it. She was taking it out on everyone else but the person she really wanted to fight. It didn't take a genius to figure out why. Killian had tried so hard to make sure the kid was nothing like her, but she'd obviously passed on her abandonment issues.

"He offered to help me raise you," Killian informed her, earning a surprised glance from Dash. She'd never revealed that to anyone before. "If I had, he would have been more of a father to you than Jason ever could. Look, kiddo, why don't you just tear a strip off me and get it out of your system?"

"I'm so fucking sick of people telling me what I should do." Shannon adjusted the strap of her purse on her shoulder. "I knew it was a mistake to come here. I should have known you wouldn't care. No one does." With that dramatic pronouncement, she stomped out of the kitchen. A second later, the front door slammed.

"You going after her?" Dash asked.

Killian wanted to. God, she really wanted to. She wanted to put her arms around Shannon and make it all better, but she couldn't. And she couldn't let the girl manipulate her, either. She didn't know what the right thing to do was, but she knew it was time to take a hard stand, no matter how painful it might be for her, and for Shannon.

"No," she replied, cutting into her steak once again. She didn't care that it was getting cold. "This time I'm letting her go."

SEVEN

It was a photo posted on Instagram that made Killian get into her car and drive all the way to Ilyana's house in Riverside—one of the richest zip codes in Connecticut—an hour earlier than she was expected.

The neighborhood made her itch. So much pretension. So much flagrant flaunting of wealth. But that wasn't really what pissed her off. What annoyed her was her own reaction to it—how in awe she was of the homes and the cars and the lawns. What would it be like to have a pool—and someone to clean it? To have a lawn, and then someone to mow it? It all seemed so far out of reach, and she wondered how much the people who had it really appreciated it.

She wondered how many of the owners were white, and how many of the people working for them weren't.

Ilyana's home was a sprawling structure of Spanish inspiration. Cream stucco with dark wood doors and a long, curving drive. It looked almost modest compared to some around it—not that there was another house for at least a couple of acres.

She had to get past the guard at the wrought-iron gate, then the butler who answered the bell. The old guy gave her the kind of once-over most people reserved for mice carcasses or road-kill, before closing the door and leaving her on the step while he went to check with Ilyana if she was safe to allow inside. A few minutes later, he returned—still looking at her like she was shit on his shoe. Maybe her skin tone wasn't light enough for him. But he let her inside and led her into the parlor where Ilyana and Raven were having a meal.

"Thank you, Monroe," Ilyana said with a smile. "You may leave us. Killian, what a surprise. Join us for lunch?"

Killian knew enough not to air the dirty laundry with the help in the room. She also knew she hadn't really been invited to join them. Nor was she welcome, judging from the look on Raven's face. She didn't care.

"I need one of you to explain this, and someone wasn't answering my texts." She set her phone on the table between the two of them and directed a pointed look at Raven, who ignored her.

It was from one of those Hollywood gossip sites—the kind that was always talking about who was wearing what and who was dating whom. The headline accompanying the photo asked, "How Does Ilyana Feel About Daughter Dating Her Ex, Miguel?"

"So?" Raven asked, brow puckering.

Ilyana blinked up at Killian. "I don't understand. It's a photo of my daughter and Miguel Vargas, a family friend. What's the problem?"

"That photo was taken yesterday. Clearly Dylan isn't a prisoner anywhere."

"Not all prisons have bars," the actress said in a cool tone. "Or perhaps you were in a cage too long to remember that."

It was shitty bait, and Killian knew better than to snap at it. "What I know is that you failed to mention that Dylan was involved with your ex. Is that why you hired me to find her?"

"Of course not," Raven interjected, but she didn't look her usual confident self. "Killy, it's exactly how I told you it was."

Killian shot her a dark look. "Okay, well, how about this: Why didn't you think to tell me that the son of a known drug lord was involved? That's information I should have been given, Rave."

Miguel Vargas, son of Rafael Vargas. Vargas was "allegedly" the leader of the Desierto Cartel, one of South America's most ruthless and powerful suppliers of meth to the US. A few months ago Vargas sent the head of one of his rivals to the man's children as a present. He was a sick son of a bitch and not the kind of person Killian wanted to get within ten miles of. He masqueraded as a legit businessman and his charm and money made it easy for him. There were plenty of Americans—and Europeans—delighted to take his money and be seen socializing with him, because for all his cartel connections, he was known for putting wealth back into the economy. He owned at least two resorts that brought a lot of tourists and a lot of money into his country. Also, he gave funds to orphanages and children's hospitals—ensuring he always had a steady supply of kids who owed him a debt and were already loyal to him.

"Because Miguel is not involved," Ilyana answered smoothly. "It's Magnus and Shasis who are blackmailing my daughters, not him. If he is there, then I'm glad. It should be all the easier for you to convince Dylan to leave."

"Really, because I hear that his old man has been to several of the Incarnyx 'experiences,' as have his wife and much of his family. But there's no link, huh?"

"None."

The woman was a bald-faced fucking liar, but it wasn't any wonder she had a crap-ton of Oscars. She was a good actress, and she sold it like her life depended on it.

"So, you have a problem with your daughters taking sex photos but not hanging out with cartel brats?"

"I never saw any sort of criminal activity when I visited the Vargas family at their home."

Killian tilted her head. "If he's so awesome, and you have no problem with him banging your daughter, why didn't you just ask him to get the girls out? If he's got an in with Incarnyx, wouldn't it make more sense?"

Ilyana smoothed the napkin draped over her lap. "I didn't want to involve him."

"Were too pissed that he rolled you over for your kid to talk to him, you mean."

"*Killian.*" Raven's eyes flashed with anger. "Back off."

Shrugging, Killian rocked back on her heels. "Hey, I'm more than happy to give you a refund and walk away from this right now. Even I'm not stupid enough to get between the feds and the cartel."

"Please," Ilyana pleaded, gazing up at her with so much vulnerability Killian wanted to stab her with a fork. "I just want my daughters back."

She jabbed the screen of her phone. "Dylan looks perfectly happy."

The actress reached out for the phone but then stopped, curled her fingers into a fist. Jesus, she deserved every one of those awards. "Because Magnus allowed her to spend time with a man she's known for years."

"They're holding hands, Ilyana."

The blonde shrugged. "They've always been friends. It was Dylan who introduced us. At first I didn't care about the age difference, but it soon became apparent that we weren't well matched." She glanced at Raven. "I'm sorry I didn't tell you, darling. It just didn't seem to matter. I don't care about *your* past relationships."

Oh, hell no. Killian glared at Raven, who at least had the grace to look uncomfortable. Raven had told this cow about them? Why would she do that? They hadn't been a couple, for fuck's sake.

"Save the lovers' spat for later," she told them. "What I want to know is why some photographs are worth me risking getting my damned head cut off."

Raven stood, put her hand on Killian's arm. "Killy, come on. There's nothing here. It's just a coincidence. Vargas has nothing to do with Incarnyx."

Or he was a partner and the cartel was using it to traffic girls. Or drugs. Or both.

Either Raven had been taking acting lessons, or she really believed it. She believed in her girlfriend. Killian wanted to slap her hard upside the head. If this was prison, she'd mock her for being blinded by pussy, but it wasn't even something she could bring herself to say in this fancy house.

"You give me your word?" Killian asked, knowing it would only be worth something if she survived.

Raven inclined her head, smiled that little smile. "Of course. If Ilyana says Shasis and Magnus are who we have to worry about, then that's the truth. Just go to the next class, see what Dirty T's got going on, and get those girls out of there. Just today I saw someone on a site allege that Magnus sexually abused her during her time with the organization. It's not going to be long before they're raided. Dylan and Lyria can't be there when that happens."

"Right, because Dylan recruited other women." She was beginning to think there was more to it. It couldn't be a coincidence that Vargas was connected. It just couldn't.

Killian turned to Ilyana. "You went to some of these seminars and classes, didn't you?"

Ilyana nodded. "I did. I was the one who first introduced the girls to them. If I'd known what would happen, I would have stayed far away."

"So what do they have on you?"

"I beg your pardon?" She didn't do shock as well as she did vulnerability.

"For blackmail material. If they have stuff on your girls, and every other woman who signs up, what do they have on you?"

The older woman laughed. "Oh, nothing. I left before they even dreamed of asking me for anything like that. No, it seems to be the young ones they get their claws into that way. You know this generation, they don't think anything of sending nudes of themselves to people."

Killian didn't know that. "Right, so I won't look for a file with your name on it, then."

Ilyana laughed. "Well, as far as I know, it does have my last name on it—it's the girls' last name as well. It's a flash drive with their photos, and yes, they may believe they have material on me as well, but I guard my privacy. It will be nothing of consequence. All that matters is getting my girls out of there."

She didn't like this woman, with her white-on-white outfit and her manicured nails that were pointed like dragon claws. Raven let those hands touch her? Let them inside her? That seemed like an infection waiting to happen.

She wasn't jealous. She wasn't. She just didn't trust Ilyana, and that made her not want to trust Raven. Her cellie was obviously infatuated with the white woman—why, Killian couldn't comprehend. Maybe it was the money. Maybe she had a tongue piercing.

"I'll go back to New York, and I'll do what I can. But if I find out the cartel has their hands in Incarnyx, I'm out of there. And I hope you guarded your 'privacy' as well as you hope." She picked up her phone and shoved it into her pocket. "Enjoy your lunch. I'll see myself out."

Raven tried to stop her, but Killian waved her off. She wasn't in the mood to hear any more excuses or promises. And she'd be damned if she'd ask Raven to look into the parole thing now. She just wanted to get the hell out of there. Unfortunately, Monroe wouldn't give her the satisfaction of an exit. He walked her all the way to the door.

"Wanna check me for silverware?" Killian asked as he held it open for her. "Make sure I don't have a candelabra in my pants?"

Silent, he stood there, looking straight ahead. Killian resisted the urge to flick his Adam's apple as she walked by. Sanctimonious little prick.

She got into her car and started the engine. A glance through a window revealed Raven and Ilyana in the parlor. Raven stood while her lover remained seated at the table talking. She held one of Raven's hands like she was some kind of delicate princess. Yeah, right. As delicate as a brick. God, she thought Raven was better than that.

As she drove down the long drive, Killian hit speed dial on her phone. A familiar voice picked up. "Hello?"

"Hey, Story," she said with a grin. Story Jones had become one of her closest friends over the last couple of months— her only friend, really. They were also work colleagues. Story was an extraordinary woman who could give the impression of being nothing special at all. She could morph herself into a drab little mouse or become a glamorous diva, and no one would ever know the two were the same person. She was a professional driver, and she was just fucked-up enough that Killian felt comfortable with her. Story was good people, dependable and loyal.

And she could drink like a damn fish.

"Kiki-Dee, to what do I owe the pleasure?"

"I need your help. How do you feel about backing me up on a job?"

"What's it involve?"

"Possibly a sex cult, maybe trafficking, and possibly a cartel, but hopefully just a cult. You've heard of Incarnyx?"

Story whistled. "Girl, you always throw the best parties. Incarnyx is that self-help group, yeah? The one with the slick Southern dude in all their press?"

"That's the one. He calls himself Magnus. Turns out I was inside with his partner."

"This keeps getting better and better. Does Raven know about it?"

"She's the one who hired me. Her GF's daughters are involved. Wants me to get them out."

"Jesus, this is better than *General Hospital*. I'm on my way back from Boston right now. When do you need me?"

"Tomorrow morning." She turned right onto another street. "Meet me at Dash's?"

"You got it. You need me to bring anything special?"

"Just your sweet self. Thanks so much, babe."

"Oh, I'm not doing it out of the kindness of my heart. You know you're giving me a cut."

Killian grinned. "I know it. And, hey, what do you know about the Desierto Cartel?"

"I know there's a bounty on Rafael Vargas's head of about fifteen million pesos. Is he involved? Because I'll have to make sure I bring a vehicle with a big enough trunk."

Killian grinned. Story had a way of making their twisted world seem like a big adventure. "Maybe. His kid's around."

"Miguel? He's almost as bad. I wonder how much I could get for him."

"You do the math. I'll see you tomorrow. And, Story? Bring lots of guns, okay?"

"Don't you worry, baby. Auntie Story's got you. Okay, I gotta go. The guy in the trunk's making noise. I have to find a rest stop and knock him out again. Love you, bye."

Shaking her head, Killian disconnected the call and turned her focus solely to the road. Having Story backing her up made her feel a lot better about heading back to New York the next morning, but she wasn't going back to Incarnyx for Ilyana Woodward or either of her daughters. She was going back for Maryl, because there was no way she could leave the woman alone with Dirty T and a frigging cartel.

Parole had just become the least of her worries. If she lived to see Memorial Day she'd consider herself lucky.

Story kept her promise—just like always.

Shortly after nine in the morning, a red Chrysler pulled into Dash's driveway. Story got out of the driver's side dressed in jeans and a white button down, with her brown hair back in a ponytail. She looked like she could be any age between twenty-five and thirty-five, and just about any nationality.

Killian met her at the door. "A rental?" she asked, noting the bar codes in the car's windows.

"Nah, it's one of mine. It just looks like a rental. I slapped New York plates on it to sell my story."

Her story? "Which is?"

"The woman whose invitation I stole is from LA looking to relocate. It explains why no one has seen me at any events in the area before."

"You set that up already?"

"Yesterday after I took care of my delivery."

She was impressed. "You get him to stop making noise?"

"It took a little persuasion, but, yeah." She stepped inside. "Hey, Dash."

Dash smiled, melting Killian's heart a little bit. No man should look that good after just crawling out of bed. "Hey, you. Thanks for having Kill's back."

"Always."

"Nice to see the two hundred getting some use." There was a teasing edge to his voice. "I only tricked her out a million years ago."

"Stop it," Story chided with a grin. "Not like this is the first time I've had her out."

Killian had no idea just how many cars Story actually owned, but each one served a specific purpose. They were as much a part of her cover as her hair or the clothes she wore. Dash was responsible for the customization of most of them, and the two of them had become good friends.

"Are you going to have your phone?" Dash asked as he pressed a to-go mug of coffee into Killian's hand.

"Probably not, but I'm going to sneak in a burner."

"How?" he asked.

Killian smiled sweetly. "Don't ask, babe."

Story laughed. "Oh my god. I didn't need to hear that. C'mon, felon, let's go." She walked out the door.

Dash kissed Killian before she left. "You call me if you get in trouble," he murmured. "And for Christ's sake, stay safe."

"I will. Promise." They both knew it wasn't a perfect promise, that she'd stay as safe as possible, but Dash knew the risks of her job. He worked for the Initiative as well, had been the one to bring her on board, so he wasn't kidding himself in any way. He just needed to say it, and she needed to hear it.

Story stayed behind her almost the entire way, turning off the highway just before Killian's exit to grab a coffee so they didn't show up at the same time.

When she arrived at the main house, she had to buzz in at the gate, where a guard checked her ID. A security camera stared her in the face. As she drove up the long lane, she noted landscapers mowing the lawn and caring for the perfectly manicured shrubs. Must be nice.

The guard at the gate had told her where to park—a small lot behind the house near what probably used to be a stable. Killian got her suitcase out of the trunk and started in the direction of the main building.

She was met at the door by a smiling Mina. "Killian! How good to see you again. Please come in and I'll help you get settled."

"Thanks," Killian murmured as she walked into the cool interior. The house was even more ornate than she expected. So much marble and glass. It was a little gaudy, she thought, but not like anyone had asked for her opinion.

"First thing I need to do is ask you to surrender your cell phone and any electronics you might have."

Killian pulled her phone—securely locked and wiped—out of her pocket and handed it over. She watched as Mina placed it into a baggie with her name written on it.

"Is that all you have?" the woman asked.

Killian smiled. "I'm a bit of a Luddite."

Mina didn't look convinced. "We do conduct room searches from time to time."

"That's intrusive, don't you think?"

"Shasis and Magnus have had their teachings leaked before. Their intellectual property is very important to them."

And they don't want anyone seeing how much they've ripped off other people, or risk people finding out about their "sexual healing" crap.

"Well, you can search my room all you want. The phone is all the tech I have."

Mina still looked dubious, but Killian didn't care. Unless the woman snapped on a pair of gloves and got *really* intrusive, she wasn't going to find anything Killian didn't want her to. "It's fine. The Wi-Fi is password protected."

Like she'd trust their network anyway. "Again, Luddite. I welcome the quiet."

"I'll take you to your room. Follow me."

Mina's kitten heels echoed in the cavernous hall as she led the way to the grand staircase. It rose straight up and then split left and right. Mina took the right set, and Killian followed her, carrying her suitcase and trying not to gawk like the rube she felt like.

Upstairs was just as decadent, but the floor was covered with a thick carpet that muffled the sound of footsteps. Good to know for when she had to sneak around. Mina took her to the end of the corridor—last door on the right. She knocked on the dark, heavy wood.

"Come in," called a familiar voice.

Mina opened the door into a bedroom that was larger than most hotel suites. There was a queen-size bed against either side and a private bathroom. There was another door against the left wall, presumably that led to a balcony, and a television between the large windows against the back wall.

Sitting on the bed nearest the balcony was Maryl. As soon as she saw Killian, she tossed aside the book she'd been reading and jumped to her feet to greet her. "Hey, roomie!"

Killian didn't have to force the grin that curved her lips. "Hey, yourself." At least now she'd be able to keep an eye on Maryl and watch out for her. She was exactly the kind of person Shasis would set her sights on as easy prey. Magnus, too, probably. Would the big man make an appearance this week?

Mina stepped back into the corridor. "I'll leave the two of you to get settled. There will be luncheon at one downstairs in the dining room. The program begins after that. Killian, your orientation package is on the bed." She smiled brightly once more. "We're so very happy to have you as part of the Incarnyx family."

Killian kept her smile frozen in place until the door shut; then she let it slip away. She turned to Maryl. "She creeps me out."

"Shh." But the other woman laughed all the same. "I'm so glad we got put together. I was terrified they'd put me with Belle."

Killian carried her suitcase over to the wardrobe on her side of the room. "Belle's not so bad. Nothing a jab to the throat can't fix."

"Oh God. I'd try it if I thought it would actually shut her up."

"Do it right and it would," Killian replied, unzipping her bag. She and Maryl made small talk while she put away her clothing. She didn't ask about Joe but was told that Maryl had avoided seeing him when she went home to get her things. She'd come here straight from the hotel.

"He's called me easily a dozen times. I haven't answered, but he's left voice mail. At first he was angry, but the last couple have been him pleading for me to come home."

It was obvious that Maryl liked his pleading. "I'm sure he misses smacking you around."

Maryl's jaw dropped. It took Killian a second to realize that strangled sound was laughter. "Maybe you should be Belle's roommate instead of mine."

"She'd be dead before morning," Killian quipped, setting her now empty suitcase inside the wardrobe and closing the door. Then she went to the bathroom and removed the RF detector from her toiletry bag. Mina really wouldn't get very far in security. She quickly scanned the room for feedback. Nothing. No cameras, then. Chances were, no listening devices, either, but she turned on the taps just to be safe.

Killian carefully retrieved the condom-wrapped mini-phone from where she'd hidden it. It wasn't much, but it would allow her to at least text Dash, and that was all she needed. Removing the device from the condom, she quickly sent a message to Dash using the private cellular network the Initiative utilized, just to let him know she was there. Then she silently hopped up onto the vanity and slipped the phone behind the mirror, securing it on a small ledge. Satisfied it wouldn't be found, she jumped back down, flushed the condom, washed her hands, and went back out into the main room.

"I'm going to take a shower before lunch," Maryl announced. "Do you mind?"

"Of course not. I'm going to chill with some TV." Killian watched her enter the bathroom and close the door. It was the oddest thing, but she couldn't help but wonder if Maryl was hiding something as well.

Adriana Morales-Vargas didn't much like her husband, but she loved him dearly.

Rafael had always been a man of loyalty—provided it didn't involve his penis—and action, which was all the better if it involved his penis. He had been loyal to her in his heart for thirty-five years. His loins were another story. It was fine. He bought her lovely gifts, never forgot her birthday or their anniversary, encouraged her career in medicine, and was completely blind to the fact that she had her own lovers.

He never noticed, because her lovers were all women, and it never occurred to him that she might find pleasure elsewhere than with him.

So, when Rafa got involved with this Deacon Ford and his Incarnyx group, she didn't bat an eye. She knew "Magnus" supplied her husband with women as agreeably as he trafficked her husband's drugs. While the two of them did their business over drinking and tomcatting, she was left with Shasis and a bevy of other desirable women to conduct business of her own.

Whenever he had Incarnyx business, she always went with him, or opened their home to Shasis and Magnus. What was good for the gander was also good for the goose.

They had separate bedrooms at Magnus and Shasis's extravagant home. That had been Rafa's idea. He said it was so he wouldn't wake her when he came in late from meetings, but she knew the truth. It was fine. Her room was across the hall from Shasis's.

"Bisexuality," she'd once heard her lover say to a group of women, "is a societal construct. In reality, humans are pleasure-driven animals. The female of the species understands that better than the male, and because of male hang-ups, we are able to explore our sexuality with much more freedom. We caress each other, kiss each other, hold one another, with so much more abandon and joy than men do. That's why we live longer." The remark was met with soft laughter. A couple of the women argued that they were straight, that the idea of being with a woman was repugnant to them.

Those were the women Adriana was drawn to. She befriended them, opened up to them. She shared wine and marijuana with them, and she started slowly—a whisper here, a whisper there. A touch here, a touch . . . there. Sometimes it worked and sometimes it didn't, but the thrill was in the seduction itself. She had learned that from her father—not that Manuel had ever touched her. He'd been a good father and faithful husband. He had also been a ruthless "businessman." Rafa had taken over when he was murdered and inherited a spot in both the cartel and Manuel's family. It had been divine interference that he and Adriana had also fallen in love.

But Rafa was not her father, and she was not her mother. Her mother still wore black to this day, mourning the man she'd lost more than thirty years ago. She prayed to God that he would take her to Heaven every day, but God had yet to answer those prayers. There were days when Adriana prayed he would take her mother as well, if for no other reason than it would put an end to her suffering.

Adriana took a nap before lunch so she would be fresh and alert. She touched up her eye makeup and applied a fresh coat of lipstick before dressing in a dark red sheath dress that showed off her impressive chest and toned arms. She worked hard to have those arms. The boobs came naturally, but they'd required a little assistance after three children. It was the best thing she'd ever done for her self-confidence, and Rafa loved them.

So did Shasis.

High-heeled sandals and gold bracelets finished the look. She spritzed some perfume and smoothed her hair. Perfection. She wanted people to notice her, not her effort to get them to notice. She needed to look sensual but polished. Intimidating but warm and friendly at the same time. Rafa used to tell her she was the most beautiful girl in all of the world. He still did—on their anniversary or her birthday. Not like he used to say it, but that was okay. He meant it when he did, just as she meant it when she said she loved him.

She went downstairs five minutes after the scheduled time—not enough to be obnoxious, but enough to not be eager. It was a large gathering, which was good. More people talking meant fewer people would notice her husband and his men. Thankfully, Rafa had sent most of them away for the meal and only had two of his guards with him—José and Oscar. They were the two best actors, the ones who were good-looking and charming as well as cold-blooded killers. They would flirt with the women, but not too much. They would also make sure the trip went smoothly as far as the drugs were concerned. As much as she made the trip her own, she must never forget what it was really all about—maintaining the family name and power.

As soon as Shasis saw her, she approached. The woman was magnificent in head-to-toe white. Her skin glowed and she smelled of ripe peaches and ginger.

"Adriana," she said, holding out her arms. "I'm so glad you could make it."

She stepped into the embrace, pressing her body tight against Shasis's. "Thank you for including me." God, she felt good.

Taking her by the hand, Shasis led her toward the table. "Let me introduce you to our newcomers."

Most of the women were well dressed and attractive. They tried to look polished and put together, but there was one who stood out from the crowd. She was fairly tall, with a tanned complexion and dark brown hair that hung in tousled waves around her shoulders. Her eyes were what? Green? Hazel? Brown? It was hard to tell in this light, but she had one of the most arresting faces Adriana had ever seen. She was beautiful like a jaguar is beautiful—you want to pet it right until you realize it could tear your arm off. She wore slim black pants and a knit top that weren't designed to flaunt her figure but simply couldn't help it. The woman was built like an Amazon, with tattoos and an attitude.

"This is Killian Delaney," Shasis said.

Why did that name sound familiar? Adriana wondered as she extended her hand. Then, out of the corner of her eye, she saw Rafa's head snap up. He recognized it, too...

She was the woman who destroyed Rank Cirello, their previous "product manager" on this coast. The fighter. The woman who refused to die no matter how many were sent to kill her. Rafa had sent two of their own people to do the job. Both had come back broken failures.

There was no bounty to collect now, but her husband might still decide to kill this magnificent creature out of some sense of loyalty or pride. He wouldn't do it right away, however—not while there were so many people present. So that gave Adriana plenty of time.

By the end of the module, Killian Delaney would be hers. And then maybe she'd convince Rafa to spare her life.

Or not.

EIGHT

Are you okay?" Maryl asked as they sat down at their assigned spots at the dining room table.

"Fine," Killian replied with forced lightness. She wasn't the kind normally given to panic, but her pulse pounded in her throat at an uncomfortably violent pace. This was a potential complication she did not need.

Rafael Vargas and his men had looked at her like they wanted to skin her alive—slowly. Vargas's wife looked like she wanted to eat her alive—*very* slowly. It was obvious the woman was having an affair with Shasis, and that was something she did not want to get in the middle of. Frankly, she'd rather deal with the guys with guns.

She didn't know how they knew her, or what their grudge was, but if she had to guess, she'd say it had to do with Cirello. God, the guy was dead, get over it. If she had more ego she'd assume they'd sniffed her out as a fellow predator, but she didn't see herself that way.

This was exactly what she'd been worried about when she confronted Ilyana about her involvement with Vargas's son. The feds poking around was bad enough. Being this close to a cartel was bad enough, but to have both, along with all the other craziness of the situation, was pushing too much to handle. It was like trying to take a dump on a toilet full of dynamite and hoping to finish before it went off.

It meant she wouldn't have the time to get to the girls and the blackmail that she initially thought she would. She was going to have to do this quickly and as quietly as she could, and hopefully she'd make it out alive.

"You don't look fine," Maryl continued. "Is it because of the Mexican guys? They're kind of cute."

Jesus Christ, the woman had a thing for predators. She didn't correct her that they weren't Mexican. "No, it's nothing, seriously. I'm good." Thank God Story was with her, because she was going to need the extra hands and eyes to keep Maryl and the other women safe as well. What if the frigging feds showed up during the retreat? What if someone started shooting?

"Why do you think they're here?" Maryl whispered.

Killian glanced at her. There was a strange glint in the other woman's eyes, like she already knew the answer to that question. What would someone like Maryl know about South American cartels? Or even Vargas as a person? It wasn't as though he was a media darling. His son was much more in the public eye, but even then the press tended to refer to Miguel as a *businessman*—his father as well.

"Maybe they're looking for enlightenment," Killian quipped. Thankfully, she was seated far away from Vargas and his men, because there was part of her that was tempted to tell them the feds were watching, just to get rid of them. They were seated at the end of the table reserved for Magnus himself, while she was only two chairs away from Shasis at the opposite end. It put her diagonally across from Mrs. Vargas and beside Mina. Shasis must have been serious about wanting to bring her in. Good. It might be the only thing that kept her alive long enough to finish this damn job.

In the middle of the table, across from each other, sat Dylan and Miguel. Oh yeah, they were definitely into each other. They couldn't stop looking and smiling at one another. Lyria, however, was nowhere to be seen. Just guests and the necessary peons, she guessed.

Unlike her sister, Dylan looked the very picture of health. Her skin glowed; her hair shone. There was even a fullness to her face that hadn't been there in the photographs Killian had seen. Was Incarnyx responsible, or the man staring at her like she was everything? She didn't care what Ilyana said; it had to chafe, seeing your ex with your kid, regardless if they were closer in age.

The last person to enter the room was a very tanned man with dirty blond hair and sparkling blue eyes. He wore sandals and loose-fitting pants with a billowy shirt, open just enough at the throat to show off his muscle tone. He was incredibly good-looking, and he knew it. He also had to work incredibly hard at it to have a body like that, so Killian wasn't going to diss him for doing it, even if he did look like an ad for men's cologne.

A broad grin revealed his perfect, brilliantly white teeth as he opened his arms to greet Vargas. A quick male hug and some clasped arms later, and Magnus worked his way down the table.

He stopped at every chair and welcomed every guest—flirting with the women. He knew all their names, but then they were written on the place cards. When he got to Killian, he gave her an appreciative once-over.

"Miss Killian Delaney," he drawled. Was that accent for real? "So pleased you could join us. I wonder if you might indulge me and join me in some sparring tonight?"

WTF? Killian blinked. "You want to fight?"

He squatted down beside her chair so they were at eye level. Everyone at the table watched—Killian could feel their gazes. "I want you to help me show the kind of personal power that comes with physical strength and agility. Don't tell me it doesn't take you to a higher plane when you've reached the limit of your endurance. All those endorphins—it's exhilaration at its zenith."

Killian frowned. Was he hitting on her? What would happen if she said no? Hell, what would happen if she said yes? She'd never turned away from a fight in her life. And for all his charm, this guy was just another posturing rooster who thought he could beat her.

"Yeah," she said. "Okay."

Magnus grinned. "Excellent. Nine o'clock in the gymnasium." He rose and continued on to Mina.

Killian caught Maryl staring at her with a "What was that?" expression on her face, eyes wide. All she could do was shrug. Not like she'd invited the attention.

"This ought to be interesting," Shasis remarked, lifting her wineglass to her glossy lips. Her eyes glittered with amusement.

Killian couldn't help but smile a little. She didn't trust the woman at all, but if nothing else, Shasis knew what she was capable of.

"I promise not to go too hard on him," Killian joked, earning a few chuckles from other guests—including Adriana.

"Go as hard on him as you'd like," Shasis replied. "I won't mind." Then she winked, making it seem like more of a joke, but Killian saw the truth in her eyes. There was a divide between the two of them that hadn't been there before. She wouldn't be surprised if Shasis was pissed because of the cartel connection. She seemed to like having this veil of respectability around her con, but even two cartel strongmen at her table ruined that.

Lunch was high-end, the salad course crisp and flavorful, accented with exotic fruit and nuts. The appetizer was vegan, and the main course offered a choice of meat or plant-based protein with healthy carbs and fats as sides. It was healthy as well as delicious, something Killian appreciated.

"Magnus will be pleased that you enjoyed the meal," Shasis told her. "He makes most of the menus himself."

"I haven't met too many meals I didn't like," Killian replied with a humble tone.

"Well, I'm stuffed," Maryl commented—she'd barely touched her entree, while Killian's plate was clean.

"I do like to see a woman with an appetite," Adriana announced in that lyrical, throaty voice of hers. "There's a primal sensuality to be found in the act of eating, which I've always enjoyed."

Okay, so it was no wonder Incarnyx had a reputation as a sex cult. Everyone there was a complete and utter horndog.

"I've always thought of food as fuel for the body," Killian

replied. "But if it's something the body needs, why not take pleasure in it?"

Adriana's dark eyes lit up. "Exactly. Oh, Shasis, darling. I'm so glad you invited us to this gathering. So many wonderfully interesting new people."

"I thought you'd be pleased," Shasis replied. There was no jealousy in her expression, so both of them were either secure in their affair or had no claim on each other.

They were served fruit for dessert—beautifully ripe and juicy. Killian was completely aware of Adriana's attention as she ate but pretended not to notice. If flirting with the wife of the *teniente* helped keep her out of the crosshairs, she'd do it.

After lunch, there was an orientation ceremony. Unsurprisingly, Vargas and his men weren't present. Magnus wasn't, either. Shasis had them all pick out tunics and yoga pants from a room stocked with all sizes, sealed in bags fresh from the manufacturer. They wrote down their sizes on slips of paper that were then given to staff who would make sure that a fresh set would be delivered to their room every evening for the following day. Killian, who spent most of her time in leggings or other clothing with a good amount of freedom of movement, appreciated the uniform.

"I feel like a Moonie," Maryl whispered to her as they stood with the others in the gym.

Killian choked back a bark of laughter. "Well, you look like Doug Henning," she replied.

Maryl giggled. The fact that she didn't ask who Henning was made Killian like her even more.

Shasis had also changed into the same outfit as the rest of them, but she made it look fabulous, of course. "I want you all to lie down on a mat," she instructed.

Killian and Maryl approached the circle of plush white mats laid out in the center of the room. Most of the woman rushed toward the front, filling in the top section, forcing everyone else to the outer edge. Killian didn't mind. As she sat down on the mat, she wasn't the least bit surprised when Adriana sat down beside her.

Maryl arched an eyebrow. Killian shrugged.

"Lie back, please," Shasis said. "Get comfortable. I want you to lie so that your feet and hands touch those of the person on either side of you."

Oh, fabulous. Killian slowly reached out until she encountered Maryl and Adriana. Maryl's grip was light. Adriana's was more intentional.

"Close your eyes and take a centering breath. In through your nose and out through your mouth. Nice and controlled."

Killian did as instructed. Next, Shasis walked them through some relaxation techniques. Slowly, tension eased from her limbs, neck, and jaw.

"You're part of a circle," Shasis went on. "You're all connected through touch, the most necessary of human senses. Feed your positive energy outward, giving it to everyone else in the circle. Feel the energy of everyone else connected to you coming back and filling you with warmth and positivity."

Maybe it was a bunch of BS, but Killian's nerves tingled. Lying there on the floor, she was vulnerable to attack, her muscles loose and relaxed. She was surrounded by strangers, the wife of a drug lord, and at least one other ex-con; she should be alert and on guard, but she felt safe and secure.

Adriana's thumb stroked hers—lightly. It might be something, or it might not. She ignored it and it didn't happen again. Her own fingers twitched against Maryl's. The other woman gave her hand a light squeeze. Funny, she knew it was meant as supportive, while Adriana's was obviously interest.

Maybe she wanted Adriana to flirt with her. Maybe she was attracted to predators as well. Maybe she liked attention.

Maybe *gay for the stay* took a while to wear off.

Or maybe she trusted Maryl and not Adriana. Maybe it was the twenty-first century and she should stop worrying about her sexuality and focus on getting her ass out of the mess it was currently in.

She had to find Lyria. And she had to find a way to talk to Dylan, but the older Woodward daughter seemed to be sticking pretty close to Adriana. Maybe one, if not both, of them would be at the big fight that night.

Jesus, what had she been thinking? Maybe it would just be some innocent sparring, but no one associated with this frigging place gave even the slightest illusion of innocence.

They stayed on the floor for a bit, breathing and soaking up positivity. They were told to be aware of the hands and feet touching theirs and take strength from them, giving love in return. Killian didn't have a lot of love to give, but she'd take all the strength she could get.

After the exercise was finished, they all sat on their mats and introduced themselves one by one. It was a little bit like AA, Killian thought, except hardly anyone declared themselves a drunk. Everyone made *some* kind of declaration, though. Divorced, menopausal, widowed, addict, sexual abuse survivor, afraid, alone. It was different for each and every one of them. Killian declared herself an ex-con. Admittedly, part of her did it just to see the reactions it got. Honestly, she was a little disappointed. No one really seemed to care. She'd expected at least one horrified glance but got nothing. Huh.

After an hour of yoga—something Killian had never been particularly good at—she felt like she'd gotten her workout in for the day. Shasis then invited them all to make use of the pool if they wanted, and since it was a gorgeous day, most of them did.

Dylan announced that she was going to take a nap, and Killian seized the opportunity. Smiling, she said, "That's a great idea. Mind if I walk with you?"

"Of course not," the younger woman replied with a slight smile.

Neither of them said anything until they were out of the room.

"How are you enjoying the retreat so far?" Dylan asked.

"Food's good," Killian replied, getting a chuckle from her companion. "If nothing else I'll leave here with my downward dog in good form."

"I know my mother sent you," Dylan murmured as they approached the main section of the house. "My sister told me."

"Where is Lyria? I haven't seen her."

"Probably in her room. She doesn't like Miguel." This was said with enough bitterness that Killian didn't pursue it. "Look, we need to talk. Privately."

"Let's talk, then," she suggested as they climbed the grand staircase together.

"Not now. There are too many people around." At the top of the stairs, Dylan stopped and turned to her with an expression of practiced serenity that didn't reach her eyes. "I'll find you. Enjoy your nap." Then she turned down the left corridor—the private wing—leaving Killian with little choice but to continue on to her own room. It wasn't a complete wash. At least now she'd have time to search through Maryl's stuff. She couldn't shake the idea that her roomie was hiding something. Maybe it was a distrust she'd picked up in prison, but it didn't hurt to follow through. She liked Maryl, but she'd liked Raven, too, and she'd been a plant.

Once inside the silence of the shared room, Killian did another RF sweep. The room was clean.

She lifted up the mattress of Maryl's bed—nothing. She looked under the bed, behind the headboard, behind the nightstand. She searched the other woman's wardrobe—still nothing. Then, out of paranoia, she searched her own. Nothing, of course.

She retrieved the phone from its hiding spot in the bathroom and checked for messages. Dash had sent one to check in. Smiling, she texted a quick reply before hiding the phone once again. Then she lifted the cover on the toilet tank. It was the first place most people would think to hide something.

Nothing.

Nothing under the sink, either, or at the back of any shelves. She stood there, hands on her hips, looking around the room. Her instincts were usually pretty good, but maybe she'd been wrong about Maryl.

Her gaze fell on the fake plant between the toilet and the vanity. It was a tall thing—like bamboo or something. Very realistic until you touched it. Grabbing it by the stalk, she carefully pulled it out of the pot—the fake soil came with it.

She peered into the planter. Nothing. Then she turned the column of plastic soil and looked inside it.

There was a large square of felt secured to the "ceiling" of the column. There was definitely something underneath it. Killian peeled back the edge of the fabric...

Well, shit. Maryl had something to hide after all.

It was a Glock. Who the hell was she planning to shoot?

Killian didn't ask Maryl about the gun when she returned to the room later that afternoon, for a couple of different reasons. Firstly, she might need the Glock herself at some point, and she didn't want to risk Maryl moving it. Secondly, she knew it was none of her business. It did make her wonder what else people might have smuggled past Incarnyx's lame-ass security, but that wasn't her problem, either.

"I'm going for a smoothie," she told her roommate when Maryl came out of the shower. That would be her excuse, of course, if anyone noticed her snooping around. "Want anything?"

"I'm good, thanks. You could probably get a swim in now if you want—everyone's in their rooms getting ready for dinner."

Killian hesitated just for a moment. It almost felt like Maryl was giving her a "coast's clear," which was impossible. "I'm probably not going to swim, but I might do a little yoga. I want to be limber for tonight."

Blotting the water from her hair with a towel, Maryl sat down on her bed. Killian couldn't help but notice how defined her calves were beneath the hem of her robe. Maryl never mentioned working out, but it was obvious she did. "Are you really going to fight Magnus?"

Killian shrugged. "It was his idea. He wants to make it a learning experience, remember?"

Maryl smirked. "Try not to break anything important—like his ego."

"Are you asking me to throw a fight?" She was all mock offended.

"God no! Just don't hurt him too bad. He's nice to look at. Plus, I paid a lot of money to hear him speak. If you break his jaw, that goes down the toilet."

"Understood," Killian replied with a smile.

Maryl was right—the place was quiet. At the bottom of the stairs, Killian took a moment to look around. There didn't even seem to be any security cameras in place. That didn't mean they weren't there, though. Shasis was definitely the hidden-camera type. In the interest of paranoia, she kept her expression open and curious as she slowly ventured away from the more public part of the building, down a corridor behind the stairs. At the end of it, a large man stood outside one of the doors. Rafael Vargas was obviously in that room. Was it Magnus's office, though?

"Killian," said a familiar voice. "What are you doing down here?"

She turned to Mina with a practiced sheepish expression. "I'm looking for the smoothie station, but obviously I'm in the wrong place."

The other woman looked only slightly dubious. "The kitchen is at the other end of the house. Come, I'll show you."

"Thanks." Any other response would arouse suspicion, so Killian followed Mina to the kitchen and the amazing smoothie bar.

"You want one?" she asked as she began to put her own together. "I make a pretty mean smoothie."

Mina smiled—probably the first genuine one Killian had witnessed. "No. Thank you, though. Enjoy yours—and you can use the kitchen area whenever you want. Magnus will be so happy to know someone appreciates his attention to health."

"Mm." Killian didn't know what the hell to say. She blended herself a smoothie while Mina watched.

"Shasis has requested that you join her this evening after your *exercise* with Magnus. Please don't make other plans."

Killian rinsed the small blender and put it in the dishwasher, as per instructions left on the smoothie station. "Yeah. Okay."

The other woman left her with a curt nod. What the hell did Dirty T want? It was either business, or a threesome with Adriana, or she wanted to kill her. Each of those was equally possible.

Killian took a sip from the glass as she left the kitchen. She really did make a good smoothie. Being pseudo-forced into making one was more treat than punishment for being caught snooping. It backed up her theory about hidden cameras, though. It hadn't taken Mina long to find her. She'd have to be more careful later.

Slowly, she wandered toward the sound of voices—the sliding doors that led out to the pool area. The dress she wore—one of the few she owned—was long and gauzy and perfect for lounging.

"Psst."

Stopping, Killian turned. At first, she saw no one, but then she saw a face peeking out of a doorway across the hall on her right. It was Lyria.

Killian took a quick glance around to make sure no one else was nearby who might have noticed and hurried toward the room. It was one of the "open" areas so it was unlikely anyone would come asking what she was doing. Lyria had already ducked back inside.

"I've been looking for you," Killian told her in a quiet voice as she closed the door. The room looked to be a library. Shelves upon shelves of books lined the walls, surrounding comfortable-looking chairs and sofas. "Where have you been?"

"Hiding," Lyria explained. "I'm spending as much time in my room as possible while Vargas and his goons are here."

"By choice?"

The girl nodded. "One of Vargas's guys got handsy last time they were here. He would have gone a lot further if Magnus hadn't walked in."

"You're hiding so you won't get assaulted?"

"Pretty much, yeah."

A familiar burn simmered at the base of Killian's skull. "Which one is he?"

Lyria shook her head. "You don't have—"

Killian's teeth scraped together. "*Which—one—is—he?*"

"Rosary tattoo that curls around his left arm onto the back of his hand. Long hair. Good-looking if you like cold-blooded."

Killian had seen him earlier with Vargas. He'd been one of the guys at lunch. She'd admired the tattoo. "I'll keep an eye on him. If you want to join the others, you should. You can stay near me. I won't let him touch you."

"What are you going to do?" the girl asked with a nervous chuckle. "Kill him?"

Killian shrugged. "Break his hands for a start."

Lyria swallowed. "You know, you're kind of scary."

"That's why your mother hired me."

"Yeah, about that..." She shifted her posture. "What exactly did Ilyana tell you?"

"You call your mother by name?"

"*Mom* makes her feel old." The smile she wore was a sad one. "What reason did she give you to come here?"

"She's heard rumors of an FBI raid and she wants me to get you and your sister out of here before that happens. She also wants me to retrieve the blackmail material Incarnyx has on you."

Frowning, Lyria leaned back against one of the sofas. "Blackmail on me?"

"And Dylan."

"What kind of blackmail?"

"Photos and video of an...intimate nature of both you and your sister with Magnus and others."

Lyria's eyebrows rose. "I don't know anything about that."

"I saw photos of your sister with Magnus."

"Yeah, they used to bang before she hooked up with Miguel. Dylan's not big on denying herself whatever or whoever she wants."

Confusion and suspicion mingled in Killian's gut. "You mean Incarnyx hasn't blackmailed you and Dylan into remaining loyal?"

"No." Lyria laughed. "Shasis and Magnus don't need to do that. In case you haven't noticed, they're pretty much all about doing whatever makes you feel good. I feel better with them than I have in years."

"Then why do you look exhausted and stressed?"

The girl laughed again at her blunt tone. "Because I've been recovering from drug addiction and an eating disorder and sometimes I'm exhausted and stressed from trying not to abuse myself."

Killian frowned. "Your mother didn't mention that."

"I don't think she noticed, to be honest."

Right. *Right.* "Well, she hired me to get the two of you out of here."

"Because she thinks there's going to be a raid?"

"Yeah. Whatever else she is, she's worried about you two."

Another chuckle, accompanied by a shake of Lyria's pretty head. "You know if there's a raid it's because of her, right? Mom probably gave them everything she had on Miguel's family out of spite."

Ilyana never mentioned having dirt, but it stood to reason that she might. It also explained how she knew there was going to be a raid soon. Ilyana hadn't told her any more than she felt Killian needed to know, apparently. Bitch.

"So, your mother knows about Vargas's drug business?"

"And the girls, yeah."

Wait. "Girls?"

Lyria shook her head with a disgusted expression. "She didn't tell you anything, did she?"

"I guess not. What girls?"

"Every class or retreat Incarnyx holds, Vargas sends a couple of girls. They go through the program and then they're shipped somewhere else. I don't know where, but they don't go back to South America. I think they're trafficked, or, at best, willing to set up as high-end prostitutes in the city."

The "city" being New York. Killian's mood soured quickly. "So Shasis is turning out girls."

"I don't know if she even knows about it."

That stopped Killian hard and fast. "What? How could she not know?"

"Mina takes care of all the registrations. She makes it look all aboveboard. All Shasis sees is the money, and on paper everything looks legit."

"Wait. You're telling me Mina is in on this? 'Butter wouldn't melt in her vag' Mina?"

The younger girl laughed at that. "Yeah. She's been bouncing back and forth between Magnus and Rafael Vargas for months now. I'm not sure how she keeps their attention, and I'm pretty sure I don't want to know."

This place just kept getting more and more fucked-up the deeper she looked. "Is that what Incarnyx has on your mother? That she knows about this shit?"

"Mom brought some younger actresses with her to a few retreats. Those girls are making more money on their backs than they ever made on-screen. She got kickbacks or a 'recruitment incentive' for bringing them in, so she essentially made herself a pimp. She tried to get Dylan in on it as well."

Recruitment, Ilyana had called it, fucking bitch. "A good lawyer could work around all of that."

Lyria smiled wryly. "It's not the law she's worried about. It's the press. It's what it will do to her reputation and career. She doesn't mind being seen with a cartel daddy, because it makes her seem like a badass, but she doesn't want anyone to find out she did business with him."

"She's covering her ass."

The girl shrugged. "Knowing Mom, yeah. In her defense, I'm pretty sure she really does want to protect me and Dylan, too."

"Right." If it made the kid feel better to think that, whatever. "Okay, I really don't want to be here when the feds arrive. Will you leave?"

Another shrug. "I don't want to leave my sister with them."

"Earlier she told me she wants to talk, so maybe she'll be open to the idea." If not, there was always the option to knock her the fuck out. Killian didn't want to spend any more time there than she had to. Her skin was already tingling with the anticipation of danger. "How deep is Miguel into all of this?"

"I don't know. I figure he has to know at least some of it, right? But Miguel says he wants a different life. He talks about wanting to get into legitimate business here in the US. It's not him you have to worry about; it's his father. If Vargas is here to do business, it's not going to be easy for any of us to leave before he does."

Killian nodded. "It would also be a great time for the FBI to show up." Ilyana should have told her about squealing on Vargas.

"I can't believe Mom would endanger me and Dylan like that, though."

"That's why I'm here, kid." And of course, Ilyana couldn't just tell the girls to get out, because there'd be a hit out on her if Vargas found out what she'd done.

"Yeah, well, if you can get Dylan to leave, I'll go. I'm not leaving her here alone, though. Mom can just fucking deal."

Killian nodded. She could relate to that. She'd do anything for Megan. She rarely spoke to her mother. "Do you think Dylan will leave?"

Lyria shook her head. "Not without Miguel. Not willingly."

"Do you think he'd let her go if shit goes sideways?"

"I don't know. He'd want to protect her, I think."

One thing at a time. "Okay, first we need to get the truth from your mother. Find out how long we have. Then we'll figure out what to do about your sister."

"Okay," the girl said with a nod. "But this place doesn't have a landline."

"Let me deal with that. What room are you in?"

"When you come up the main stairs, stay left, then turn right down the hall. I'm at the very end on the right. Why?"

"I'll come find you tonight. That code you gave me, it's for the safe, yeah?"

"In Magnus's office, yes. Behind the bar. I got it from his phone when he was in the shower. Anything he has on Mom or Dylan will be in there." Blue eyes narrowed. "Can you really protect my sister?"

Killian liked this kid. She was ballsy and loyal to a fault. "Yes. Provided Magnus doesn't hurt me too badly tonight sparring, I'll come to you at two."

Lyria's eyes widened. "Oh, he won't hurt you. He'd never hurt a woman. He's not like that."

Tell that to all those girls he helped sell. Killian smiled. "That's too bad, because I intend to beat the snot out of him."

NINE

Before the next session, Killian managed to snag five minutes alone with Story to fill her in on her discussion with Lyria.

"Have you talked to Dylan yet?" Story asked.

"No. She said she'd find me. You think she's going to have a different version?"

"Maybe. I just don't like that Lyria's version is so different from her mother's. I get shame and privacy, but we can't do our job properly if we're being lied to." Story took a lot of pride in her work and her ability to do the job. Killian, too, though to a lesser extent. Neither of them appreciated being put in unnecessary danger.

"I don't like it, either. It feels more like I'm here in a bid to cover Ilyana's ass rather than rescue anyone."

"These Desiertos put me on edge. The fact that Vargas is walking around like he owns the place..." Story shook her head. "We're underarmed for this, my friend. Whatever happens here, it's not going to be good. If the feds show up, people are going to get hurt. Innocent people."

"Mm. I know. It's a hostage situation looking to happen."

"We need a plan to get these women out of here if things go south—not just the Woodward sisters. When I researched the history of this place, I found out it was used for hiding slaves escaping north. It was also used for rum-running during Prohibition. There have to be tunnels underneath us."

"You researched this house?"

Story looked at her in surprise. "You didn't?" When Killian shook her head, Story chuckled. "Girl, I do not know how you've managed to stay alive this long."

"Because God looks after idiots?" Killian suggested with a smile.

"You believe in God?"

"Doesn't matter what I believe in, so long as whatever's out there believes in me." Mostly she was ambivalent about religion, but there had been times in her life when she wondered if maybe something hadn't been watching over her.

Maryl entered the room just seconds before the class was to start, which was unlike her. Her hair was slightly messy and she hadn't managed to wipe away all of the mascara rings beneath her eyes. It would be worrying if she didn't have the look of a woman who had been used well and liked it.

Her roommate approached them with a smile and joined them on the cushions that had been laid out for seating. A newly familiar scent tickled Killian's olfactory memory. She shot Maryl a wry look. "Seriously?" she asked.

The other woman blinked at her. "What?"

"You have the smell of... *enlightenment* all over you." She couldn't blame Maryl for getting it on with someone other than Joe, but did it have to be Magnus the Slut? At least Joe didn't smell like patchouli.

Maryl's cheeks flushed bright red. "You can smell it?"

"I can't smell a thing," Story assured her.

Killian was stopped from saying anything else by Shasis's call to start the class, so she just patted Maryl's leg and turned her attention to the front of the room.

"Ladies, I trust you've been having a good day so far?" Shasis began, smiling at the answering applause. "I want to begin this afternoon's session by talking about the way women are conditioned to behave in our society and what we can do to repel and break that conditioning."

"Down with the patriarchy," Story whispered. Killian flashed her a grin.

"How many times have you looked at a woman who stayed with a partner who treated her badly, and thought she was weak?" Shasis asked, her voice ringing through the room. "How many times have you said, 'I wouldn't put up with what she puts up with'? How many times have you criticized the way another sister was dressed, or looked? How often do we judge each other in our minds? By the uncomfortable expressions on your faces, I know it's a lot.

"I'm guilty of doing it as well. In fact, there was a time when I enjoyed nothing more than tearing another woman down in order to lift myself up. That's what real weakness is, ladies. I was so full of hate for myself that I had to reduce all other women to the same state just so my rage had somewhere to go outside of me. I was so angry I had to hurt others, but in actuality it was just another way to keep myself low. I made myself the bad person I believed myself to be."

Killian frowned. This all sounded pretty honest and raw and not at all the Dirty T she remembered from prison.

"If I saw a woman with bruises, I'd mock her for letting a man do that to her. I'd make her less than me, because obviously I wouldn't stay with someone who beat me and treated me worse than a dog." Shasis smiled sadly. "You see, I didn't realize I was already being abused like that—by myself."

A couple of women audibly gasped. It was a good line—Killian would give her that.

"But the difference between me and that woman was that I was also the abuser. It's so easy for us to say she should have left when what we need to work on is that it is completely unacceptable to treat anyone—especially yourself—with that degree of cruelty. You see, I realized that woman was a lot stronger than me, because she stayed because she had children to take care of and she couldn't do that on her own. He was a good father, despite being a terrible husband. I didn't have that. I was just stuck with myself." As she spoke, Shasis slowly paced in front of the seated group, making eye contact with as many of the women as she could without it getting weird.

"There is no shame in doing what you need to do to survive, or to feed your children. It takes real strength to hold on to your self-confidence in the face of oppression—to do what needs to be done despite overwhelming adversity. To allow yourself to suffer so that those you love might have a better life is not weakness. It is the purest expression of love, but we as women agree that we shouldn't have to make that choice. So why, then, do we despise and mock those who do instead of gathering our support? Why do we abuse ourselves instead of turning that love inward?"

Story leaned closer. "I am about to give her an amen."

Killian nodded but didn't speak. She didn't want to miss what came next.

"Too often women are taught that we're in competition with one another. I think this must be because historically there were so few options open to us that we had to fight each other for them. Today I want to talk about making your own opportunities, giving yourself options, and having the confidence to believe not only in yourself, but in the women around you. It's time we started lifting ourselves up rather than putting each other down."

Killian watched Shasis's face as she spoke. It wasn't all a con. You didn't drag yourself up from being someone who sold women and turn yourself into someone who empowered them without doing some work on yourself. This woman was not the same one Killian had met in prison. She still wouldn't trust Shasis to not put a knife in her back, but there was no denying how far she'd come.

That's what happened when you drank your own Kool-Aid, she guessed. Still, she preferred this incarnation to what she'd been in prison. She really hoped Shasis didn't know about the girls Vargas ran through this place, because Killian didn't want to have to mess her up over that. She'd already decided to look into it on her own.

The woman at the front of the room smiled at each and every one of them, clasping her hands in front of her. "Now, I want you all to stand. We're going to mix the group up a bit and start with some metaphorical trust falls before moving on to more physical ones. Killian, would you mind assisting me, please?"

The other women were going to start hating her for being singled out by both of their hosts in one day, but that was the least of Killian's worries. She had no doubt she could catch and support Shasis's weight if the woman fell—that was a given. What she didn't think she could do was trust Shasis to catch her.

After the session—during which Shasis had indeed caught her in midfall—Killian returned to the room to find not only tomorrow's tunic and leggings on the bed, but another set as well. This one was black. There was a note with it that read, "Just in case you draw blood. These will be easier to clean." It was signed with a simple "S."

It had been one of the longest damn days of her life, and it wasn't anywhere near done yet. She still had to spar with that fucking idiot later. She'd be more annoyed if she really thought he was out to hurt her. More like he was out to make himself look like the big man, and cop a feel while he was at it. But just in case, she wouldn't let her guard down around him.

Since Maryl was still downstairs, Killian took the opportunity to do some stretches and call Dash, filling him in on what was going on.

"I don't like this," he said. "You and the cartel are a mix that's going to end up exploding. Get the fuck out of there."

She didn't bristle at his tone—he was right. "I haven't spoken to Dylan and I have to find the blackmail material; otherwise the job is a bust."

"So bust it. You don't need Raven's fucking money."

Dash was one of the best men she'd ever known, but there was an edge of jealousy to his voice that surprised her. She didn't need to overthink it, just acknowledge and move forward.

"I'll get out as soon as I can, promise."

"I can come up there if you need me to."

"No. Story and I are good. At least for now, we are. I'm hoping we'll all be out of here by tomorrow night."

"So, you don't have plans to try to bring down the Desiertos single-handedly?"

Killian made a scoffing sound. "Babe, I might be slightly crazy, but that's just full-on fucking nuts."

"Slightly?" There was laughter in his voice.

"I'll get out of here as soon as I can."

"I still think you should just drop it."

"I owe Raven. Without her I wouldn't have survived prison. You know that."

Dash sighed. "Yeah. I know. Your sense of loyalty scares me sometimes."

"Me too." She let a moment of silence pass between them. "I'll call or text you later, okay?"

"Sure. By the way, Shannon's been quiet. Going to school and behaving. I'm not sure I trust it."

Laughing, Killian shook her head. "I wouldn't. Right now, I'll take it as a win, though."

A few moments later, after saying goodbye for a second time, she hung up and hid the phone once more. Then she used the room intercom to request a light dinner in her room and took a quick nap. She was just finishing her meal when Maryl burst through the door.

"You missed karaoke!" she exclaimed as she plopped down on her own bed. "It was so much fun! Belle sang 'These Boots Were Made for Walkin'.' It was hilarious."

Killian was actually sorry to have missed it. "Maybe she'll do an encore another night." She checked the clock on the bedside table. It was eight thirty. "Guess I'd better get ready for the big match."

"He doesn't really want to fight you, does he?" Maryl looked worried. "I mean, he said it was to demonstrate personal power, but he wouldn't... he's not like Joe, do you think?"

Aw, hell. Killian hadn't even thought about how this little exercise might trigger Maryl—or any of the other women at the retreat. She'd bet a hundred bucks ole Magnus hadn't given it a thought, either.

"No," she said. "I don't think he's like Joe." He was worse, but she didn't say that.

In the bathroom, she brushed her teeth and pulled her hair back into a messy bun. She changed into the black tunic and leggings, cracked her neck, and returned to the main room.

"You look like Audrey Hepburn," Maryl commented with a smile. "If Audrey had tattoos and, you know, a record."

Killian laughed. "Incarcerated at Tiffany's."

Maryl chuckled. "Thanks for not taking offense. It was a pretty thoughtless thing for me to say."

Killian really wanted to ask her about the gun. Was she worried Joe would come for her? Or was she scared of something else? But it wasn't her business, and she hated people prying into her life, so she knew when to keep her nose to herself.

She slipped her feet into a pair of sandals—she'd be barefoot in the ring—and made her way to the door. "See you down there?" she asked.

"Wouldn't miss it," Maryl promised.

On her way downstairs, Killian bumped into Shasis, who was coming up.

"Killian," she greeted her. "Black looks good on you."

"Yeah, thanks." She leaned in. "What the fuck are you doing with the Desiertos?"

Shasis smiled. "*I'm* not doing anything with them, but now you know why Magnus is making me reconsider my life choices. I am not going back to jail for that cracker."

That was probably the first completely honest thing the woman had said to her—ever—and a crack in her newly acquired veneer. "What's your backup plan?"

Shasis glanced around—two women approached the stairs from the other end of the hall. "Come to my room at midnight. I'll explain it."

"Bitch, please. I am not showing up at your bedroom at midnight."

She laughed. "Fine. Meet me by the pool." With that, she climbed the stairs, leaving Killian no choice but to continue down.

There was a group already gathered in the gymnasium—and more coming in behind her. The boxing ring that had been in the corner earlier had been shifted toward the center of the room, and there were chairs placed in a semicircle around it.

Huh. Not bad. When she'd first started out she'd fought in less professional setups.

"Killian!" Magnus's voice carried like a stage actor's. He came toward her with a warm and welcoming grin—no malice at all. "I cannot thank you enough for indulging me in this, darlin'."

She shrugged. "You said it would help you demonstrate personal power, or something?"

"Exactly." He took her by the arm and led her toward the ring. "At Incarnyx we see so many people, but very few of them know the strength of their minds and bodies, let alone how the two are connected. It wasn't until we had one of the Chrises come visit—you know, one of those Marvel boys—that I realized what an amazing teaching opportunity physicality can be."

Jesus, he actually made sense—kind of. She ignored his name-dropping. "It's a known fact that just learning self-defense can make women much more confident and less afraid."

"I knew you'd understand," he enthused. "So many of these ladies have no idea of their sensual or physical power. I want them to leave here with their spines straight, confident in themselves and looking to only get stronger. Fitness, as I'm sure you know, is as effective as any medication against depression and mental illness. I believe it can cure physical and sexual ailments as well."

He talked just a good enough game to be dangerous, she thought. He had so much natural charm and charisma that it was easy to believe the words that tumbled out of his mouth. If it wasn't for the fact that she automatically distrusted practically everyone she met, she might be sucked in by him just like everyone else.

"So how do you want to do this?" she asked, slipping into professional mode, even though it had been years since she'd been in a fight that had been for glory and not her life. "Mostly grappling, or do you actually want to throw some punches?"

"Both. I have no desire to actually strike you or be struck by you, but I'm not going to ask you to pull your punches. I'm going to try to hit you and I want you to stop me. These women need to see what a woman's body can do."

There was still the creepy realization that he was probably going to jerk off to this later, but for now her muscles hummed with anticipation. "Got it." She smiled. "I'll try to avoid your face."

He grinned in return. "Hands off my moneymaker, if you please."

Jesus, he really made a person *want* to like him. Even knowing that he was a douche who exploited women, she still wanted to return that smile.

They both climbed into the ring at nine. Magnus pulled his shirt over his head, earning some whistles of appreciation from the audience. He grinned, loving the attention.

"Are you wearing a sports bra?" he asked.

Killian frowned. "Yeah." Duh.

"Will you remove your tunic, then, please? Seeing musculature is important in this exercise."

Yeah, whatever. Killian wasn't ashamed of her body. It was strong and muscled. Once a woman commented on the size of her thighs with a sneer, but Killian shrugged it off. She didn't need chicken legs to feel good about herself. She yanked the tunic over her head. It would have only gotten in the way and made her overheat anyway.

She got a few whistles of her own.

"That's an interesting tattoo," Magnus commented when she turned to face him.

She didn't have to ask which one he meant. He meant the one everyone always meant—the seven crows in flight across her back.

"I like crows," she said. And that was all the answer he'd get. Seven crows for a secret she never meant to tell. She'd broken that vow.

Killian warmed up while Magnus welcomed everyone and explained the reasoning behind this display of flesh. Maryl gave her a thumbs-up from the front row.

It was apparent once they got started that this was just for demonstration purposes. Posturing, even. While it was obvious that Magnus had trained—a lot—it was just as obvious that he'd never been in a *real* fight in his entire life. He was all about the choreography, the flow and exchange. He wouldn't know what to do if she tried something street on him. He'd make a good stuntman, though. His timing was great and his agility was impressive. He was just a little too over-the-top for her. She'd known other fighters like that—they were more about putting on a show than proving which one of them was the better fighter. Killian never much cared about the show.

Still, it was good for her muscle memory, for her body. She

blocked his punches and kicks, rolled with it when he took her to the ground. He liked to stop and explain things when he was lying between her thighs, or had her in some odd position, but then she'd gain the upper hand and put an end to it.

The next time they grappled, he surprised her by whispering in her ear, "My South American friends don't trust you."

"I don't trust them." She jumped off him and offered him a hand up.

"You need to be careful."

Right. Vargas was in the audience right now with a couple of his men, watching with interest. She knew better than to poke a bear, but she wasn't about to cower before a bully. Killian executed a move that was a lot of flash—the kind of thing they did in movies. She whipped her body into a handstand and used her legs to wrap around Magnus's waist, then, with him off guard, lunged upward, twisting onto his back to get him in a choke hold. He wasn't the only one who could get theatrical. Gasps echoed throughout the room.

"Bring it," she whispered. She held him for a second longer, then let go and dropped to her feet.

Magnus turned to their audience. "I concede. Isn't she magnificent, my friends? What a gorgeous example of feminine strength."

Feminine? Killian's eyes narrowed despite the applause. *Strength doesn't have a gender, asshole.*

"Tomorrow afternoon," he told her. "Two o'clock, my office." Then he offered her his hand.

She took it. Sweat ran down her face and back, pooled in

her bra. He'd given her a good workout regardless of his finesse fighting. Had this all been a ruse to warn her about the cartel? It seemed a little much.

"I'll be there," she told him. Fuck, she was going to need a secretary to remember all these meetings. She'd never had a job with this much juggling involved.

A meeting with Magnus. Would Vargas be there as well? Probably, and with his backup. Shit. Killian wiped sweat from her brow with the back of her hand as she stepped from the ring. Dash was right.

She needed to get the fuck out of there.

Midnight came quietly in the paying-guest wing of the mansion. Killian slipped out of bed—already dressed—and padded across the carpet to the bathroom. She grabbed the burner phone, then crept toward the door.

"Killian?" came Maryl's sleepy voice.

Shit. "Yeah?"

"Are you going out?"

"I'm just going down to the kitchen."

"Okay. Be careful."

Be *careful?* "Sure. Thanks." Quietly, she opened the door and eased out into the gloomy hallway. There were soft lights plugged in near the floor at intervals, so it wasn't completely dark and she could see where she was going—helpful for all the nighttime screwing around that seemed to happen in the place.

Killian crept downstairs, keeping to the shadow near the wall as much as possible. She could hear voices coming from

the game room and the unmistakable sounds of someone playing pool. Probably some of Vargas's men. She made a mental
note to stay as far away from that room as possible.

Other than that, the house was quiet. Soft music played outside by the pool—discernible only because the sliding doors
to the patio were open. Killian stepped outside, out of the air-
conditioning, into the warm summer night.

Lights sparkled and shimmered on the pool's surface. A
woman—Adriana—cut through the water like a shark. Another
woman, whose name Killian didn't know, sat on the edge of the
pool with her feet and shins in the water. Her torso swayed lazily
to the music.

Shasis sat in a lounger, facing the pool. She wore a white
crocheted cover-up over her equally white bathing suit. In her
hand she held what looked to be a piña colada. She glanced up
as Killian approached.

"Hello, darkness," she quipped. "Still high on your victory?"

Killian shrugged. "Not much of a victory when your opponent gives up."

"Yes." She drawled the word out into two syllables. "Sit
down. Wine?"

This time Killian accepted the offer. "What's that sound?"

"White-noise machine." Shasis winked. "You can never be
too paranoid. You understand, yeah?"

"Yeah." She watched as the other woman poured her a glass
of wine, the pale liquid glittering under the patio lights. "I'm
more paranoid on the outside than I ever was in."

"Me too. Sometimes I just don't feel safe with all this space around me." She laughed, and then: "What did he say to you after the fight?"

For a second, Killian considered lying. "He wants to have a meeting tomorrow afternoon. Me, him, and probably Vargas. I don't know."

Ex-cons were some of the hardest people to surprise, but Shasis arched a brow. "The fuck he want?"

Killian ignored the slip into rougher speech. It would be too easy to fall back into it herself. "I don't know. He made it seem like Vargas wants to make sure I'm not going to be trouble. He could be looking to slit my throat."

"Not here." She took a drink from her glass, leaving a glossy imprint of her lips on the rim. "I bet he's going to offer you a job."

"The kind I can't refuse?"

"You think Vargas has any other kind of employment opportunities?"

Killian chuckled at that. She glanced over at the women in the pool. Adriana stood in the water, her hand on the other woman's knee. "She's a bit of a horndog, isn't she?"

"Starved for affection," Shasis replied. "She won't admit it, of course. Thinks all that money and success of hers make up for the fact that the only person who thinks she's worth a damn is a retired pimp."

"That would be you, I assume?"

"You assume right. Sad, isn't it? That I'm the only one who sees her worth."

"You're in love with her."

A sad smile lifted Shasis's mouth. "Feels a little ironic, doesn't it? Turned my life around just to fall in love with a gangster's woman." The smile faded as she held Killian's gaze. "Why are you really here, Che-che? And don't tell me it's because you want to be a better person. You like yourself just as you is."

"Che-che." Killian shook her head. "No one's called me that for years. Not since Ronnie died."

"I was sorry I didn't get to see her before she died. I meant to. She was the original TAB."

"Tough-ass bitch." They shared a grin. "She was always good to me."

"She was good to everybody until she wasn't." Shasis topped up both of their glasses. "Answer the question."

Oh, what the hell. "Ilyana Woodward hired me to come here and remove her daughters from your evil clutches."

Shasis's fingers tightened around the stem of her glass. "She ratted, didn't she?"

Killian shrugged. "I don't know, but she did indicate that time was of the essence."

"Bitch," Shasis murmured. "I'll give you a million to kill her."

Killian choked on a sip of wine. "I'm not a contract killer, T. I'm only telling you this because I don't trust her."

"You don't trust me, either."

"I trust you more than I trust her." She folded her arms on the table. "Did you know Vargas was running girls through Incarnyx?"

There was no faking her surprise. Shasis genuinely looked like she'd been punched. "You're lying. Magnus moves his drugs, that's it."

Killian shook her head. "That's not what I heard. Hasn't he brought girls here before? Girls that just disappeared afterward?"

The other woman's striking features hardened. "Son of a bitch." She turned her attention toward the pool. Adriana looked up, said something to the other woman in the pool, and then slowly climbed the ladder out of the water. Her companion got up and walked into the house. Adriana slipped her arms into a silky kimono and padded toward them.

"What is it?" she asked in her husky voice.

"Did you know your snake of a husband is using us to run girls?"

The older woman let loose a string of something under her breath. "No," she said finally. "I did not. He promised me he was done with that."

"He lie to you a lot?" Killian asked, lifting her glass.

"Enough," came the reply. Then, to Shasis: "My darling, I am so sorry. I didn't know."

"The drugs are bad enough," Shasis remarked bitterly. "But I can separate myself and Incarnyx from that if need be. But skin trade? No one will buy I'm not part of that once they've got my prints. If Ilyana Woodward went to the feds, we're in trouble."

Adriana took her hand. "We could leave. Get out while we can."

Killian couldn't say she was surprised by the suggestion. Anyone with half a brain would want out. "You think the Desiertos will just let you walk away?"

Adriana glanced at her. "There's not a man in that cartel who will lift a hand against me."

"Not even your husband?"

"Especially not him. Not if he wants to live." Then, to Shasis: "We need to make a plan."

Shasis patted her lover's hand. "We will." She glanced at Killian. "I appreciate you being straight with me, so I'm going to be straight with you. Ilyana Woodward doesn't give a shit about her daughters. Those girls have been free to leave whenever they want, and they'd rather be here."

"I get why Dylan sticks around, but Lyria doesn't seem particularly happy."

"Yeah, well, that little girl's more trouble than she looks. Magnus keeps her around 'cause she'll do whatever he wants if he keeps her supplied. Why do you think I don't want her around the other women much?"

"She told me it was because one of Vargas's men was grabby." Shit, was Lyria really an addict? That called her trustworthiness into question.

"Because they know she'll give it up for a hit. You take that girl off my hands and I'll thank you for it."

"Dylan won't leave," Adriana joined in. "And even if she would, she's carrying Rafa's grandchild. He won't let her go far."

Killian nodded. This was getting more and more fucked-up and less and less worth the risks involved. But she couldn't just walk—not without something to take to Raven. The woman had saved her ass so many times. If Ilyana was what Shasis said, Raven deserved to know.

"Magnus wants to see Killian tomorrow," Shasis told Adriana. "Has your husband said anything?"

Adriana took a drink from Shasis's glass. "He's worried you are a threat. Maybe you were sent here by a rival? Or maybe you are here to make trouble because Magnus has taken over Rank Cirello's place as distributor."

Killian frowned. "What I did to Cirello had nothing to do with his business. He killed someone important to me. Last year he went after my niece. It was personal. Feel free to tell him that."

"I think it's better if I let you tell him, but perhaps I can soften his paranoia."

"Thanks." After a moment, Killian rose to her feet. It was obvious her companions wanted to talk privately. "I'll let the two of you make your plans," Killian said.

Shasis stopped her. "Thank you, Che-che. If things start to go sideways, I'll come for you."

Killian nodded, then left the two of them alone to return to the house. She was getting tired, and she still had work to do.

The corridor to Magnus's office wasn't lit like the upstairs, so the far end was almost pitch-dark when she reached it. Her hand curled around the doorknob and turned. It wasn't locked. Some people would think that lucky, but to Killian all it said was that Magnus kept the stuff he didn't want anyone to find well hidden.

Silently, the door swung open. She slipped inside and closed herself in before groping in her bra for the RF detector she'd hidden there earlier. She moved clumsily in the dark, but she made sure there weren't any hidden cameras in the room before turning on a light.

The top of the desk itself was clear except for a blotter and some pens. No phone, of course.

No computer, either, which meant he probably used a laptop and kept it locked up as well. He was smarter than he looked.

Behind the bar, there was a large abstract painting of a naked woman. At least, she thought it was a naked woman. It could just as easily be a dead manatee. It was just the kind of obvious that seemed to fit Magnus's personality. Prying her fingers under the edge of the frame, Killian tugged until it swung away from the wall. There it was—a large, glossy black safe.

She'd memorized the combination, so she quickly turned the knob from one number to the next. When she heard that audible release of the lock, she breathed a sigh of relief.

Inside were stacks of envelopes, files, and money. There were also thumb drives, CDs, cell phones, and various tapes. His passport was there—with his real name, of course—and a bunch of stock certificates. There was also a semiautomatic pistol.

According to the information Raven had given her, Magnus had a thumb drive containing all the dirt he had on the Woodward family. Fortunately for her, he was the kind of guy who liked to label everything, and he didn't seem to be big on using codes or cyphers. In the little organizer that held the drives, there was one labeled "I.W." How very convenient and helpful of him.

Killian grabbed the drive and shoved it in her bra—the opposite cup from the electronics detector.

She started to close the safe door but hesitated. *Is that . . .* She opened the door again. He had a file labeled "Washington, T." Killian took it from the pile and opened it. There was no way the file belonged to Shasis, so Magnus had to have it as power over her. Power that Shasis didn't know he had. Magnus was a pimp, a dealer, and a blackmailer.

She shoved the file into the waistband of her yoga pants and arranged her tunic over it. Then she moved the painting back into place, turned off the light, and crept out into the hall.

She managed to make her way back to her room without being seen, and breathed a sigh of relief.

As she opened the door, the light from the corridor illuminated just enough of the room that she could see a shadowy figure leaning over Maryl's bed.

It was too big to be Maryl.

"Who the fuck are you?" she demanded.

He charged her.

TEN

Maryl waited until she was certain Killian was gone before slipping out of bed, still wearing the clothes she had worn during the day.

What a coincidence that both she and her roommate had late-night plans. Whom was Killian meeting and why? She'd been tempted to follow, but Killian wasn't her target and she needed to remember that. It didn't matter what the other woman was up to, so long as she didn't get in Maryl's way.

She wanted all of this over. Being around Vargas and his people—even though they set themselves apart—set her teeth on edge. It was like waiting for one of those windup jack-in-the-box toys to pop. She wasn't usually one for nerves, but apparently sharing a roof with a drug lord was where her threshold ended.

She checked the hall before leaving the room. It was empty, of course. The corridor was too well lit to allow for much cover, but she didn't anticipate running into anyone, except maybe Killian and whomever she was with.

At the bottom of the stairs, she glanced toward the back patio and saw the pool lights were still on. Adriana Vargas was in the pool talking to another woman, who sat on the edge. The sliding doors were closed, so she couldn't hear their voices or any music. Was Shasis out there, too? Was Killian?

As if on cue, Killian walked into the hall as if she, too, were trying to go unnoticed. Maryl ducked behind a large potted plant and waited for the other woman to pass before continuing. The corridor to Magnus's office was darker than the rest of the house, and she knew for a fact there weren't any security cameras down here. There weren't security cameras in much of the house—no place that might be useful to anyone other than a voyeur. Magnus and Shasis were big on their own privacy, to the point where they didn't want their own security to know what they were doing. You couldn't incriminate yourself if there wasn't proof, she supposed.

The door opened easily—thankfully. She wasn't too surprised because she'd tampered with the lock earlier when she'd had sex with Magnus on the desk. It had actually been pretty good, but still embarrassing when Killian teased her about it. The woman would have made a good detective if she hadn't decided to take the law into her own hands when she was younger.

Maryl used the light from her watch to find her way through the dark room. She planted the recording device under the edge of the desk, between it and the wall. It was the one place she thought it had the least chance of being found. Of course, it wouldn't do her much good if he had an app or something that could detect or interfere with it, but he struck her as being too arrogant to think he might have a spy in his own house. He certainly wouldn't suspect one of *his* women of doing anything of the sort. He thought his dick was too magical for that.

God, he was such a scumbag. A scumbag capable of being incredibly charming and a very good liar—the worst sort. Her father had been like that. She was glad for the other women, the fresh meat at this retreat, because his interest in her was already waning.

If they could just screw and not talk it wouldn't be so bad, but it was her job to get him talking. That he talked incessantly about himself would normally be a good thing, but most of his breath was spent talking himself up, or demanding compliments on his sexual prowess.

Satisfied that the bug was well hidden, she left the office, checking the corridor before stepping out. No one was around, so she slipped out of the room. Old habits made her wipe both knobs free of prints with her sleeve before closing the door.

This time when she looked out into the pool area, both Adriana and the woman were gone, or at least had left the water. She couldn't really see anything else except a few empty lounge chairs.

Maybe Killian really had gone to the kitchen for a snack. Maybe she wasn't lying, or involved in what was going on at Incarnyx. Maybe she was just what she seemed.

Maybe Maryl was just trying to justify the fact that she actually liked Killian. She shouldn't like her. Shouldn't like anyone who consorted with bikers and criminals and had served a prison term for assault. If Killian were a man, she'd stay as far away from her as possible. Hell, she'd look for a reason to despise her. She hated knowing she had a double standard when it came to violence, but she did. Of course, she wasn't alone. It was why it had been so easy to sell her cover as an abused woman.

When she reached the upstairs hallway she noticed the door to their room was open.

Shit. She'd left the Glock in the bathroom. She glanced about for anything that might be used as a weapon...

A man fell out of the room onto the hall floor. Actually, *fell* wasn't the right word. It was as though a giant, invisible hand reached in and yanked him from the room and dropped him onto the carpet. It didn't even look like his feet touched the ground.

Killian came out of the room after him, fists clenched at her sides. Maryl watched as she swung her leg in a high, fast kick. Her opponent managed to block the kick and punched her in the stomach, but Killian didn't fall. She backhanded him hard and then grabbed him by the Adam's apple. The man went still. When Maryl was young her father, a marine, had given her tips on dealing with boys who might think she was an easy target. The first thing he told her was what a delicate thing the Adam's apple was.

"What's going on?" she asked, hurrying forward. Jesus, she wished she had that gun.

"Not sure," Killian replied, not taking her gaze off the man. "Might want to ask him."

By this time, other people had heard the noise and were coming out of their rooms. Shasis and Magnus were there as well.

"It's all right, everyone," Shasis said, assuming control. "We'll take care of this. Please return to your rooms."

The women hesitated but slowly retreated, closing their doors.

"What the sweet hell is going on?" Magnus demanded as he approached. "Were you ladies hurt? Who is this man?"

"We were in the kitchen," Maryl blurted. "We wanted a snack. When we came back, we found him in our room."

Killian met her gaze and held it. Maryl didn't feel uncomfortable that often, but she felt it at that moment. And now Killian had something on her.

"Yeah," Killian said, backing her up. "I came in first and found him looking through Maryl's things."

Her things? What the...? She had assumed the man had been there for Killian, but now that she was right there, Maryl could see the man's familiar eyes peering out from behind the ski mask he wore. Her heart sank.

"Joe?" What the hell was he doing there? He was going to ruin everything.

His wide gaze rolled toward her. "I had to see you," he rasped.

"You could have knocked, asshole," Killian snarled, still holding him by the throat as she pulled off his mask. "Just what was the plan, huh? Were you going to hit her? Maybe rape her?"

"No! Of course not. I'd never—" Whatever he was going to say broke off into a strangled mess as Killian squeezed.

"Don't lie, Joe. It's not very manly."

Maryl would never admit it out loud, but the world needed more people like Killian Delaney in it.

What Killian didn't know was that the world also needed people like Joe.

"How did he even get in here?" Shasis demanded, hands on her sari-wrapped hips.

"I . . . jumped the gate when the guard wasn't looking," Joe confessed. "Came in through the delivery entrance."

"Killian," Maryl began. "Please, let him go. He's not going to do anything."

Killian glanced up at her. "Seriously? You're going to call the cops, right?"

"No police," Vargas barked. When the hell had he arrived? Killian glared at him. He was one of the biggest, most ruthless cartel bosses in the world, and she looked at him like he was gum stuck to her shoe. Jesus. Just the sight of him made Maryl's throat tight.

"No, we don't need the police," Maryl agreed. "Just let me talk to him, and then he'll go. Right, Joe?"

He nodded—as much as he could with Killian holding him.

Killian didn't want to let him go; that was obvious. And Maryl didn't like thinking that maybe the situation made Killian think less of her, but it had to be defused—quickly. Joe couldn't be there.

"Fine," she said, rising slowly to her feet. Joe waited until she backed away to stand himself. Even though he was several inches taller than Killian and at least forty pounds heavier, he regarded her with wariness. He was smarter than he looked.

"I don't think you need to talk to anybody," Magnus said. Maryl glanced at him in surprise. He wasn't getting all possessive and alpha on her, was he?

Joe looked surprised, too. "What?"

Magnus stepped forward. He was almost the same size as Joe, and he had the cartel for backup. "I think you should just leave, sir. You're not welcome here. This is my house and Miss Maryl is under my protection, so you will leave and you will leave quietly, or there will be hell to pay, understand?"

There was nothing of the charming Magnus in this man's expression. His features were hard, his gaze sharp. If Maryl had thought him a good-ole-boy con artist before this, she was now very much aware that he was much, much more.

Of course, he would have to be. The Desiertos didn't align themselves with idiots or cowards. Snakes and cretins, but not idiots.

"I'm sorry," Joe said, clearing his throat. "I got tired of waiting. I'll go. But, Maryl, when you're done here, please look for me."

She kept her shoulders relaxed even as the muscles in her core clenched. She'd heard him right; she knew she had. It was all there in the intensity of his gaze.

She nodded, mouth dry. "Okay," she replied, and she didn't have to fake the slight tremor in her voice. Things were progressing much faster than they'd planned.

"I'll walk you out," Magnus offered, gesturing for Joe to walk ahead. Vargas, on the other hand, wasn't so inclined.

"We'll discuss this lapse in security tomorrow," he said, to whom Maryl wasn't certain.

Slowly, Vargas retreated to the other wing as Joe, Vargas's man, and Magnus went down the stairs. Only Shasis remained.

"Are you all right?" she asked. "Adriana is a doctor if you need attention."

Maryl nodded. "Thanks. I'm more shocked than anything else."

"How about you, Wonder Woman?"

Killian flexed her fingers. "I could use some ice."

"There are ice packs in the mini-fridge in your room. And several kinds of pain relievers in the bathroom vanity."

"Then, I should be good."

Shasis turned back to Maryl. "I'm sorry this happened. There's no excuse for our lack of security. I will personally reprimand our head of security and set the alarm myself once he is off the grounds. Of course we'll understand if you choose to leave tomorrow and will give you a full refund."

She wanted nothing more than to leave that place as soon as possible, but that wasn't an option now.

"Thank you, I don't think that's necessary, but I'd like to sleep on it, if that's okay?"

"Of course. Would you like to be moved to another room?"

"No." Maryl glanced at Killian. "I think I'm in the safest room in the house as it is."

"Indeed," Shasis agreed, giving Killian a once-over. "Very lucky for you. Well, then, try to get some sleep. I'll see you both in the morning."

Once inside the room, Maryl immediately went to her bed and lifted the blankets. Nothing. She thought maybe Joe had left her a message.

"Anything new or missing?" Killian asked. "Any creepy gifts?"

She shook her head. "Nothing. Look, I know you're not much of a hugger, but I'm going to hug you now, if that's all right."

"Uh, okay."

She didn't wait for Killian to change her mind, just grabbed her in a hard but quick hug. "Thank you."

Killian patted her shoulder a little awkwardly. "Sure. Listen, I'm pretty wired right now. I'm going to run a bath. Do you mind?"

"No, go ahead. I'm going to take a pill and go to bed. I'll be dead to the world by the time you're done, probably."

Killian looked at her for a second before nodding. "Okay." She didn't ask why Maryl had lied about being with her, and Maryl knew she wouldn't say anything unless Maryl volunteered an explanation.

"Just let me get in there long enough to brush my teeth." Inside the bathroom with the door closed, she checked to make sure the Glock was still in its hiding spot. It was, but now it had two extra magazines of ammo with it. Joe must have thought she might need it. Shit.

She used the toilet, washed up, and brushed her teeth, then turned the room over to Killian.

Once she heard the water start filling the tub, Maryl changed into her pajamas. She'd lied to Killian about taking something to help her sleep—she rarely took any kind of drug unless she had to, and she needed to be sharp from now on.

Maryl turned out the light and closed her eyes. She knew she could put herself to sleep fairly easily by thinking about pleasant things and telling herself that everything was going to be all right. Insomnia was an occupational hazard sometimes in her line of work.

I got tired of waiting… Look for me. Those weren't the words of a penitent man, or even a manipulative one. It was a heads-up, and it was a promise. It meant that he would be coming for her soon.

And that he wouldn't be alone.

Before getting into the bath, Killian grabbed an ice pack for her knuckles and hid the USB drive where she'd hidden the phone.

Once in the hot water, she texted Raven to tell her that she had the blackmail evidence and that she was planning to leave ASAP. Every instinct she had told her to run, especially now that Joe had shown up. There was something sketchy about that, though she couldn't quite figure out what.

If she couldn't convince Dylan to leave, it was out of her hands. She had a really bad feeling about this situation and she was going to get the fuck out of it.

There was something about Joe and Maryl that was totally off. He hadn't acted like an abuser. He hadn't raged and fought and screamed at Maryl. He hadn't fought like a woman hater. He'd acted desperate, like someone worried. He'd told Maryl to *look* for him. Weird word choice, unless it was a message of some kind.

She had the uncomfortable feeling that Maryl had lied about who she was. Uncomfortable enough that she ditched meeting with Lyria. There were too many people awake. Too many prying eyes. When she texted Dash from her bath, she asked him to check Maryl out and asked him to check with Raven about Joe's license plates.

When the alarm went off in the morning, she felt like she hadn't slept much at all. Maryl didn't seem to have fared much better.

"You okay?" Killian asked her.

"Yeah," she said with a slight frown. "I think so. It just kind of seems so surreal, you know? I really didn't expect him to come here."

"Yeah. I'm just glad you weren't here when he showed up," she lied. If Maryl had been here, maybe Killian could have gotten some answers.

Or maybe Maryl would have used that Glock on her. It had extra ammo with it now, she'd discovered.

"Mm."

She clearly didn't want to talk about it. Huh. She'd been really keen to talk about Joe before this, when she'd been trying to convince Killian he was an abuser.

They went downstairs to breakfast together a little while later. Maryl was still subdued but not quite as quiet has she had been earlier. As soon as they entered the dining room, people started coming up to her and asking her how she was doing.

Killian told Maryl to sit while she went to get them food from the buffet.

"It was magnificent what you did to that man last night," murmured a voice near her ear.

She turned her head to meet Adriana Vargas's smoldering gaze. "If you think that was good, you ought to see where I can pull a rabbit out of."

The older woman laughed. "You are a delight. I do hope you

will join us at the pool again tonight? Perhaps linger a little longer this time?" There was double meaning in her tone.

"I wouldn't dream of denying you and Shasis all the details of my meeting with your husband—provided I walk out of it alive."

Adriana tilted her head, thick dark hair spilling over her shoulders. "You'll walk out of the meeting. You may even walk out of this house. Afterward..." She shrugged. "Rafa doesn't defecate where he eats, if you'll pardon the expression."

"It's only good business," Killian agreed.

The other woman regarded her with a curious expression. "You're not the least bit afraid of him, are you?"

"It's not an insult. I'm not afraid of many people." The only thing that scared her was losing—or failing—the ones she loved.

"I'm not sure if that makes you very brave or very stupid."

There was no insult in her tone, but Killian wouldn't have cared if there was. She shrugged. "I haven't figured that out, either."

That drew a smile. "I find you incredibly attractive."

"That will fade once you get to know me."

"Perhaps. Perhaps not. However, it would be wrong of me to find out while I have someone else in my bed."

Killian nodded. "I noticed. I'd tell you to be careful if I didn't think you could eat her alive."

Adriana chuckled. "Indeed. Do you want me to talk to my husband, *querida*? Assure him you aren't a threat? I will do this for you."

"Thanks, but no." She glanced down at the tray. "Now, if you'll excuse me, I promised Maryl I'd bring her some breakfast."

"Of course. Until tonight, then." The other woman nodded slightly and drifted away. Killian was glad to see her go. Intense people like Adriana made her edgy. Even when they were relaxed, they had a dominant energy that assaulted everyone around them.

When she returned to the table, Maryl had an intent expression on her face. "Where do you suppose the staff is going with all that extra food?"

Killian turned her head to see one of the young women she recognized from the previous retreat—Heather or Hollie or something—wheeling a cart of what appeared to be bread, fruit, and coffee across the room through a doorway.

"I don't know. Maybe some of the higher-ups are having a breakfast meeting." It did seem weird, though, because Mina was at a table not far away. It reminded her of what Story had said about there being tunnels under the house. Maybe that was how Vargas's people were able to come and go.

"Maybe." Maryl didn't sound convinced. "That Vargas woman seems pretty hot for you."

Killian choked on her coffee. Wiping her mouth with a napkin, she took a sip of water to ease the coughing. "Warning next time."

"Sorry." Maryl chuckled. "Don't tell me you hadn't noticed."

"Oh no. I noticed. I just didn't realize it was that obvious. I think she sees me as a trophy or something."

"You mean like a white rhino?"

"Only slightly less horny." Killian smiled when it was Maryl's turn to cough. "You know who her husband is, right?"

"Yeah, he's some big-shot businessman."

"With rumored cartel ties." There was no need to tell her they weren't "rumored."

Maryl's eyes widened. "Really? What are they doing here?"

Fuck. Killian had to fight to hide her disappointment—in both herself and Maryl. She hated playing games. She shrugged. "Maybe he felt they needed a little self-actualization. Or maybe he's looking for American businesses to invest in."

"Do you think Magnus and Shasis know about the rumors?"

"You'd like to think they've checked him out, right?"

"Oh, they must have." Maryl frowned. "I hope they have. I'd hate to see them get into trouble for trusting the wrong people."

It was all Killian could do not to laugh, but she wasn't ready to confront Maryl just yet.

After breakfast there was a workshop on the terrace, directed by Dylan, that involved making your own blend of essential oils into a personalized perfume that made you feel empowered.

"I love the smell of lavender," the young woman informed them from behind the table that had been set up. "But this little guy *hates* it." She put her hands on her stomach. "I can't wear it anymore!"

Some of the women commiserated about the weird peculiarities of pregnancy. Killian said nothing. She just kept blending sandalwood and vanilla until she found the balance she preferred. If nothing else, she'd have a new perfume to show for her time in Incarnyx.

It was all just so fucking ridiculous. None of this had been worth the time and hassle. She would think twice before ever taking a job from Raven again.

The perfume class was followed by guided meditation—led by Mina—and then Magnus led them in a workshop called "Woman as a Sensual Being."

"I don't mean sensual as in necessarily sexual," he said with a rakish grin, "but rather sensual, as in a creature awakened and delighted by her own senses." He went on to talk about the pleasure in simply paying attention to one's surroundings, the grounding of it. Most of the women in the class seemed to hang off his words—except for Maryl.

Careful, Killian wanted to advise her. *Your mask is slipping.*

The man was all about his dick. At least Shasis was in it for the money—and put the work into actually offering something in exchange. This guy charged a crap-ton of money for his "teachings" and then used them to screw as many of his students as he could. And then he moved drugs and girls for the cartel on top of that.

Asshole. She was ashamed of having had five seconds of begrudging like toward him. Now, because of him, she had to sit down with a Desierto lieutenant and hopefully walk out of there alive. Christ only knew how that was going to go over.

After listening to Magnus bullshit for forty minutes, it was time for lunch. Killian realized she marked the passing of time by meal breaks—the one upside to this whole experience.

Once again she saw staff pushing a cart of food through that same door. It couldn't be for Incarnyx members because it looked to be sandwiches, or something rolled in foil. Killian hadn't eaten a sandwich since getting involved with the group. It wasn't their style.

"We're going to have to check that out," Story whispered from beside her.

"I'm surprised you haven't already."

"My roommate's a light sleeper." She took a bite of salad. "What was all that about last night?"

"Not sure."

Her friend watched her for a moment. "I don't like it."

"Neither do I." She gave Story a meaningful look. "I'm meeting with Vargas and Magnus at two."

"I don't like that, either."

Killian shrugged and made sure no one was listening. "Let's check out those tunnels later."

"You got it."

Maryl joined them a moment later, ending their discussion. It was clear there wouldn't be any more talk of plans as the time crept nearer to two.

"Where are you going?" Maryl asked her when she got up from the table.

"I have a meeting. I'll see you after." If she lived, that was.

A normal person would have been afraid as they made the walk to Magnus's office, but Killian was more weary than panicked. When she knocked on the heavy wood door, a Latino man answered. She hadn't seen him around before this. He was dressed in a nice suit, with his hair neat and tie straight, but no amount of prettying up could do anything about the nasty-ass scar that cut across half his face—including his left eye.

"I'm expected," she said.

"You're early," he replied.

Killian arched a brow. "You want me to come back?"

"Let her in, Diego," came a deep, rich voice from behind him. Diego stepped back and held the door open for her to enter.

Killian looked inside first. Other than Diego, there was Magnus, Vargas, his son, and one other person in there—a tall, powerfully built woman Killian hadn't seen before. Her odds would be better if they weren't armed, but that wasn't a bet she was stupid enough to take.

She stepped inside and Diego closed the door behind her.

Miguel Vargas moved toward her. "Miss Delaney, thank you for coming. Please, won't you sit? Would you like a drink?"

"No. Thank you." Killian angled one of the chairs in front of the desk so that she had a good view of everyone in the room, and the door. She sat down and looked at each one of them, silent.

Rafael Vargas sat in a wingback chair like it was a throne and his ass was royal. His thick dark hair was starting to gray at the temples and his eyes glittered like black stones. "You don't look afraid, *niña*."

"I'm not," she replied calmly.

"Not even when you are outnumbered and your life possibly resides in my hands?"

"Not even." It wasn't a bluff.

The woman inclined her head to one side in contemplation, watching her. Killian had to resist meeting her gaze. It would be a mistake to take her attention from Vargas.

"Then you're either a liar or incredibly brave."

"Not much for lying—too much to remember."

He smiled slightly—patronizingly. "Then if I ask you about the spy in our midst, you would tell me their identity?"

"Spy?"

"Yes, a spy. But first, why are you here, at this place?"

"I was invited."

He chuckled softly—it reminded her of a dog's growl. "Touché. What brought you to Incarnyx in the first place?"

Well, she'd already said she wasn't a liar, but truth could bend. "I heard you guys were running a cult—a very lucrative one. I came to check it out. Shasis and I go way back and I want in."

Vargas turned to Magnus. "A cult, my friend! You are Charles Manson now?"

Magnus laughed. "Whoever told you that exaggerated my charisma, Miss Delaney. Incarnyx is not a cult."

"No," Killian agreed. "Just a front. It would be more convincing, though, if you didn't have a representative from one of the most notorious drug cartels in the world sitting in your office."

"I am a humble businessman looking to invest in my good friend's aspirations."

Killian smiled. "You don't have to spin that tale with me, Mr. Vargas. I don't give a flying fuck about why you're here. I just wanted to get in on the action."

"Well, I'm afraid you're going to be very disappointed," Miguel stepped in. "Obviously there is nothing remotely cultish going on here. No 'action.' Incarnyx is exactly as it presents itself, but by all means, you may discover that on your own."

Killian didn't even look at him. "My bad. Well, I guess I'll just be on my way." She made to stand.

Diego pushed her back down into her seat. Killian grabbed his fingers and snapped one of them like a pretzel. The sound of his pain resonated throughout the room—less than a cry, more than a moan.

"Don't fucking touch me," she told him.

He raised his hand to strike her, but suddenly the woman was there. She caught his arm. "Enough. You are stupid. Leave."

Diego glanced at his boss. Vargas dismissed him with a wave. The woman retreated only when the door closed behind him.

"My apologies," Vargas said. "Diego has much to learn. I am afraid, however, that we cannot simply allow you to leave."

"Why the hell not?"

"Not without proof that you have no intent where our interests are concerned."

"Does it have to do with your mysterious spy?"

"Indeed. There is a federal agent in this house."

That sense of unease grew. "How do you know that?"

Magnus held up a small listening device. "I found this when I did my sweep this morning. It wasn't here the day before."

Killian shrugged. "Okay."

Vargas steepled his fingers in front of his chest. "We want you to find the agent for us."

"And if I decline?"

"You can die with her." He smiled again. "And Lyria, too. And maybe that attractive friend of yours. Come on, *niña*. You know how this all works, yes?"

Of course. Fucking piece of shit. Killian didn't doubt for one minute he'd do it. "Find her and then what?"

He opened his hands in an expressive gesture. "And nothing. Just find her and tell us who she is."

And then turn her back so Vargas or one of his goons could kill her. *Shit.*

"Fine." It wasn't. Nothing about this was fine, and she had no fucking intention of leading a federal agent to her death. Nope. "I'll see what I can do."

"No see. Just do." Another smile. "And then we will all be friends."

"Friends," she repeated. "Right." She rose to her feet and started for the door. Suddenly, Vargas was there. He moved fast for a man in his fifties. He braced his arm above her head, leaning in like he was going to kiss her.

"You want to have me for a friend, *niña*. I'm a much better friend than enemy."

Killian looked him in the eye, her jaw tight. "So am I."

He laughed, displaying teeth that must have cost the people of his country a fortune. "I like you. We're going to work well together." Then he tapped her on the nose. It was the singularly most patronizing thing anyone had ever done to her.

If he was anyone else he'd be pissing blood for the next week, but even she wasn't impulsive and crazy enough to take on the Desierto Cartel.

Vargas stepped back, allowing her to finally open the door and make her escape. She stomped down the corridor, fists clenched at her sides. Asshole thought he could control people because he knew their weaknesses, and he was fucking right. She hated him for that—and grudgingly respected him.

There was no running from the cartel. If she left now, they'd hunt her, and she knew they'd go through Shannon and Megan to get to her. They were all the same.

Killian would also bet her entire savings account that they already had an idea who the fed was. She did, too.

She just hoped she was wrong.

ELEVEN

Killian was not going to be responsible for the death of a federal agent—especially not one trying to bring down Vargas and his operation.

Especially not one she suspected to be Maryl. It didn't matter if the other woman had played Killian as part of her cover. Didn't matter if the whole abused-woman thing was a lie. Killian hadn't exactly been entirely truthful about why she was there, either. And it didn't matter that one wrong move where Maryl was concerned could land her in a lot more trouble than just a parole violation.

What it boiled down to was that she wasn't one of Vargas's flunkies and she wasn't about to let him think she was. But she couldn't let him hurt anyone she cared about, either. She'd deal with Vargas on her own, but first she had to make sure there was a way to get Story and the other innocent women at the house out before the FBI arrived and the place became a war zone.

And she knew the FBI was coming, because she'd glanced out the window of her room and saw an old battered pickup half-ass parked behind the stable. She knew that truck—she'd asked Raven to run the plates.

Funny how Raven hadn't gotten back to her on that.

Joe hadn't been released, which meant he was still on the property. Hopefully he was alive, but it would only be a matter of time—possibly hours—before some of his coworkers came looking for him.

Story met her in the room where she'd talked to Lyria the day before.

"Vargas's men are acting snaky," Story informed her. "What did he want from you?"

"He wants me to find out which of the women here is a fed."

Story's mouth thinned. "Maryl?" When Killian nodded, she asked, "What are you going to do?"

"We're going to check out those tunnels and then you're going to get as many people out of here as you can—tonight."

"What about you?"

"I'm going to deal with Vargas."

An expression of alarm took over Story's features. "You can't kill a cartel boss, Killy. The entire operation will come for you."

"I'm not going to kill him. I'm just going to make sure he doesn't escape." And if that didn't work, then she'd kill him. He had threatened Story, her only friend. There was no way she'd let that go. If she had to, she'd take out Miguel, too. And Magnus—and everyone else who had been in that room when Vargas made his threat.

Her friend didn't look like she completely believed her. "I need you to make sure Maryl gets out of here alive. I don't know what kind of information she's collected, but she needs to live."

"Fine." Story sighed. "Let's go. If I'm right about that door the servants were using, it should take us down to the tunnels."

It was siesta time, so some of the women were out at the pool, while others took advantage of the time to rest. The house itself was relatively quiet.

"What if we're caught?" Story asked as they walked.

"I'll tell them I'm looking for a way out. No one's going to think I want to be here when the feds show up."

"So, you're going to tell them the truth."

"I'm not a great liar."

When they reached the door, it was Killian who tried the knob. It was unlocked and opened easily.

There was nothing more exciting on the other side than a servant's corridor. She and Story exchanged a glance before starting down it. There were a couple of rooms labeled as the laundry, the pantry, and a staff room. Then, at the end of the corridor, they found a door marked WINE CELLAR. It opened right onto a set of stone stairs that led down.

"This is it," Story whispered.

Killian led the way as they crept down the stairs, ending up in an open space several degrees cooler than the main house, with a state-of-the-art wine cellar to the left and another door straight ahead. It was obvious the door had been there for a long time. It was little more than a heavy slab of wood on a rail.

Killian approached the door and listened. She couldn't hear any voices coming from the other side. Slowly, she grabbed the handle and pulled the door to the side just enough to slip through the opening. It slid easily along the track with a soft whisper of metal on metal. Someone had taken the time to maintain it.

There were more stairs, but these were rougher, hand carved. The air smelled of dirt and moisture. Once upon a time this would have been the root cellar, maybe even the summer kitchen.

The steps only went down a couple of feet. Dim electric lights were strung along the stone walls. They were beyond the foundation of the house now, as evidenced by the dampness and the darkness that could only come from being completely underground. The old shelves were empty, covered with dust. Old tables and machinery had been abandoned here to seize up and eventually rust in the moisture. For anyone else, it would be a good place to turn around and go back.

But Killian couldn't, because ahead? One more fucking door.

She opened it and stepped inside, Story behind her.

Three guns were pointed at them, held by men playing cards at an old table, sitting on mismatched, rickety chairs. So this was how they treated the help.

"Lower your weapons," commanded a husky voice. It was the woman from the office earlier. Killian was glad to see her— her high school and prison Spanish might not be good enough to talk herself out of a bullet.

The men did as she told them—a good sign. Killian nodded at her in thanks.

"What are you doing down here?" the woman asked.

"Would you believe we're looking for a bottle of chianti?" Killian asked, closing the distance between them. Story hung back. The men went back to their game, but she heard one of them mutter, "Come coños," to his buddies.

"No." The woman then slapped the man who had spoken upside the head hard enough to knock him out of his chair. Killian didn't blame her. *Cunt eater* wasn't meant as a term of endearment. "I don't think you're here for wine, since you obviously walked past it to get here."

"True. What's your name, anyway?"

She blinked. "Why do you want to know my name?"

Killian shrugged. "You know mine."

"Rosario."

"Nice to meet you, Rosario. I'm down here looking for the federal agent your boss is coercing me into finding for him."

"What makes you think they'd be down here?"

"What makes you think they wouldn't be?"

Rosario's brow furrowed heavily. "Because we are here."

Good answer. "These tunnels are public knowledge. You guys know that, right? I mean, if I know about them, you can be sure the feds do, too. Say, what happened to that guy last night?"

The larger woman looked confused. "The crazy boyfriend? He was let go."

"Then why is his truck parked, hidden—pretty shittily, by the way—behind the stable? Did you kill him?"

"I don't understand you. He was taken away. Now, go back up to the house." She gave her a nudge, but Killian stood her ground.

"Did he tell you who his partner was before he died?" Killian shifted her stance, in case Rosario shoved her again. "That's what this really is, right? You don't need me to find the fed; you just want to see if I'll actually turn her in. Your boss wants to know where my loyalties lie before he decides if he wants to kill me or not."

"I could kill you now."

"You can try, sweetheart." Rosario was bigger than her, but Killian had fought bigger before. A good part of being a good fighter was being able to talk yourself up. You'd never beat anyone if you didn't believe you could.

For a second, she thought Rosario might actually give it a whirl. "Go back upstairs."

"No. Show me what's down here."

"Why, so you can escape?"

"Where am I going to go that your boss can't get me?" And then she pointed at Story. "But if the two of us are picked up by the feds, I'll sing like a fucking canary."

Rosario's frown deepened. "You would endanger the people you love?"

"I'd beat your precious Rafa to death with a toothbrush to protect the people I love, but I'll sing to keep my ass out of jail, yeah. I'd rather die than go back there." It was truth enough that it wasn't really a lie. And while she believed Vargas meant his threats, Killian also knew that Dash wouldn't let anything happen to Megan and the girls. Vargas wouldn't touch them.

So, now it was just a matter of doing what she needed to do, and what she'd just decided she needed to do was end Rafael Vargas.

The other woman considered that. "Come on, then."

It wasn't much—a large area where they obviously ate and slept on cots, plus a couple of bathrooms and showers, then a more roughly constructed tunnel about five feet wide and seven feet tall that led on into blackness.

"It goes out to an airfield behind the property," Rosario explained. "I'm not showing you that. Once you are there, you are on your own."

Killian was surprised she'd given her this much. "Thank you."

"Don't thank me. I do not wish to have your blood on my hands, or the blood of innocent women. I was against this visit."

"Why did your boss come if he knew the feds were watching?"

"He refuses to be seen as a coward."

Killian understood that.

Rosario walked them back to the wine cellar.

"Just do what Mr. Vargas asks," Rosario advised her. "It's easier that way."

Killian could tell her she rarely did things the easy way, but there seemed little point. "Thanks."

She and Story returned to the main house in silence. It wasn't until Killian was sure they weren't followed that she turned to her friend. "If Joe was FBI, how long before they show, do you think?"

Story shrugged. "Tomorrow at the latest."

"We need to talk to Maryl."

"*You* need to talk to Maryl," Story corrected. "I don't have any intention of spending more time with her than I have to. I'm going to take care of some other matters."

Killian didn't ask what those matters were. At this point, she wasn't sure what the best course of action was, but she wanted to minimize bloodshed as much as possible. Maryl was in the position to do that. And she trusted Story to do whatever she thought was best. "I'll find you later."

When she opened the door to her room she found her room-mate on her bed, reading. Since the book was on exactly the same page it had been on the last time she saw Maryl with it, she assumed her roomie had been doing something else before her arrival.

Killian decided to go with the direct approach and save them all a lot of wasted breath.

"Vargas knows you're a fed, Maryl. They tortured Joe and he broke."

All the color ran from her roommate's face as she sat up. "What are you talking about? Why would they hurt Joe?"

Sighing, Killian sat on the edge of the mattress. "Listen to me, and don't bother trying to play me, okay? I think Joe's dead. He gave you up. And now I'm supposed to give you over to Vargas."

Maryl stared at her. "You're serious."

"You're fucking right, I'm serious. Jesus, Maryl." She ran a hand through her hair. "You have to get the fuck out of here. There's a secret passageway under the house, but it's filled with Desiertos."

"You've seen them?"

"Yes. Do you have keys for Joe's truck? They stashed it behind the stables."

"I do, and I know." Killian could actually see her pulling herself together in real time. "Did you see his body?"

"No, but they're not the kind of people to let someone walk away, especially a fed."

"Why are you telling me this?"

"Because I like you, and I'm not a killer." Not if the person didn't deserve it.

"Are you in league with them?"

"What do you think?" Killian challenged.

"My gut tells me no, but why are you here?"

"Ilyana Woodward hired me to come here and get her daughters out before you lot could raid the place."

"You know we suspect Woodward of being in on Magnus's trafficking operation?"

"I just found out about that, yeah."

Maryl continued. "I know you were locked up with Tara Washington."

"If you know who she really is, you know she and I were never friends. You also know she's been clean since she started this place. It might have started as a scam, but she's trying to have a better life."

"With a cartel boss's wife."

Killian shrugged. "I don't know anything about that, really."

The other woman's gaze narrowed. Gone was the sweet, naive woman of whom Killian had felt so protective, replaced by the career agent. "Why should I trust anything you say?"

"I don't give a shit if you trust me or not. What I care about is not having your fucking blood on my hands. You need to get out of here and tell your people to move in, and fast. And you have to warn them that there's an army hiding beneath the house."

"How do I know you're not setting me up right now?"

"If I was really your enemy, that Glock of yours would be in my hand and not hidden under a fake plant in the damn bathroom. Yeah," she continued when Maryl's mouth dropped open. "I found it. It's not that great a hiding place."

"Neither is a ledge above the vanity," the agent shot back.

Killian smiled. Then chuckled. "Jesus, this is fucked-up."

Maryl chuckled, too. On a sigh, she sobered. "If I run, they're going to know you warned me."

"So, we'll have to make it look like I tried to stop you."

"No one is going to believe I could beat you up."

"Probably not, but they'll believe you could pistol-whip me."

The other woman cringed. "Jesus."

Shrugging, Killian didn't see the problem. "I've been knocked out before, by bigger people. You don't have to smash my skull in, just make it look good. Go get your gun. And when you leave, take the phone. Call your boss, and then do me a favor and call Dash. His number is programmed in."

Maryl hesitated. "This doesn't feel right."

"Woman, they killed your partner. I don't even care that you sold me some terrible abused-woman crap—that's how real this is. You need to get the fuck out of here or your entire operation is going to go down the damn toilet."

She nodded shakily. "You're right. I know you are. Okay, give me the phone."

Killian handed it over.

"It's tiny."

"It's a piece of crap, but it will get the job done. Now, you go get your gun."

Maryl did as she instructed. When she returned to the room, Killian had shifted how she was sitting on the bed, her back slightly turned toward the bathroom.

"You know where to hit me, right?" she asked.

"I can't believe you're asking me to do this."

"It's the only way we both stand a chance of getting out of this. Now, shut the fuck up and—"

She didn't get to finish the sentence. Her skull exploded into an array of stars and expanding spots like fireworks behind her eyes. She fell off the bed onto the carpet, and then everything—everything—went black.

Her husband had lost his damn mind.

"You tortured an FBI agent?" Adriana repeated. "Here?"

"I needed to know what he knew about our operation. Don't worry, *querida*. He's in no position to cause trouble for us."

She knew that smile. That was the smile he always wore when he killed someone he thought of as a trophy.

Her mind spun. "We have to leave. Now."

He actually chuckled. "Be easy, my love. I have the situation under control."

He couldn't truly be so foolish, so arrogant. Their son's relationship with Ilyana Woodward and now her daughter had brought them a degree of celebrity in this country—celebrity they did not need. Now people who would have believed Rafa to be a wealthy businessman knew there were rumors that maybe weren't rumors at all. And gossip magazines made them easy to find. There were pictures of Miguel and Dylan in one just recently, showing them out and around in public. If the press knew where they were, and the FBI did as well, then so did every other law enforcement agency in the country.

And they were already watching.

"You forget where we are, Rafa," she said softly. "We are not at home where we have friends to protect us."

"Relax. The rest of the shipment will arrive tonight. Magnus and I will conclude our business, my men will leave, and even if agents come here, they will find nothing. *Nothing.* Once again, I will have made them look stupid."

Years ago she would have believed him, trusted him, but she no longer did.

"Why don't you go for a swim or do some yoga?" he suggested. "Have a drink by the pool and forget all of this."

God, he really was a fool. He believed himself to be untouchable. Smarter than anyone else. "Perhaps I will," she humored him. Then she kissed him lightly on the lips. "Go, finish your business. I will be fine."

As he left, she wondered what her father had seen in him. What she had seen in him. He'd changed since they first fell in love. Back then she was his everything. The cartel was his family, and he guarded it like one.

He'd once hidden out in the mountains for days—living in a cave, wearing the same clothes. He valued those close to him. Now he couldn't stand having a scuff on his shoe, and he thought loyalty was something he could buy or, worse, coerce. He'd lost some of his edge, and with it, her respect. Her father had trusted him with his business and his daughter, and Rafa was taking too many risks with both.

Her mother would be looked after if anything happened to Adriana—her younger sisters would see to that. And Mama had many friends who would rally around her.

"It is time," she murmured to herself. Time to shit, as they said, or get off the pot.

Adriana reached under her bed and pulled out a small suitcase. Inside were several stacks of American cash, a new passport, ID, a bank card, and a credit card. They were all in the same name—an alias she'd picked out a long time ago should she have need of it. She'd been secretly putting money away into the account for years through friends her husband didn't know—friends all over the world. Shasis had been the most help. She knew people who made the most perfect papers.

There was also a handgun—registered to her alias—and a box of ammo. Everything she needed for an escape.

She put the case back in its hiding spot. Just looking at it had eased much of her anxiety. She had a plan.

Like Shasis, she'd grown up surrounded by men—and women—who earned their living on their own side of the law. It had been Shasis, though, who showed her the kind of success that could be found through legitimate means. It didn't matter if it was moral; it was legal.

And if that didn't work out, they had plenty of money

between the two of them, and plenty of talents to fall back on if that ran out.

Adriana ran herself a bath and rolled a joint. She smoked as she soaked, letting the herb and hot water drain the tension from her body. She could think better when she wasn't in full-flight mode. She needed to think, and to plan.

By the time the water began to cool, she was pleasantly stoned and did, indeed, have a plan. She rose from the tub, moisturized and dried her skin, and then padded out to her bedroom to find something to wear to dinner.

But first...she used her phone to send a text. Then she pulled on her favorite silk kimono and unlocked the door to her room. Then she sat on the bed and waited. It wasn't long before she heard the knock.

"Come in."

The door eased open to reveal her visitor. Rosario—gorgeous, fierce Rosie—walked into the room. "You wanted to see me?"

"Close the door," Adriana said. "Lock it."

The other woman didn't hesitate. When she turned to face Adriana again, her gaze was bright and full of hunger.

Adriana rose to her feet. "We need to talk, my friend. But first, I need to know where your loyalty lies." She eased the kimono off her shoulders and dropped it to the carpet.

"My loyalty is with you, Riri," Rosario replied as she approached. "As always." Then she sank to her knees.

Easing her hands into the other woman's hair, Adriana sighed. Her husband might have forgotten how to choose those he kept close, but she hadn't.

*   *   *

Fuck, her head hurt.

Killian came to on the floor, mouth dry, vision a little blurry. She touched her fingers to her head—not at all surprised when they came away sticky with blood. Maryl had cracked her good.

Slowly, she pushed herself up into a sitting position. Her skull throbbed, but no nausea. Good sign. She leaned back against the side of the bed. She just needed...a minute. Not like she was in a hurry. She probably hadn't been out that long, and she wanted to give Maryl as much of a head start as she could.

Vargas might kill her for letting Maryl get away, regardless of her cracked head. After killing a fed, it would be easy to snuff out an ex-con.

She should have stayed at the club. Bartending and security hadn't been that bad. She'd hated it, but at least she never had to worry about getting killed or arrested. When Maxine came to her with her offer of a job, she should have turned the bitch down.

Killian sat there for a long time, zoned out, working on pushing the pain away. It was a meditative technique her fighting coach had taught her years ago and was one of the singularly most useful things she'd ever learned in her entire life. Mind over matter was a real freaking thing.

Finally, she knew she couldn't sit there any longer. Using the bed for support, she stood up and carefully made her way to the bathroom. She grimaced when she saw herself in the mirror— blood matted her hair and stuck to the side of her face. Maryl had hit her in the temple: a good choice when wanting to not only knock someone out but make sure the wound was visible as well.

Now the question was, should she clean it up and try to hide it, or go downstairs like this looking for Vargas?

Cleaning it up would look like she didn't want to attract attention and didn't want to look like a victim, so she retrieved the first aid kit from under the sink and set about doctoring herself up. When she was done, she stuck a couple of steri-strips over it and stepped back to survey her handiwork. Not bad. It was going to look worse once the bruising bloomed, but for now it looked just fresh and ugly enough.

She swallowed a few Tylenol at the sink before changing her clothes, then leaving her room. No more time for sitting around.

She made her way to the Incarnyx wing, found the right door, and knocked.

"Who is it?"

"Killian." When the door opened, she looked Lyria in the eye. The girl looked like shit. "You picked a great time to kick the habit."

Dylan appeared behind her sister. "That's what I told her. Come in."

Killian stepped into the room, catching a whiff of Lyria's body odor as she brushed past the girl. From the look of her, she was still in the early stages of withdrawal.

"Has she started feeling paranoid yet?"

"Just anxious," Dylan replied.

"I can speak for myself," Lyria informed them both in a raspy voice as she closed the door.

Sitting in a chair by the window was Miguel. Killian was surprised to see him there. "Doing some market research?" she asked. "Let Daddy know how effective his product is?"

Miguel wasn't that much younger than Killian, but at that moment he looked years older. "No. What happened to you?"

Shit. "I got hit."

His face brightened. "The fed. You confronted her."

Killian scowled. "That's what your father wanted, wasn't it?"

"He wanted to see if he could trust you."

"We're hoping he can't," Dylan interjected, stepping into Killian's line of sight once more.

She looked at the girl. It was true what they said about some pregnant women glowing. "Explain."

Dylan and Miguel exchanged glances. When her baby daddy shrugged, Dylan continued. "I know Mom sent you here under the pretense of 'rescuing' me and Lyria, but we want to hire you ourselves."

Killian frowned. "For what?"

Dylan moved to Miguel's side and put her hand on his shoulder. He lifted his own to twine his fingers with hers, but his gaze was on Killian. "We want out," he said.

Killian's attention moved to Dylan. Lyria had drifted to the bed and sat on the edge of the mattress. "Why didn't you just go to Raven with this?"

"She's being used by my mother. I can't trust her."

Raven wasn't the kind of person who was easily duped, but either Ilyana had fooled her, or Raven was in on it with her. Either way, the girl was probably right. "What is your mother, exactly?"

Dylan shrugged. "Insecure? Power hungry? She isn't as famous as she used to be and it freaks her out. She doesn't want to lose the lifestyle she's had for the last twenty-five years."

"So she got into bed with the Desiertos?"

Miguel nodded. "She wasn't in love with me. She just wanted a path to my father. When Dylan and I got together she thought that would solidify the familial connection."

"But it didn't?"

"I don't want anything to do with crime," Dylan told her. "Neither does Miguel."

Killian looked him in the eye. "I'm willing to bet you haven't mentioned that to your father."

"I'm not going to, either. My grandfather built an empire. It might not have been built on a sense of morality, but there was respect. My father used to share those ideals, but now... he's getting sloppy. Not even my mother respects him anymore. Soon, he'll lose the respect of the men, and then he'll be destroyed."

"You don't want to be there when that happens?"

Miguel shook his head. "I've started my own business—a legitimate one. I don't want to go down with him, or be left trying to clean up his mess." He glanced at Dylan. "I have more important things to think of."

Killian turned to Lyria. "What about you, sunshine?"

The girl shrugged. "I'm just tired."

Dylan left her lover to go to her sister, kneeling before the younger girl. "I'm going to get you out of here, sissy. I'm going to take care of you."

Killian's chest tightened. Years ago, she'd sat in a hospital bed, freaking out because she was afraid of giving birth. What if she'd done something to the baby? What if there was something wrong with it? Megan had held her hand and told her it was going to be okay, that she was with her no matter what.

"What do you want me to do?" Killian asked.

Miguel looked her in the eye. "I want you to kill my father."

TWELVE

It wasn't the request, the money they offered, or even the temptation of both that lingered as Killian made her way downstairs. It was the image of Lyria, sitting on that bed, exhausted and caught tight in the clutches of withdrawal, that swirled around in her head and refused to go away.

Her pulse jumped a little as she walked the hallway to Magnus's office. If he was alone, maybe she could just break his neck and blame it on someone else. Or maybe she'd get even luckier and Vargas would be in there alone and she could snap him in half and blame that on Magnus, let Vargas's men take him out.

She didn't knock, just opened the door and walked in. She didn't know what she expected to find, but Magnus, leaning back against his desk, eyes closed, with three-quarters of his dick buried down Mina's throat, was not it. They were so into it that they didn't even hear her come in—or they just didn't care.

What the hell was up with these people? Everyone was just fucking everyone else and it didn't seem to matter who or where, and certainly not when. How did they ever get any work done with all the screwing that went on?

It was creepy AF to just stand there and let them finish, but that's what she did. She just leaned her shoulder against the wall and waited. It didn't take long.

Magnus noticed her first. When he finally opened his eyes, his fingers were still clenched in Mina's hair. Killian was the first thing he saw.

"How long have you been there?" he asked, unbothered.

Mina, on the other hand, leapt to her feet. She looked mortified as she wiped her mouth with the back of her hand.

"Put your dick away, Magnus," Killian suggested. "Nobody wants to see that withered little thing now. Mina, don't look so nervous. I don't care who you do. I'm actually looking for Vargas."

"He's in a meeting," Magnus told her.

"You'll have to do, then." Honestly, it was a relief. She wasn't worried about either of them. Vargas, on the other hand, was something to worry about.

Magnus zipped his pants and smiled at Mina. "Run along, darlin'. I've got business to attend to."

Mina looked from him to Killian and back again. "But if it's got to do with—"

He actually gave her a little shove. "Go on, now."

The woman gave him a narrow glare as she begrudgingly made her way to the door. Personally, Killian would have punched him in the throat for being so patronizing, but whatever.

"He's all yours," Mina said sweetly.

"I don't do leftovers, but thanks." She watched her leave the room before returning her attention to Magnus. "I found the fed, but you already know who she is because Vargas tortured her partner."

Magnus's eyes widened a fraction—just enough to show surprise. "Where is she?"

"I was hoping you could tell me." She pointed to the wound on her temple. "She pistol-whipped me."

"She had a gun?"

"Yeah," Killian replied. "And she stole the burner phone I brought with me. Your attempt at security in this place sucks, by the way."

"She can't have gotten very far on foot," Magnus commented. "In case you haven't noticed, we have security and Desiertos all over the place."

"She had a set of keys for the truck stashed behind the stables. You might want to check to see if it's still there." God, she hoped it was gone.

Magnus immediately pulled a phone from his belt and called someone on it.

"Yeah," he said sharply, Southern drawl all but gone. "That half-ton—is it still behind the stables?" A few moments later his face fell. "No, I didn't tell anyone to fucking move it."

He didn't say anything else, just ended the call and swiped a hand over his face. "Vargas is *not* going to be happy. The truck's gone."

Yee-fucking-haw.

For the first time since she met him, Magnus's face lacked some of its smug composure. He glared at Killian. "She was your responsibility."

"Yeah, well, how was I to know she had a gun, huh? By the way, she knows all about your plans, apparently. And she has a pretty good idea her partner is dead."

Magnus swore. "How the hell did she know that?"

"You tell me. You were the one sleeping with her." At his startled expression she laughed. "Does Vargas know you were fucking a fed?"

"I didn't know she was a fed at the time," Magnus shot back.

"Did you check your bedroom for bugs?" Killian asked. "'Cause if she planted one in your office…"

He turned white beneath his tan.

Killian smiled. "I hope you've got a plane waiting on that private airstrip, too, buddy. Yeah, I found the tunnel. It's nice. Just one question: What's the deal? You guys setting up a lab here? Or was Vargas planning to run more girls through? Or both?"

"What the fuck are you talking about?"

Killian smiled. "Shasis and I go way back. Didn't she tell you? I knew her back when the only woman she wanted to empower was herself. By the way, the cartel is a really good way to diminish any credibility."

Magnus shook his head. "Fucking bitch. How much did she tell you?"

"Don't blame her for the mess you're in. You're the one who made the deal with Vargas and decided to get into drugs and trafficking, asshole."

He smirked. "You think she didn't know anything about that?"

"I know she didn't. If she was with you, I would never have gotten the invite to come here. She wouldn't have let me any-where near her business because she knows what I think of pimps."

"Doesn't matter why you're here. Your little friend Maryl will roast you along with the rest of us if she gets the chance. Who's going to believe an ex-con? Same with Shasis when they run her prints. They'll find out who she really is and I'll be the one pleading ignorance."

Killian had just about lost her patience with this guy. She was going to regret that five seconds of almost liking him for the rest of her life. "You really think you'll live that long? Var-gas isn't going to let you out of this alive, idiot." He must have considered that—unless he really was stupid.

Magnus's fingers curled into fists. He looked at her like he wanted to kill her.

"Bigger men than you have tried, Deacon. Couple of them are dead, but go for it."

He lunged for her. "Fucking cun—" Killian cut him off with a sharp chop to the vagus nerve on the side of his neck. It was a good hit—crumpled him to the carpet like a discarded sock.

She gave him a solid kick to the kidneys just for spite. There was nothing like pissing blood for a day or two to give a person perspective.

Then she turned and sashayed out of that office like she damn well owned it. Now, to find Story and get a plan in motion so they could make sure the rest of the women in the place got out of there with as little injury as possible. It was the most triumphant she'd felt since dropping off that pimp a week ago. It wasn't a win, not yet, but she'd take it.

Maryl continuously checked the rearview mirror as she sped away from the Incarnyx campus. It felt weird, driving Joe's old beater. It smelled like him, had his junk strewn all through the cab. Tightness coiled in her chest with every reminder.

He was dead.

She blinked back tears as the tiny phone on the seat beside her rang. She didn't recognize the number, but it was a Connecticut area code.

"Hello?"

A moment's hesitation. "Killy?" The man's voice was smooth and low.

"She can't come to the phone right now."

"Is this Maryl?"

"Who's this?" she countered.

"Let's just cut the shit, *Agent Rogers*, and you can tell me what's going on."

A chill ran down Maryl's spine. "This is Dash, isn't it?"

"Yes."

"How do you know my name?" Her *real* name.

"I made it my business to find out," he explained without any edge to his tone. "Where is Killian, please?"

It was the *please* that got her. He couldn't hide his worry in that one word. Killian trusted him, and she was going to have to as well.

"She's still at the Incarnyx house. My cover was blown so she gave me this phone and told me to get out. I was supposed to call you when I got somewhere secure."

"Is she in trouble?"

Her job demanded that she lie to him, tell him it was under control and to stay where he was, but Killian had probably saved her life, and every instinct Maryl had told her that if she didn't want Incarnyx to end up a massacre, she needed to take a different approach.

"I think so, yes."

"Thanks."

Maryl opened her mouth to say more, but he had hung up. She thought about calling him back, then changed her mind and checked the rearview again. Nothing suspicious.

Her thoughts returned to her partner. How was she going to face his mother? His girlfriend, Sarah, already disliked Maryl for seeing more of Joe than she did. How was she going to explain that she let him get killed?

That flicker of guilt almost immediately gave way to anger. What the hell had he been thinking showing up like that? She didn't need him checking in or giving her messages. He ruined everything by showing up. Jesus, he almost got her killed, too.

Unless... Maryl blinked. Unless Joe had done it on purpose. Done it knowing they'd drag him away and figure out who he was. But why take such a chance? Why risk his life? Why get himself killed?

Unless he wasn't dead. Killian hadn't seen a body. Maryl hadn't seen one, either. They had nothing but the word of a criminal that Joe had been killed. Maybe he was still alive.

That was the thought ping-ponging off the sides of her brain when she heard the siren. She glanced in the rearview and saw flashing red and blue lights behind her. Right behind her.

"Balls," she muttered as she flicked the signal indicator. She slowed down as she pulled onto the shoulder and came to a stop. She had no ID on her—nothing legitimate. The last thing she needed was to get hauled in by the cops.

She rolled down the window as the trooper approached.

"Good afternoon, Officer," she began.

He removed his sunglasses. "Agent Rogers?" he asked.

Maryl hesitated. Did Vargas have cops on his payroll? Had he called in a favor?

She reached beneath Joe's jacket on the seat beside her and closed her fingers around the comforting weight of her Glock.

"Yes," she said.

"Officer Ed Reid," he replied. "Special Agent Thomason said it would be either you or Agent Riley driving this vehicle. I'm to escort you to where the Bureau has set up headquarters."

He knew her name. He knew Joe's. More important, he knew her direct supervisor's name. Still, that was all information Joe could have revealed under torture.

"Did Agent Thomason give you a message for me?"

Reid took a black notebook from his uniform breast pocket and flipped it open. " 'Wherever the corpse is, there the vultures will gather.' " He closed the pages. "That make sense to you?"

Matthew 24:28. It was a quote Thomason was quite fond of, but not something Joe would ever think to reveal.

"It does," she replied as her fingers relaxed around the gun.

She wasn't going to have to shoot a cop after all. "Lead on, Officer Reid."

"Yes, ma'am." He turned to walk back to his cruiser but stopped and tapped a knuckle against the side of the truck. "By the way, you got a busted taillight you might want to get looked at."

She should have asked Maryl to leave her the gun, Killian thought later that afternoon as she tried to formulate a plan.

She wasn't good at plans; she knew that. She was more of a react-as-things-happen kind of person, a trait that served her well as a fighter, but not so much when it came to outwitting federal agents and the cartel.

It would be so much easier if all these other people weren't involved. She honestly didn't know how to protect all of them. Getting them out was all she could think of, and she had no real idea how to do that without getting Shasis and Adriana involved.

So, that's what she did. But she collected Story first and the two of them went to Shasis's room, where they found her and Adriana together, talking.

"Maryl's gone," Killian informed them. "The FBI will be here at any time and your son just offered me a large sum to kill his father. Apparently Rafa sucks as a dad, too."

Adriana arched a brow. "If my son has turned on his father, then there is honestly no hope for Rafa. Miguel has always idolized his father." She shrugged. "Did you accept?"

"No, because I don't have a death wish."

"You didn't have the same reserve where Cirello was involved."

"That was personal. Honestly, I don't give a flying fuck what you all do to each other."

Her lips curved into a slight smile. "When you speak like that, I see why you and my queen get along as you do. Alas, I met her first." She cast a glance at Shasis, who rolled her eyes despite wearing a smug smile. Killian frowned. Being compared to a pimp was not her idea of a compliment.

"I'm all for a good romance," Story spoke up, "but we need to figure out a plan. How do we get all of these women to safety?"

"The tunnels," Shasis offered. "When Vargas and his men are moving their product."

"But the tunnels lead to the airfield," Killian countered.

"One of them does. There's another that leads out to the old stables, which is now the garage."

Killian and Story exchanged glances. "We'd still have to get through security at the gate," Killian said.

Story shook her head. "You think those rental cops get paid enough to stand in front of a moving car? And if anyone does stand in our way, he won't be there for long. Doesn't matter, though. Even if we only get the women to the wine cellar, it should keep them safe from any gunfire."

At that moment, Lyria wandered out of the bedroom area, into the sitting room where the four of them were gathered.

"I'm thirsty," she said, voice thick.

Adriana got her a sports drink from the mini-fridge. "Here, darling. Drink this. It will make you feel better."

"You doing okay, kid?" Killian asked. She'd never been

addicted to any drug, but she'd known far too many people who suffered under it.

Lyria nodded, like her head was several pounds too heavy for her neck. "I will be." There were tears in her eyes, though. Adriana put an arm around her shoulders and gave her a gentle squeeze.

"She's worried about what's going to happen to her and her sister," Shasis added with a grim expression. "Apparently some of the recruitment missions Magnus sent them on weren't just for Incarnyx members, but other *business opportunities*."

Lyria broke away from Adriana and slowly sat down on the sofa. "He told us we were helping them." She shook her head. "And then I got to a point where I didn't care because all I wanted was the high he promised me."

If Killian had any say in it, Magnus was going to pay for what he'd done. She looked at Adriana. "Any idea where these girls might have been sent?"

The other woman's lips thinned. "I assume New York City. My husband knows I would not approve of the flesh trade, so he has never spoken to me of this."

Men. Some of them were just oxygen-wasting parasites. It made her appreciate the good ones all the more.

Killian sat down on the edge of the bed. "Lyria, how many girls did you recruit?"

A shrug. "I don't know. A few."

"What about Dylan?"

"She brought in a few more. They liked her better."

Don't ever apologize for not being a good bottom bitch.

Lyria picked at the cushion beside her. "I heard they became real party girls, you know?"

"Yeah, I know. Did Magnus ever try to get you to party?"

"Once, but Miguel stepped in. He told Magnus Dylan and I were off-limits. This was when he was still with my mom." She frowned. "I don't want to think about how much she knows about all of this."

"Hey, my mother married a pedophile."

Blue eyes widened. "Your dad?"

"Step. She kicked him out when she found out what he'd done, but the damage had already been dealt. She has to live with that, you know?"

"Are you two close?"

"Nah. I think the guilt makes it easier for her to avoid me."

"That sucks."

It was Killian's turn to shrug. "Some people find out too late they weren't meant to be parents."

"I've already figured that one out." She slipped off the sofa. "I'm gonna go lie down again."

Killian watched her go with a heavy heart. Hopefully the girl would be okay.

"You really have to do something about your poker face, Che-che."

Killian turned to her. "Aren't you the least bit worried about a raid?"

"My hands are clean."

"But Magnus's aren't."

"I'm not involved in any of that."

"Guilt by association."

"I have a really good lawyer. And, honey, I will tell those feds everything I know about Magnus to save my own hide."

"You going to snitch?" She made a tsking sound with her tongue. "What would the girls back in Niantic think of that?" Niantic was the town in Connecticut where they'd been locked up.

"I do not care. Never have, never will. If I don't look out for number one, ain't no one else going to do it."

Killian smiled. That was the Dirty T she remembered. "I guess I don't have as much faith in my lawyers as you do."

"You can always run," Adriana suggested. "I know people—"

Killian held up her hand. "Thanks, but I don't run."

Shasis grinned at her lover. "She's never been terribly bright. Instinct is her strength."

"What's your instinct telling you, Killian?" Adriana asked.

Killian met her gaze. "That you have something you want to tell us."

Sighing, Adriana looked away. "That is true."

For the first time, Shasis looked concerned. "Adri?"

Their gazes met. There was an intimacy between them that made Killian uncomfortable. It wasn't just sexual. Somewhere along the line, these two women had come to mean a lot to one another. They were lifelines to each other. They were in love, whether they wanted to admit it or not. The way they looked at each other made her uncomfortable because she knew she looked at Dash the same way.

"Rafa wants the agents to come. He wants there to be a huge

bloodbath. You will not get those women to the cellar. He will hold them hostage. He will hold all of you hostage."

Shasis swallowed. "To what end?"

"I think he knows he has been losing the confidence of his men. He has this stupid idea that if he gives blood to Santa Muerte, she will favor him again. He will be feared once more."

"She'd probably like him better if the blood was his own," Story muttered for Killian's ears alone. Killian arched a brow but said nothing.

"How do you know this?" Shasis asked.

"One of his guards has more loyalty to me than to Rafa."

"Rosario," Killian spoke, filling in the blanks.

Adriana nodded.

"The male FBI. Did Rosario tell you if he's dead?"

"She hasn't mentioned it, but I can find out easily enough."

Killian nodded. "Do that." If Joe was still alive, he might be a help to them—especially if they managed to rescue his ass.

She turned to Story. "Do I need to kill Vargas?"

"Uh, no," her friend replied. "But maybe if we put him out of commission for a while…"

Right. Killian turned to Adriana. "You're a doctor, right? What do you have with you for meds?"

"Oh, I have painkillers and sleeping pills, antibiotics, epi-nephrine…You want to knock Rafa out?"

"I sure as hell do."

"I can do that, easy. When?"

"Christ, as soon as possible, I would think." She thought for a moment. "Do you have enough to knock out his men as well? We could put the drugs in their food."

"I don't think..."

"I have a bottle of sleeping pills," Shasis spoke up. "Between the two of us we probably have enough."

Slowly, Adriana nodded. "Enough to knock them all out. Then what? Let the feds come?"

Killian nodded. "Who has access to the food?"

"I can get into the kitchen," Shasis said. "That won't be hard at all. The others we can dose with their drinks."

"And what happens when my husband wakes up and realizes what has been done?"

Killian glanced at her. "You pretend you were drugged, too."

"He'll know he was set up. My husband is a vengeful man."

"Your husband will be in prison."

"This is crazy," Story said. "We're talking about knocking out a drug lord and his entire entourage."

"Our only other choice is to let it play out, and I don't trust that motherfucker," Killian replied.

"What about when Vargas sends people after you?" her friend challenged. "Weak or not, I have to think he has more reach than Cirello did. You know who he'll go for. We need to think about this and form a real, solid plan."

Suddenly, a loud popping noise echoed outside. Killian froze, then slowly turned. "What the hell was that?"

Story's expression was grim. "Gunfire."

THIRTEEN

Too late. No time left to make a plan.

It wasn't just a single shot. It was a lot. And it wasn't just one-sided, either. Someone had fired at someone else, and those shots had been immediately returned.

"What's going on?" Lyria asked, wide-eyed and pale as she stumbled in, clutching her sports drink.

"I don't know," Killian told her, "but it's not good. Stay here."

Story grabbed her arm as she tried to leave. "You really think this is a good idea?"

"I won't go far."

She didn't have to. Halfway down the stairs she ran into Rosario—armed and serious. "What's going on?" she demanded.

"A federal agent pulled a weapon on one of our men," the larger woman replied, her tone soft. "Mr. Vargas sent me up here to gather everyone and bring them to the main hall."

Killian's lips thinned. "You realize if he takes control, this whole thing is going to go to shit fast?"

Rosario nodded. "You also realize that fighting him is the quickest way to get yourself and everyone else killed?"

Good point. "What's the FBI thinking? There are innocent people here."

"It wasn't FBI. It was DEA."

Shit. "Well, the Bureau won't be far behind them now." The entire situation had just spiraled completely out of control.

"Go get the other women," she told Rosario. "I was with Adriana and Shasis. I'll get them."

Rosario hesitated, then gave a sharp nod. "Mrs. Vargas will know what to do."

Killian didn't respond. She hightailed it back to Shasis's room. "Vargas is having everyone herded to the main hall. They just shot a DEA agent."

Story swore and Lyria turned to Adriana with a frightened gaze. "Are we all going to die?" she asked in a dramatic whisper.

"No," Killian replied before anyone else could. "You are going to get the fuck out of here." And then to Story: "And so are you."

Her friend gave her a "Hell, no" look. "I'm not leaving you here alone. They'll gas this place now."

"But innocent people…" Lyria protested.

"Since when has that ever mattered?" Shasis challenged, ignoring the girl's terror. "We've also got a major player for the Desiertos."

A major player who killed an FBI agent. Had Maryl done this? No, Killian couldn't believe it. Maryl wouldn't risk the lives of all the women who were just here for a retreat.

"What were you thinking?" she challenged Shasis. "Having a retreat the same time Vargas is here?"

"Magnus thought it would be the perfect cover."

"Yeah, fucking perfect. I'm sure Vargas is happy to have all the hostages."

Adriana and Shasis exchanged glances, as if the idea hadn't occurred to either one of them before this moment.

"Oh, come on," she continued. "You had to know your husband would want his escape guaranteed. Hostages give him the chance to play the big bad and give him enough time to make his escape. Didn't the two of you plan an escape if this all went to hell?"

The look the two women exchanged answered her question and said so much more. Killian didn't know to what end, but she was sure the two of them had hoped for something like this and already had a plan in motion.

Her main concern was making sure innocent people didn't die—mostly Story and Lyria. Then she'd worry about the others. Her own ass came a distant third, though she was tempted to just bolt.

They might actually believe her cover story, especially if Maryl went to bat for her, but she couldn't count on that. This, along with the parole board investigation, would ensure not only that she returned to prison, but that she served more time.

"The tunnel that leads to the stables," Shasis suggested. "Let's go."

"Now?" Adriana asked, incredulous. "We'll be shot."

"If we don't go now, they'll round us up with the others and we'll never get the chance," Killian argued. "This chaos is the perfect cover."

"Okay, then," Adriana said. "Let's go."

They gathered up what they needed and went to the stairs, staying just out of sight of the entry hall in case anyone came through.

"Lead the way," Killian said.

The hall was empty. The five of them hurried across it toward the nearest servants' door. The house was one of those built with a separate corridor within the walls so the maids and help didn't have to be seen. These days there weren't so many servants, but it explained why the cartel goons were able to come and go without being seen by guests.

Lyria's palm was damp against Killian's as they hurried along through the warm, narrow space. It certainly wasn't as nice as the rest of the house. If they ran into one of Vargas's men, they were screwed—unless someone had a gun.

Sweat trickled down Killian's back. What kind of asshole didn't provide AC to the people who worked for them? The bleak lighting and confined space felt like prison, jacking her heart rate.

She really didn't want to go back there. She could survive, but fuck, she didn't want to go back.

This wasn't the time to worry about prison. She'd deal with that when it happened. Right now, she had to worry about getting these women to freedom.

At the end of the corridor, there was a stairwell leading down. Thankfully the air was cooler down there. The lighting was just as shit, but it was more comfortable. They were underground now, Killian could tell from the smell.

They went on for what seemed like forever.

A sound echoed around them—a door slamming. The five of them crammed themselves into a corner behind a door, each one of them holding her breath.

One of Vargas's men ran past, carrying an automatic rifle. He didn't even glance in their direction, he was so intent on his mission.

They waited a moment to make sure there weren't more behind him. Then Killian motioned for them to keep going. She stepped out first, pushing the others ahead in case the guy came back.

There was a set of stairs at the end of this corridor as well. This one led up. Carefully, Shasis opened the door and peeked out. She gestured for the rest of them to follow.

They stepped out into the stables/garage. There were several high-end cars parked there, along with some that weren't so eye-catching. The sight of her old, beautiful Impala brought a lightness to her heart—hope. It was an obnoxious, bright beacon among the rest of the vehicles. God, she loved that car.

She loved Dash, too. The sudden rush of emotion wrapped around her throat, threatening to choke her. She had no time for this kind of crap. She pushed the feelings down until they were nothing more than an annoying itch in the back of her mind.

"Now what?" Adriana demanded as gunshots continued to ring out in the darkening evening. "If we try to leave, we will be shot."

Killian turned to Story. "You got a phone in your bag?" She kept her tone low.

"Yeah. Who do you want me to call?"

"The burner phone I had." If anyone could get them out of there, it was Maryl. Killian knew it was stupid, but she trusted the woman as much as she could bring herself to trust any federal agent. Maybe a little more.

Suddenly, there came a sound from behind them. They turned in unison.

Rosario. Shit. She looked disappointed—and pissed.

She said something to Adriana in Spanish.

"I don't care if my husband wants me," Adriana replied in English. "One of us has to get out of here alive. Please, Rosario."

Rosario pointed the gun at her. "I have orders to shoot anyone who tries to escape." There was no real threat to her tone, but when she turned to Adriana, there was genuine fear. "Please, come back inside, Mrs. Vargas. I won't tell anyone where I found you, but you are needed in the gymnasium. There's been...an accident."

Killian's gaze narrowed. "What kind of accident?"

"I can't say."

"Just tell us, Rosario," Adriana commanded. "And I'll come quietly."

The tall woman sighed. "Miguel's woman has been shot."

Beside Killian, Lyria gasped. "Dylan!" she cried, and before Killian could stop her, she began running for the door back to the house.

"My grandchild," Adriana whispered. Her expression horrified, she turned to Shasis. Killian watched as Shasis took her hand and walked with her toward the entrance as well.

Rosario pointed the weapon at Killian and Story. "Let's go."

"Make that text," Killian whispered as they started walking.

"Already on it," she replied.

As they hurried back the way they'd come, Killian could feel the *sicaria* behind her. "Thank you," Rosario said.

"For what?"

"For not trying to fight me."

"Dylan's life is more important than escape. I think we all just proved that." She wasn't even pissy about it, not really. Family always came first.

"I don't want to kill you," Rosario went on. "I want you to know that."

"That makes two of us," Killian replied with a tight smile. "I don't want to kill you, either."

The taller woman's gaze locked with hers. "But I will, if I need to. I will do anything to protect those whom I serve."

Killian nodded. "Then we understand each other, because if it comes down to it, I will fight to survive."

"Then let us both hope it doesn't come to that."

Killian said nothing, walked on in silence. There was nothing to say. She'd spent a lot of her life around various gangs, and the cartel was just like them. You could hope all you wanted, but it always came down to kill or be killed. It was just the way it was.

The DEA thought it was going to be an easy takedown. They'd been watching the compound and were convinced Vargas only had a handful of minions with him. Since neither Maryl nor

Joe had been able to clarify that there were indeed more, the DEA decided to take a chance and move in.

Maybe it was posturing against the Bureau. Maybe it was eagerness. Maybe they were afraid Vargas would get away if they didn't bolt. Whatever, it was fucking annoying, because they'd decided to move in despite Thomason urging them to wait on Maryl's debriefing.

The FBI wasn't really interested in Vargas; they wanted Magnus, aka Deacon Ford. They wanted him bad on racketeering charges, linked to his association with Vargas, but if Vargas was in custody, it might make the case against Ford all the tighter, so, sure, they said, go get your fella.

Jesus, what a shit show.

She'd arrived at the makeshift headquarters only a few miles away from the Incarnyx compound, thanks to her statie escort, and found herself in the middle of an uproar. Telling Thomason that she believed Joe to be lost was one of the hardest things she'd ever done.

Her superior laid a gentle hand on her arm. Special Agent in Charge Thomason was a tall woman with salt-and-pepper hair and bright blue eyes. She'd been with the Bureau for more than twenty years and Maryl respected her as both a woman and an agent.

"We're still getting a signal from him. It's weak, but it's there."

Maryl's heart leapt into her throat. "How is that possible?"

"Subdermal tracker, very well hidden."

"Why did he come to the house? It couldn't have been to warn me."

"He thought it would force Vargas's hand and he's right. The man's a time bomb. Even his own people know it. He was also worried about you."

Anger mixed with relief. "I think I've proven I can take care of myself."

"He mentioned Killian Delaney. He said she was a wild card and he didn't like it."

"If it wasn't for Killian Delaney I wouldn't be here right now," Maryl confessed. "She was the one who let me know Vargas had made me."

Thomason's brow furrowed. "She's not with Vargas, then?"

"No, ma'am. The only reason she was there was because… because she was checking in on a friend." She didn't like lying to her superior, but Killian deserved at least a little discretion.

"You sure you want to trust an ex-con? She and the Washington woman were locked up together in York."

Maryl nodded. "I know. She told me."

Thomason looked surprised at that. "Just so I'm clear— Killian Delaney told you about her connection to Tara Washington and helped you escape?"

"Not only that, but when she thought Joe was abusive, she took me in. Got me a room at her hotel. She knew I'd lied to her and she still helped me. I honestly don't believe she is involved in any wrongdoing."

"Just wrong place, wrong time."

"Or maybe right place, right time. Like I said, if not for her, I might be dead right now."

"How did she know to warn you?"

"Vargas found out about her criminal past and gave her the choice of turning me over or having innocent blood on her hands. He has to know she betrayed him by now. We need to get those women out of there."

That had all happened when she first arrived. Now, two DEA agents had been critically wounded, three more had been hit in less serious areas, and one was unaccounted for.

Fabulous. The DEA was pissed. The FBI was pissed, and Maryl was trying really hard not to say anything. It wouldn't go over well.

And then there was Joe. Poor Joe. He was still alive, but for how long? She didn't want to think about what they'd done to him, and she didn't want to think about what they might have done to her if not for Killian's interference. It might not immediately endear Thomason to Killian's side, but it did Maryl, so when that little tiny phone in her pocket began buzzing, she made sure she was alone before checking it.

It was a text from a number she didn't recognize, but the message was clear: *V grouping everyone like hostages. DW wounded.*

DW. Had to be Dylan Woodward. The girl was pregnant with Miguel Vargas's baby.

Hostages? Shit. This was what she'd been afraid of.

What the hell had Joe been thinking? She knew what he'd been thinking. He'd been thinking that she couldn't handle herself. Asshole. He was a good friend, but still an asshole.

She held the phone in her hand and went in search of her boss. The DEA had retreated for now, regrouping.

"Vargas has hostages," she told the special agent in charge.

"There's easily twenty innocent women in that house. And I've just gotten word that Dylan Woodward's been wounded in the firefight."

"Ilyana Woodward's girl?" Thomason asked.

"Yes, ma'am. She's pregnant by Miguel Vargas."

Thomason raised a brow. "How'd you come by this information?"

"I believe it's from Killian Delaney, ma'am."

That brow remained up. "And how did she relay this message?"

Sighing, Maryl offered her the little phone. All of the previous messages on it had been deleted, and she had no doubt they'd be impossible to retrieve, even by the agency. Whatever, or whoever, Killian worked for, they had impressive tech—the kind meant to foil people like her.

Thomason read the text and, of course, looked to see if there was anything else. There wasn't—just those two phone numbers that probably reached phones just as disposable as this one.

"That's all there is?"

"Yes. I think she had the phone with her in case of an emergency. Regardless, I'm glad she had it."

"Yes." Her boss hesitated for a second before giving the small device back to her. "You should hang on to this, I suppose, in case she has another message for you. You seem to have her trust as much as she has yours."

"Yes, ma'am." It was a risk and she knew it, but Killian had taken on Joe, thinking he was an abuser, and had taken him down. That wasn't the kind of person who ran with a man like Vargas.

"All right, then. Exactly how we got this information is just between you and me for the moment. I'll get in touch with hostage negotiation. The Woodward girl just might be the leverage we need."

Maryl nodded. "Do you want me to respond?"

"Not yet. Let me talk to the director. Then we'll proceed."

"Of course." Maryl turned to leave.

"Good work, Agent Rogers." Her real name sounded so odd after going by Blake for the last while.

"Thank you, ma'am." But it didn't feel like good work. It felt like she'd gotten off easy while Joe and Killian paid the price. It felt wrong.

And she didn't know how to make it right.

Sweet boiled hell, Dylan had been shot.

Three men carried her through the large room, dripping blood, while Adriana barked orders at them in Spanish.

Killian could see that Dylan was unconscious, which was good so far as that she wouldn't feel any pain, but she was still a pregnant woman who had been shot, so there was all the drama and potential problems that went with that. Had the bullet affected the baby? Killian wasn't a frigging doctor, so she had no idea just how bad it was, but it didn't take a genius to know being shot was never good.

It didn't matter that Vargas wanted everyone together in the hall/gym. His wife stood toe to toe with him and told him, as a doctor, that his *grandchild* was in danger and that Dylan needed to be kept somewhere quiet and comfortable.

He acquiesced without hesitation, especially when he saw the blood on his son's hands and pale face.

Killian wondered if Vargas also noticed the hatred in his son's eyes, because Miguel didn't try to hide it when he looked at his father.

Several of Vargas's men went and collected a bed and brought it to one of the smaller rooms off the great hall. This was the room where she and Magnus had had their sparring bout and where many of the large group activities were held. It had only one door and no windows, which made it the perfect place to hole up.

"The bullet is still in her," Adriana told Killian and Shasis. Shasis hadn't left Killian's side since they'd been brought back to the main house. "I don't have any surgical tools with me."

"What do you need?" Killian asked. "There's got to be bandages in the first aid kits. You can use booze to clean the wound if there's nothing better, and just about any woman here probably has a good pair of tweezers you can use."

"Prison ingenuity," Shasis explained when Adriana looked impressed. "It's like a war zone—you make do with what you've got. There's a first aid kit on the wall over there. I'll look for alcohol. Killian, you ask women about tweezers."

She didn't mind being told what to do—it was a nice change from having to make those decisions herself. She started with some of the more "high-maintenance" women. None of them were too keen on losing their expensive tweezers to bullet removal, but one did agree.

"Wait," said Belle, sitting a few feet away. "I actually have a hemostat."

Killian stared at her. "What the hell are you doing with one of those?"

"I upcycle dolls. It helps me pull the hair out of their heads."

It was a creepy image, but whatever. "Do you have it on you?"

"It's in my room."

"Go get it. Please."

One of Vargas's men tried to stop her from leaving the room, but Vargas barked something at him that made him move real quick. Killian resolved that if she survived this she was going to make a real effort to improve her Spanish, because it sucked.

Killian glanced around at all the men with guns. Some of them needed medical attention, too. She'd heard that one had been killed by an agent. They also mentioned that they had shot and killed a fed in return.

She didn't like these goons being in charge now. It was one thing when Vargas kept them hidden, but now that they felt like they could do whatever they wanted, there was going to be trouble. There were about twenty women who had come for the retreat, and then the female staff on top of that. How long before the more violent-minded of this bunch decided they should be able to take what they wanted? It wasn't that Killian had a distrust of men. Women were capable of the same kind of behavior—she'd seen it more than once in prison. People showed their true stripes once they thought there wouldn't be any repercussions for it. These guys wouldn't expect their boss—a man who sold women into prostitution—to stop them from raping if that's what they wanted to do.

Vargas probably wouldn't stop them, so then it would be up to Killian to do it. Shit.

She walked over to Miguel, who stood in the doorway of the room where his woman was being laid out on a bed to make her more comfortable.

Dylan's face was dewy with perspiration, her face contorted in an expression of pain, as she regained some degree of awareness. Yeah, it wasn't any fun being moved when you had a hole ripped in you.

"How's she doing?" she asked.

Miguel turned to glance at her before directing his attention back into the room. "I don't know. My mother will do everything she can for her, but I don't know how much that is. I ... I don't want to lose her."

People were often at their most honest when they were at their most terrified. Miguel Vargas might follow in his father's footsteps, or he might make his own path. Maybe he was a good guy and maybe he wasn't, but he loved Dylan, and he loved the child she was carrying, which put him on the right side of okay as far as Killian was concerned.

"The FBI will offer to take her to the hospital."

He looked at her again, this time holding her gaze. "What?"

"If they know she's hurt, they'll offer to get her medical attention—the right kind."

He shook his head. "I doubt my father will allow it."

"Family seems important to him. If they make the offer, talk to him. It will mean the two of you will be separated for a while, but at least she'll be alive, and probably your child, too. It will make it easier for you to get out, if that's what you really want."

"I feel like you're trying to manipulate me."

"Dude, what part of 'your woman and kid will be safe' sounds like a lie to you? Jesus. I don't care if you and your entire family fall off a cliff, but Dylan and that baby are innocent in all of this." At least for now. Maybe in twenty or thirty years Dylan would be another Adriana, and her child would be getting ready to take over their little corner of the Desierto kingdom.

"Why are you here?" He folded his arms over his chest. His shirtsleeves were stained with blood. "Really."

"I was hired by Ilyana to get her girls out of here. I guess she knew you guys were involved."

He chuckled as he shook his head. "Ilyana. There's a woman who needs to fall off a cliff. She and my father... well, let's just say they have a lot in common."

"I've figured that out, yeah. Miguel, how did Dylan get shot?"

He went still. "I...We were trying to leave. I had a bad feeling. I didn't want her here. I thought if I could get her out, she'd be safe."

Killian inclined her head as she studied him. "Well, shit. Aren't you a surprise."

Miguel's expression turned to one of discomfort. "I don't understand what you mean."

"Sure you do." He had someone waiting for them—someone he'd planned to meet. "Was it DEA who shot Dylan or did she get hit by one of your father's men as you tried to escape?"

He pushed her away from the door. "Keep your fucking voice down."

"Does your father know one of his men shot his future daughter-in-law?" She paused. "Does he know you killed his man in return?"

"No," he whispered, his expression fierce. "And I'd prefer to keep it that way."

"Yeah, you would. Don't worry about it, I'm not telling anyone."

Miguel sighed. "My father is a sinking ship and we are all the rats."

"Yeah, well, shit rolls downhill. Get out while you can and run as far as your money and friends can take you. It's the only way you stand a chance. And stay the fuck away from Magnus."

He laughed at that. "Yes. I've learned that lesson. Thank you." Then he frowned. "How do you know the FBI will offer to get Dylan out? They don't even know she was hit."

Killian patted his shoulder. "Yeah. They do." Then she left him there so he could concentrate on his family, and went to meet Belle, who had returned with the hemostat.

"What's going on here, Killian?" the other woman asked her in a low voice.

"We are in the middle of a very bad situation, Belle. I'm hoping it will be over soon."

"Where's Maryl? I haven't seen her since that fella of hers showed up. Is she okay?"

Killian nodded. "Yeah, she's good. Listen, thanks for this. You want it back?"

She made a face. "Uh, no. I'll get another one."

Killian pivoted and made her way to Dylan's room. She gave Adriana the hemostat.

"I need your help," the older woman told her as she tossed the tool into a bowl of what smelled like alcohol. "I need someone to hold her down."

"You've got to be fucking kidding me. Get Rosario to do it."

"Rosario is going to hold her legs. I need you to hold her upper body for me. I assume, given your training, you know how to restrain someone without hurting them."

Yeah, she did, not because of her fighting training, but from watching guards do it to the inmates who sometimes got out of their heads.

"Your husband's a fucking meth dealer and no one here has anything that can knock her out?"

Adriana's expression didn't change. "I can minimize her pain, but there's a chance she might feel something. I need your help. Dylan needs your help. Will you give it?"

Killian positioned herself at the head of the bed. Rosario entered the room a few seconds later and went to stand at Dylan's feet. Dylan's fine blond hair was damp with perspiration and some of her own blood. Her face was pale and shiny, her eyes glassy with pain.

"What are you doing?" she asked, turning her head toward Adriana.

"We're going to remove the bullet that is in you, *niña*," Adriana explained in a gentle tone. "I'm going to try to numb the area as much as possible. I want you to relax as much as you can, and this will all be over soon."

"They shot at us," Dylan said, turning her gaze to Killian. "I didn't even see him."

Killian nodded. "You don't have to talk," she told the girl, hoping she'd take the advice. If Dylan revealed what Miguel had just told her, it was going to start a whole new shit storm.

The girl's wide eyes rolled toward hers. "They *shot* at us."

"It's going to be okay," Killian told her, comfortable with the lie.

Adriana gestured for Killian and Rosario to hold Dylan while she applied some kind of topical anesthetic from the first aid kit to the wound. The girl hissed and writhed in pain, but Killian and Rosario kept her still. From Dylan's feet, the larger Latina met Killian's gaze. In her dark eyes Killian saw all her own concerns reflected. A lot more people were going to get hurt before this was over.

If anything happened to Story, Killian was going to rip Vargas's spine out through his mouth. Her friend was keeping watch over Lyria, making sure none of Vargas's men gave her drugs or unwanted attention.

Adriana pulled on a pair of disposable gloves and picked up the sterilized hemostat. She nodded at both Killian and Rosario before going to work.

"Take a deep breath, darling," she told Dylan.

The girl did as she was told and Adriana pressed the hemostat into the tear in her flesh.

The exhale of breath turned into a low, painful moan as Dylan arched her spine, fighting to pull away. Killian held her firmly, careful not to inflict any more pain if she could help it.

Adriana grimaced. "I've almost got it."

Dylan continued to moan. Tears leaked from the corners of

her eyes as she squeezed them shut. Having a bullet pulled out of you wasn't fun, and Dylan wasn't a freak with a high pain threshold who was used to being busted and torn up.

"It's okay," Killian heard herself whisper. "I know it hurts like hell, but it'll be over soon. You're going to be all right."

Dylan reached up and grabbed Killian's forearm. She squeezed hard as their gazes locked. Killian didn't blink. Didn't look away as Dylan's tears flowed.

"Got it," Adriana cried, triumphant.

Dylan's face contorted as the chunk of metal was pulled from her body. A strangled cry escaped her lips, but she didn't pass out.

"You were awesome," Killian told her proudly. "I've seen full-grown men pass out from less. You're a fucking rock star."

Dylan actually chuckled. "After this, childbirth's going to be nothing."

Killian didn't have the heart to tell her the two were absolutely nothing alike. She held Dylan's hand while Adriana stitched and bandaged the wound, then left her to rest.

Outside the room, she leaned against the wall, closed her eyes, and sighed. She couldn't help but think of Dash and how worried he had to be. Hopefully Maryl had been in touch with him, but if not... well, it was better that he didn't know.

Killian wasn't afraid of dying, but she'd be a liar if she said she wasn't afraid of never seeing Dash again. Part of her hated him for that.

She would miss Meg and Willow and reckless, sometimes stupid Shannon. It was times like these that made it difficult to think of the girl as her sister's kid and not her own. When faced with her own mortality, it was damn near impossible to be right with all the choices she had made.

But her choices had made her what she was, and now was not the time to second-guess any of that, except maybe her lack of Spanish or problem-solving abilities.

She drew a deep breath and opened her eyes.

The wrong end of a gun hovered just in front of her nose.

Shit.

FOURTEEN

Killian recognized the man holding the gun as one of Vargas's men who had been with him when he first arrived—one of the good-looking, semi-charming ones. Mateo, she thought. What was the name of the one who kept hassling Lyria? Was it this asshole?

Everyone else around them was so engrossed in their own business, their own worries, that no one seemed to notice that he had a weapon pulled.

"Move," he said, gesturing with the gun.

Killian did. She didn't move particularly fast or slow, just turned and began walking until he told her to stop. Right beside another door.

"Open it. Go inside."

She turned the knob and stepped inside. She could have run, but he would have shot her, she was sure of that. Those women out there were already afraid; they didn't need to see someone get shot right in front of them.

He followed her into the room, turning on the light before closing the door behind them. He locked it.

"Take off your clothes," he commanded.

Killian arched a brow. "Seriously? You want to rape me? That's a bit of a cliché, don't you think?"

"I'm going to put you in your place, *puta*."

She laughed. "With your big manly cock?" Deliver her from the arrogance of the male ego. She shook her head with a mocking grin. "You're a walking stereotype."

He glared at her, jabbing the gun at her like a finger. "I will fuck respect into you. Strip, now."

This was ridiculous. Killian wasn't a stranger to sexual violence. Like most women, she'd dealt with it more than once in her thirty-plus years. She'd never once given in to it willingly, and she had no intention of doing so now.

"No."

He frowned. Took a step forward. "I'm not fooling around, bitch. Take your clothes off. *Now*."

She shook her head, smiling at his frustration.

The backhand slap struck her left cheek hard—enough to snap her head back. Her bottom lip split against her teeth. Oh, that was a good one. The blood would be a nice touch.

"Fuck you, *maricón*," Killian taunted, licking the split in her mouth. She spat blood on the floor near his feet.

He hit her again—this time a real punch to the cheekbone. It might have knocked her out if she hadn't angled her head to take it. That would mark nicely, too. Just enough to show off.

"I won't tell you again, *puta*."

"No," Killian agreed. "You won't." Her left hand whipped out and grabbed the wrist of his hand holding the gun. She pushed that to the side as she swung with her right fist, driving her knuckles into his jaw. When his head snapped back, she punched him again in the throat. He staggered backward.

Killian followed him—he still hadn't dropped the gun. Her knee came up hard between his legs before she drove her fist into his stomach. As he doubled over, her knee came up again, catching him in the face as she wrenched the gun from his fingers.

His hand went to his nose, blood flowing over his fingers.

"Ooh," Killian mocked. "That looks broken." Putting a few feet between them, she pointed the gun at his head. "Even I know not to let someone get close enough to take my weapon, asshole. Walk."

He hesitated. She smiled. The Glock didn't have a safety to release, or she would have done it just for effect. "I'm not going to say it again, *puta*."

He had his hand to his nose as he straightened. Blood seeped through his fingers, dripping onto the front of his shirt and onto the floor. She'd done a good job on that.

He turned his back to her and walked to the door.

"Open it," she commanded. "Walk to the hall."

She followed him at a decent distance, in case he decided to attack. She really didn't want to kill him if she didn't have to—it would only complicate things.

Heads turned as they entered the large room. Easily a dozen weapons were pointed in her direction. Killian held up her hands, finger nowhere near the trigger.

"What is this?" Rosario demanded. Vargas was nowhere to be seen.

"Romeo here decided he wanted to party," Killian told her.

The strong-featured woman gestured for the others to stand down as she approached. She looked at Killian's face first. "He did that to you?"

Killian smiled. "I did this to him." She gestured at the mess standing a few feet away.

Rosario returned the smile with a slight one of her own. "I apologize for his poor manners." Then, to the man: "This is how you behave? You attack a guest of our hosts?"

He spat on the floor—a great glob of bloody saliva that landed near her feet. He growled something at her that Killian didn't understand, but his intention was clear. The words dripped with hatred.

Rosario dropped him with one punch. Killian watched her with awe. She was truly a beautiful thing to watch. Lightning fast, but graceful at the same time. It was like watching a shark attack.

Killian glanced down at the man's unconscious form sprawled on the floor. "That was incredible," she said. "Seriously, fucking gorgeous." She offered the other woman the gun.

Rosario arched a brow. "Thank you. You're not going to try to keep it?"

"More trouble than it's worth. One gun against many isn't much good."

"You make a good point."

"Besides," Killian added with a shrug. "I don't need it."

The taller woman took the weapon and stuck it in the back of her waistband. "No, I don't think you do. Much quieter and less mess to take someone down by hand." Then she turned to some of Vargas's men. "Take him below," she commanded.

The men jumped to do her bidding. It was obvious who was in charge, and that was good. Rosario could be reasoned with. Rosario had loyalty to Adriana, which meant she wasn't 100 percent behind Vargas.

Killian waited until the men had dragged their comrade away before speaking again. "You know this isn't going to end well, yeah?"

"Yes," Rosario replied, her expression grim. "But then, that's just part of life for people like us, isn't it? It never ends well, and then one day, it ends us."

"So you're a glass-half-empty kind of girl. I respect that."

The *sicaria* smiled. "You are a strange woman."

Killian glanced at the group of women gathered in the far corner of the room. Shasis was with them, trying to comfort those who were scared. "Don't let anyone hurt them," she said.

Rosario inclined her head in agreement. "I will do my best. Do I need to worry about you, Killian? Should I watch my back?"

"You?" Killian shook her head. "No, but I'll let you know if that changes."

Another little smile. "Same. How long do you think we have before they launch a full assault?"

She shrugged. "A couple of hours, tops." Probably less, but she wasn't going to give Vargas that information.

"Then I'd better go do my job. Good luck to you."

"Yeah, you too." Killian watched her walk away before

joining Shasis and the other women. She glanced at Story, noting that her friend looked pensive.

Killian moved closer to her. "You okay?"

Story nodded. "No response from Maryl yet, but I overheard a couple of the guards ask Vargas what they should do with the man in the tunnels. Could be her partner."

If Joe wasn't dead, that was a good thing. Depending on what kind of shape he was in, he might still be helpful. "What did Vargas say?"

"He said to wait, that the man might prove valuable. Is this really all just so Vargas can say his balls are bigger than the feds'?"

"Seems like it."

"That's just stupid."

"That's what the underworld is," Killian informed her. "Prison, gangs, cartels, organized or disorganized... it's all about who has the least fear and the most nerve. If you can use a person's fear against them, then you got 'em. The more people afraid of you, the more power you've got. It's simple math, really."

Story looked at her for a long moment. "You don't know how to plan an escape, but you know how to take over a cartel."

Killian shrugged. "Fear and balls I understand. Trying to save everyone is what fucks me up. If there was just one person to protect, I'd be golden, but I don't want anyone's blood on my hands."

Her friend glanced down at the blood staining Killian's fingers.

"I don't want *innocent* blood on my hands," Killian corrected before turning to the others. "What can I do?" she asked.

"Nothing right now," Shasis answered, angling so the women couldn't hear them. "Magnus has staff bringing food and blankets. Of course, they're being watched by Vargas's people in case they try to escape."

"So much for being partners, huh?"

The other woman shook her head. "I should have known he was shit," she murmured with a sigh. "Never trust a white boy."

Killian laughed sharply, then sobered. "Keep these women safe, T."

"I'm not in any hurry to have blood on my hands, Che-che," she said, echoing Killian's sentiment to Story. Shasis understood how this game was played, too. "Don't you worry. What are you going to do?"

"I'm going to get these women out of here."

"Too bad the feds didn't shoot Vargas instead of poor Dylan."

"Mm. We need a diversion, or a reason to get the others into the tunnels."

"Good luck with that. I think the best bet is to keep our heads down." She squinted at her. "That's a nasty-ass bruise you've got blooming there. That bastard really try to rape you?"

Killian nodded. "He was unsuccessful, obviously."

"He'd have regretted it anyway; that coochie of yours probably has teeth." She grinned.

"What do you mean, 'probably'?" They shared a chuckle.

"How can you laugh?" a woman from the group demanded. Killian didn't remember her name. She was a small blonde, slim and pretty. Her mascara was smudged.

"It relieves tension," Killian told her.

"I guess maybe this situation isn't so scary for someone like you, but the rest of us aren't ex-cons, all right? Some of us are decent people who just want to get home to our families."

"How very white of you," Killian replied, meeting the woman's haughty gaze with a hard stare. "Some of us just want to make sure you live to do that. Now, mind your own fucking business."

The blonde said nothing. Beside Killian, Story grunted her approval of her decision to be silent.

"Where's Magnus?" Another woman—fortyish, very attractive—asked. "They haven't hurt him, have they?"

"He's negotiating with them right now," Shasis replied smoothly. "You just sit tight, honey. We're going to get through this."

"How could you have let these people into your house?" the woman demanded.

"I didn't," Shasis fired back, finally losing patience. "Magnus did." She turned her back on the women, grabbed Killian by the arm, and hauled her to the side. "Some of these bitches are going to get themselves killed if they don't learn to shut the fuck up."

"Your veneer is slipping, *Shasis*."

The other woman stilled. Then she nodded, closed her eyes, and drew a deep breath. When she opened her eyes again, the mask was back in place. "Thank you," she said. "I'm not going to lose it. I can't afford to lose it right now."

Killian patted her arm. "Do you know where Magnus is?"

"No fucking idea. I assume he's with Vargas. I know he's freaking out because of the agent they shot."

They stood there a second before the sound of a phone ring-ing cut the silence. Shasis looked startled, then reached into the pocket of her jumpsuit and withdrew a cell phone. She answered the call. "Hello...? Yes, this is she...Uh-huh...I'm going have to call you back." She hung up, eyes wide.

"That was the FBI," she said quietly. Her gaze locked with Killian's. "They want to negotiate."

Maryl wasn't part of the negotiating process—that was han-dled by agents who specialized in hostage situations. All she could do was sit nearby with a cup of coffee and listen as her people tried to make a deal with Vargas.

Of course the goal of negotiations was to convince Vargas to release some of the women who were only on the premises for the Incarnyx class. The Desierto lieutenant wasn't about to do that, however, until the agency gave him something he wanted first. Maryl was surprised that the first thing he asked for wasn't a helicopter or something designed to waste time while he made his escape.

"Yes, Mr. Vargas," the negotiator said into the phone. "We can guarantee the safety of your son's fiancée, but you have to let us send EMTs in to get her so we all will know if she and the baby are okay...Yes, sir. We understand."

Maryl knew what that meant. Vargas had just told the nego-tiator that if he even thought they were trying to double-cross him he'd start killing his hostages. Having this kind of leverage must have always been part of the plan.

Some of the women who signed up for Incarnyx's courses were

among the wealthiest in the tristate area. They were married to powerful men—and were powerful in their own right. They had the means to give Vargas anything he wanted.

This operation couldn't go down the toilet; it just couldn't. She and Joe had spent so much time building a case against Deacon Ford. They'd worked so hard, and Joe was still in that house. He was still alive, but that could change at any second. It couldn't be for nothing. It just couldn't.

She pulled a pack of cigarettes from her bag and stuck one in her mouth as she walked away from the others. Once she couldn't hear them anymore, she stopped and flicked her lighter to life.

The first drag was divine. It always was. No matter how many times she quit, it always came back to that first puff. She intended to savor this one, because once reinforcements showed up, it might be a while before she was able to indulge in another.

There were women she knew in that house. Some of them she even liked. She didn't want any of them to get hurt. It was bad enough that Dylan Woodward had gotten shot. The press was going to have a heyday with that—didn't matter who had actually done the shooting. Their agents claimed the girl had been shot by Vargas's own men, and they didn't take responsibility for that same man being brought down, leaving Maryl to wonder just how much dissension there was in Vargas's family, let alone his organization.

They had the road blocked off for a quarter of a mile in either direction, detouring traffic, so the only vehicles on that stretch of road were law enforcement of some kind. Red and blue lights flickered in the dark, breaking the glare of headlights. She couldn't see the Incarnyx property from the road, couldn't hear anything, either. It was as if there was nothing amiss. But just a short time ago, gunfire had permeated the night. She could still smell it.

She walked down the road as she smoked. It felt good to move and stretch her legs. The coffee was finally starting to kick in, and it coupled with the nicotine from her cigarette so that energy flooded her veins. The fog around her brain was clearing.

In the distance something moved—just beyond the roadblock. If it weren't for the streetlight, she might not have seen it at all. What was that? Was it an animal or a person?

Maryl took another drag off her cigarette before dropping it to the asphalt and grinding it beneath her heel. She tossed her coffee as well—she'd collect the paper cup later.

Slowly, she drew her weapon as she carefully but purposefully strode toward the shape. Whatever it was, it was coming toward her. Her fingers tightened on the Glock.

It wasn't until she was maybe twenty feet away that she recognized what it was. A sob caught in her throat.

"Oh my God." She started running toward the figure, her heart hammering in her chest.

"Joe?"

The figure lifted its head. Then one of its hands, as if in greeting. He moved like a shambling zombie from a horror movie, dragging his right foot behind him. His left arm hung limp at his side. His shirt was covered in blood, and when she got close enough to see his face...

Oh, sweet Jesus. How had he survived? How could he even see? One of his eyes was swollen completely shut and the other looked almost as bad. His nose was bent to one side, his face split open in several places. When he opened his mouth to speak, she was certain he was missing teeth.

"Maryl," he groaned.

She caught him when he lurched forward, stumbling. Staggering under his weight, she struggled to stay upright, maneuvering so that his right arm was over her shoulders and her left was around his waist. The second her hand touched him it became soaked with blood. He leaned hard into her, stumbling yet again as he tried to walk.

"How the hell did you get out?" she asked him, but all she got was a groan in response.

"Need some help?" came a voice in the dark.

Maryl would have jumped if she didn't have almost two hundred pounds of injured male weighing her down. "Who are you?" she demanded.

He stepped out of the night. Easily as tall and muscular as Joe, he had a chiseled face that was almost beautiful in its perfection. "It's Dash."

Her eyes widened at the name. "Oh, thank Christ. Help me, please."

Dash moved quickly toward her, relieving her of the burden of Joe's weight. He bore it much easier than she did. "Where do you want me to take him?"

"Toward the lights, if you don't mind. How should I introduce you?"

"Let me take care of that."

Maryl studied his profile. "Who the hell are you people?"

He barely glanced at her. "Private security."

She had a feeling that barely even scratched the surface, but it was better than nothing at all. "Were you hired to rescue the Woodward girls, too?"

"No. My only concern is Killian."

"She's quite something."

"Yes," he agreed with a smile. "She is."

"I owe her my life."

"That's kind of her thing." Joe groaned and Dash shifted to take on more of his weight. "You know this guy?"

"He's my partner. This is what the people Killian is with did to him. They're Desiertos. Have you heard of them?"

Dash nodded, his expression stern. "Yeah. I'm familiar. Your partner's lucky to be alive, unless he was let loose to send a message."

"I think he must have escaped."

"He must be a tough son of a bitch."

"He is."

Maryl noticed bloodstains on Dash's clothes—on the opposite side that held Joe's weight, and frowned. He also had a mark on his cheekbone that looked as though he'd been hit.

They had EMTs and the local fire department on standby and one ambulance on hand since the shootout. Several agents had to be treated for minor wounds. The one who had been shot was presumed dead.

Dash practically carried Joe to the ambulance. The paramedics immediately took control of the situation, assessing his injuries and making him as comfortable as possible before taking him to the hospital.

"Where is the ambulance going?" SAC Thomason asked, her phone still in her hand.

"We found Agent Riley," Maryl informed her, trying to contain her joy. "They took him for treatment."

Her superior's mouth thinned. "We just got done negotiating with Vargas. He's letting us go in for the Woodward girl."

"Dylan?"

"Yes. Apparently his wife removed the bullet. He's allowing his son to accompany her to the hospital. So we'll have both of them in our custody."

She looked happy about that, so Maryl didn't question her. But if a man like Vargas was allowing his heir—and future grandchild—to be taken in by the FBI, he had to be pretty certain there was nothing the agency could pin on them.

Or he didn't care. Miguel wasn't Vargas's only son, and maybe Rafael wasn't keen on having a white daughter-in-law. The old man hadn't gotten as far into the Desiertos as he had by being a good man.

Thomason looked at Dash. "Who are you?"

"Eddie Brock," he replied easily. "I'm an EMT. Saw the lights and figured you guys might need help. I've got my truck just down the road if you need someone to go in and get the victim."

Maryl stared at him. The lie rolled off his tongue so smoothly she almost believed it, despite knowing better.

Thomason studied him—his perfect face marred by that one abrasion, the blood on his clothes. He was wearing something that looked like a uniform, at least.

"I'll need help," he added. "It's just me. I'm off duty, technically."

"I wouldn't have gotten Joe here on my own," Maryl heard herself say.

"Get your rig," Thomason instructed, her lips thinning. "I'll find someone to assist you. We want them taken to the hospital as quickly as possible."

Dash nodded. "Yes, ma'am." He turned to leave.

"Agent Rogers, go with him. Make sure they don't give him trouble at the blockade."

Maryl followed on Dash's heels. "Eddie Brock?" she whispered.

He shrugged. "First name that came to mind."

"*Venom* was the first thing you thought of when giving a false name to a federal agent?"

"Look, I'm not normally the guy who comes charging in to save the day, all right? I'm just a fucking mechanic."

He wasn't "just" a mechanic any more than Killian was "just" an ex-con.

"A fucking mechanic who just happened to show up at the exact moment I needed you." When he said nothing, she continued, "There's no way Joe escaped on his own in the shape he's in. You were in there, weren't you?"

Dash glanced at her, slowing his pace so she could keep up. "So what if I was?"

"Then I owe you for saving my partner's life."

"Keep as much of this off Killian as you can and we're even."

"What's the name of this private security firm you work for? Just out of curiosity in case I ever need to hire someone."

"New Amsterdam," he replied. "Knock yourself out looking into it."

She would, but mostly to cover her own ass, and if they checked out they could definitely be an asset in the future.

Maryl didn't have to follow him all the way to the roadblock. He turned down a side street and there was an ambulance parked beneath the streetlight.

"How did you get this past the checkpoint?" she asked.

Dash smiled. "Did you ask Killian this many questions?"

"What does that matter?"

Another shrug. "I'm going to need someone with me who knows what they're doing."

"That shouldn't be a problem. You didn't answer my question."

"And I'm not going to, Agent Rogers." He opened the driver's door. "Get in. I'll drive you back."

She was tempted to say no, but that was stupid, so she opened the passenger door and climbed inside.

"This is a real ambulance," she marveled, taking in the interior. "Where did you get it?"

Dash gave her a wry glance and started the engine. He didn't answer that question, either.

Maryl shook her head with a slight smile and leaned back against the seat for the duration of the short drive. Honestly, she didn't care where Dash had come from or how he'd managed all this. All she cared about was that Joe was alive and that they would hopefully soon have Deacon Ford and Rafael Vargas in custody. Anything else was just icing.

But she was definitely checking out New Amsterdam Security after this.

FIFTEEN

Plans were made for Dylan and Miguel to be taken off the property, along with one hostage as a show of good faith. The woman Vargas chose was a little woman who hadn't stopped crying since the first shots had been fired a few hours earlier. She was whom Killian would have chosen as well.

No one else was going to be released, however. Vargas would get to hang on to his collateral a little while longer, while he made his escape plans.

It would be over so much quicker if the FBI just bombarded the place, but obviously, they were concerned about casualties. Though, if they were faced with no other option, Killian had no doubt they'd gas the place and take their chances coming in. Vargas was a big fish and his capture was worth a little risk.

They were still holed up in the hall. Some of the women had fallen asleep on mats in the far corner of the room, while others kept a wary watch on the cartel boys. They were angry and afraid, and most of them still believed Magnus would somehow magically save them all. He sat with them now, yoga-style, on the floor, holding the hands of two women who clung to him like a lifeline. It didn't mean he was a good person—it was all for his ego. He wanted them to say good things about him when they were released. Of course that was how his brain worked. He needed to look like a good guy so the story would have the right spin. Killian would be more surprised if he aligned himself with Vargas from a public-relations standpoint.

She sat not too far away from Magnus and his women, her back against the wall, sipping a smoothie. They'd brought a cart of them up from the kitchen. It was a quick and easy way to keep everyone fed without actually cooking.

Adriana and Shasis were with Dylan—a convenient place for the two of them to hide. Christ only knew what they were planning. Vargas kept to himself in another room as well—his "office." His most trusted men were often with him, and sometimes Magnus, too. He only showed his face when something was about to happen, so when he entered the hall, Killian's spine straightened, pressing her shoulders against the wall.

Vargas walked toward her. Digging in her heels, Killian pushed herself to her feet. Magnus saw this and got up as well. He approached cautiously, reaching her at the same time Vargas did.

"It's been brought to my attention that you were sent here by Ilyana Woodward to bring her daughters home."

Shit. Well, not like she'd been exactly secretive about it. "Yeah, that's true."

"What?" Magnus demanded, with an outrage that seemed solely for Vargas's benefit. "I thought you were a friend of Shasis. She said you wanted in."

Killian practically rolled her eyes at his dramatics. "I can't do both?"

He sneered. "You can't be a friend to us if you're a friend to that bitch."

"She's not my friend." *And neither are you*, she thought. "And I proved myself to you by finding your fed, remember?"

"Who then conveniently escaped."

Killian took a step toward him. "Do you really want to get into a pissing contest with me, *Deacon*? After all, I know where your dick has been."

His cheeks flushed, revealing that he hadn't confessed to Vargas about having sex with Maryl. "I don't trust you."

"The feeling's mutual, sweetheart."

"Stop it," Vargas commanded. "Both of you try my patience."

Killian bit her tongue. Magnus, however, turned to Vargas with a flourish. "Don't talk to me like I'm one of your lackeys, Rafael. We're business partners. Equals."

It was clear that Vargas did *not* think that Magnus was his equal by any stretch of the imagination. "Is that so?"

Magnus didn't even have the sense to know he was in danger. "It is."

Vargas arched a brow. He didn't give a rat's ass about Magnus as a person. He was just Cirello's replacement, and if Magnus disappeared, Vargas would find another to replace him in an instant. It was painfully obvious that Magnus was ignorant as to how the drug trade actually worked, a character flaw that was not going to serve him well in that industry.

"Look," Killian began, taking charge of the conversation.

"Ilyana hired me to get her daughters. She didn't ask me to spy on you, or incriminate either of you in any way. She just wants her kids."

"And the… insurance my *partner* had on her," Vargas added. The menace with which he emphasized the word sent a shiver of unease down Killian's spine. This was not going to end well, and she did not want to be in the middle of it when it exploded.

"Yeah," she said. "That, too. She's just looking to cover her ass and protect her kids. It's what any mother would do." Not that she believed that, but whatever.

"What would you know about motherhood, *niña*?"

"Only what I've seen on TV," she quipped. Like she'd ever discuss that with him.

Vargas actually chuckled. But anything else he might have said was interrupted by one of his men, who whispered something in his ear. It was then that Killian noticed that some of the Desiertos wore earpieces. They had radios, the bastards.

"Let them in," Vargas said with a nod. Then to Killian: "We'll finish this discussion later."

She exhaled a deep breath as he walked away.

"I bet you're wishing you'd never even heard of Ilyana Woodward," Magnus commented.

Killian didn't even look at him. "Dude, that is so not what you ought to be worrying about right now. Why don't you run back to your groupies and leave me alone?"

The energy of the room changed when the EMTs were allowed in to collect Dylan. A few moments later, two men wheeled a gurney into the hall. Killian gave them a cursory glance. *Wait…*

Heart in her throat, she turned her head and looked at them again. What the fuck was Dash doing there? He didn't do these kinds of jobs. He was a legit business owner. What was he thinking, taking a risk like this? And for what, for her?

He didn't even look at her as he and the other man—someone she didn't recognize—steered the gurney down the short hall toward the room where Dylan was resting. A few moments later, she heard Adriana call her name. She didn't acknowledge Magnus before turning her back on him. Maybe it was poking the bear, but she was just so tired of men and their posturing for dominance.

Plus, Dash was there, and he took precedence over anyone else.

When she entered the room, Dash and the other man had transferred Dylan onto the gurney. She was covered with a sheet and strapped in, nice and secure.

"Dylan wants to speak to you before she leaves," Adriana told her.

Killian didn't look at Dash, even though she wanted to. She'd never noticed before just how aware all of her senses were of him. How much her heart beat faster just knowing he was near.

Jesus, she had it bad. Probably the danger heightened the situation, but even she wasn't so afraid of love that she'd go to such extremes to deny it. She loved the bastard, and when she finally got out of there, she was going to tell him just how much.

She approached the gurney and looked down at Dylan's pale face. She looked better than she had immediately following the bullet removal, but she was still pretty rough.

"You wanted to talk to me?"

Dylan nodded and licked her lips. "Will you take care of Lyria for me? Tell her I love her and...and maybe you can tell her that I'm sorry?"

"You can tell her yourself when you see her."

"Will you do it, though? Just in case?"

Killian nodded. "Sure. I can do that for you. I promise."

The younger woman smiled tremulously. It was obvious she was terrified. "Thanks."

Dash came around to the head of the gurney. When he got close, he pressed something into her hand. Whatever it was, it wasn't very thick and was wrapped in paper. Killian immediately slipped it into her pocket without looking.

"Are you all right, miss?" he asked. "Your lip is pretty swollen."

She arched a brow as she met his gaze. "You should see the other guy."

Dash's eyes narrowed just the tiniest bit. "Some ice would help with that."

Killian fought a smile. He wasn't talking about ice for her lip; he meant putting the guy who hit her on ice. It was almost romantic.

"I'll keep that in mind," she replied. Then she glanced at Dylan. "Take care of her."

He nodded, and then he was gone—pushing Dylan out of

the room as though he didn't know her and hadn't just slipped her something that would hopefully help her get out of there. If it weren't for Lyria, she'd find a window and jump out. Make a run for it and take her chances with the cartel boys.

"Where is Lyria?" she asked when she realized that she hadn't seen the girl in a while.

"She was very upset over Dylan," Adriana told her. "I had to give her something to calm her down. She's resting now." She gestured to the open door on the far wall that led into another small room.

Resting was such a whitewashed way of saying Lyria was drugged out of her ever-loving mind. The girl was so fragile— or treated as such. Killian had to wonder just what had been done to her, and how much information she had on Vargas, Magnus, and the entire operation. Maybe Dylan was right to be concerned about whether or not she'd see her sister again.

She slid her hand into her pocket and felt the object Dash had given her. She knew what it was now—a small blade, like an arrowhead, that could be worn across two fingers like a ring. It wouldn't do much damage to the trunk of a body, but that wasn't what it was designed for. It was for cutting up faces, wrists, and throats. It was for severing arteries that were close to the surface, or punching through someone's cheek.

Killian went to the women's locker room and this time opened the weapon in a stall. It had a sheath over the blade and writing on the paper in which it had been wrapped. All it said was, "I've got you, love D." She smiled. He really could be the perfect man sometimes. He hadn't come to rescue her, just back her up. He was there to follow her lead and she loved him all the more for it.

The rings of the blade fit her perfectly, as if it had been sized for her. Knowing Dash, it had been. This would be his—and her—idea of the perfect gift. She looked forward to trying it out. The only question was who to use it on first: Magnus or Vargas?

The door to the locker room opened. A moment later, Story peeked over the top of the next stall. "Was that who I think it was?"

"Yep. He brought me a present."

"Great. Look, we need to figure out how the hell we're getting out of here. I just heard a couple of Vargas's guys talking, and we need to move—fast."

Killian frowned. She sheathed the blade and slipped it back into her pocket, along with the note. "What did they say?"

Story's smile was a mockery of joy. "Oh, just the usual talk of where to put the C-four."

Now it made sense why Vargas wanted Miguel and Dylan out of there. Story was right. They needed a plan, and fast.

"He's going to blow this place up."

After the FBI called Shasis's phone, Vargas took control of it. As luck would have it, the battery also died in Story's burner, leaving them with no way to get word to Maryl or anyone else about what Vargas had planned. All Killian and Story could do was get Lyria and get the hell out—hopefully in time to warn them.

The idea of leaving all the other women behind left a bad taste in Killian's mouth, but she couldn't think of any way to get them all out at once, and someone had to escape, because Vargas obviously didn't care if any or all of them died in his bid to become public enemy number one.

"I don't get it," Story said in a low voice as they talked in the corner of the gym, a little distance away from the other women. "If Lyria knows something, why keep her drugged or locked up? Why haven't they just killed her?"

"Maybe she's leverage?" Killian wondered aloud. "Maybe she doesn't know anything, but there's got to be some reason they just don't cut her loose. Maybe she's their guarantee that Ilyana will keep her mouth shut about what she knows."

"You'd think having Dylan marry into the family would ensure that."

"Fuck it. I have no idea, but I can't leave her with them." There was something going on—a lot of Vargas's men coming and going through the great hall, throughout the night.

"I think I just saw some of them going with luggage," Story said.

"They must be planning to make their escape. Negotiations are just a tactic to buy time. Then they destroy the evidence and the witnesses."

"But you told Maryl about the airstrip. The FBI has to be sitting on it. How the hell are they going to get anywhere in a small plane? It won't get them all the way back to South America, and if they stop anywhere they'll be arrested."

"I don't know. None of this has made much sense since I

got here. But I know some people who may have answers." She nodded at Shasis and Adriana, who sat on chairs not far away.

"Why do they get chairs?" Story asked. "They tried to escape right along with us."

"Because no one knows they tried to escape. Rosario didn't tell anyone. Vargas thinks they're loyal to him."

"We might be able to take advantage of that arrogance."

"Maybe." Killian sat up straighter as two of Vargas's men approached them. "What do they want?" God, she hoped it was a fight.

"You," one of them said in a thick accent as he lifted his chin at Story. "Get up."

"Why?" she asked.

"Because the federal agents want another person set free and you are it," the other replied.

It couldn't be a coincidence that Vargas had agreed to release another hostage during all this ongoing activity. It was a distraction.

Story, smart girl, rose to her feet and didn't argue. She wasn't going to try to stay with Killian now that she had information that was useful outside. She could tell the FBI about the talk of explosives, about the secret passages beneath the house, about Lyria.

"Can I have my belongings?" Story asked.

"What are they worth to you?" the same man asked with a greasy smile.

Killian started to stand, but the one with better English pushed her back down. "Don't move. I will do more than fatten your mouth."

Right. She'd beaten up his buddy. That hadn't earned her any friends. She didn't fight him, didn't even mouth off. Didn't do anything that might affect Story getting out.

It wasn't easy.

"I don't need my things," Story said.

The other man's smile was replaced with an expression of indignation. What was the defect with some men that they expected women to jump at their offers of sexual coercion? It was like punching someone and then getting upset because they didn't say thank you.

Story glanced at her as the guards took her by either arm and pulled her toward the exit. Killian forced a smile. Anxiety wasn't an emotion she often felt, but she felt it now. Story was her friend. If anyone hurt her, Killian would rip them apart, but it wouldn't change the fact that Story had been hurt. Not being able to protect her friend scared her, but there was a part of her that would be glad to see her gone. Once Story was safe, all Killian had to worry about was herself. Shit, and Lyria. And anyone else who needed rescuing.

Of course, once Story was out of sight, she had no idea if her friend was safe or not. Those guards could do anything to her once they had her alone.

Killian's stomach tightened. She forced herself to take a deep breath and ease the cramping. Story could take care of herself. She'd seen her fight before. She'd be okay.

Still, she watched as Story was taken from the room and disappeared from sight before rising to her feet and approaching Shasis and Adriana. There were only two other guards in the room at that moment, and they stood talking and sharing a cigarette in the opposite corner. Most of the women were asleep.

"Did Rafa let her go?" Adriana asked.

Killian nodded. "You have anything to do with that?"

"I told him she would be a good choice, that she could tell people she hadn't been hurt—make him look good. I also told him it would leave you isolated and alone. He liked that."

She supposed she should thank the woman for that, but she couldn't quite bring herself to do it. "What's up with Lyria?"

They both frowned at her. "What do you mean?"

"Why is she being kept drugged and watched?"

"I told you. She was upset about her sister."

Killian stared at her. "The real reason. I thought she was a meth-head, but she doesn't have the look of a long-term user. She told me it was because one of Vargas's men had a thing for her, but no one's even tried to approach her. In fact, it's almost like she's being protected. Why?"

Adriana sighed. "Because Ilyana Woodward is a monster. She sold Lyria to me a year ago."

That wasn't the answer she expected. "What?"

"She offered Vargas his pick of either of them. My husband is many things, but he is not into little girls. Dylan is the stronger of the two, and I already saw how she and Miguel were with each other. I offered Ilyana a large sum of money to leave Lyria with Shasis. I told her the girl would be for my pleasure."

"It's true," Shasis chimed in, standing up. She looked Killian right in the eye. "When Ilyana first brought those girls here..." She cleared her throat. "Let's just say I can smell a pimp. She'd been passing those girls all around Hollywood. It's how she got them to recruit so easily. They were already broken in."

"Jesus." Killian's fingers curled into fists.

"Miguel and I put a stop to it," Adriana explained, also standing. "I don't advocate the selling of flesh. When my son was with Ilyana, he learned of what she had done. It's what ended their relationship—that and his growing feelings for Dylan."

What the hell had Raven gotten involved with? She couldn't know. She never would have asked Killian for help if she'd known. Would she?

"But why is she drugged?"

"She's fragile. Dylan's found it easier to live life, but Lyria's already tried to harm herself twice since she's been here, and that was down from many times she tried when living with her mother. She has been doing better since we got her a therapist, but she still needs to be heavily medicated just to get through the day."

"Ilyana's a good pimp," Shasis said, without a hint of respect. "She broke that girl's spirit hard. Doesn't matter what she does to her; Lyria just wants her love. We've been trying to keep her from going back. When we found out Ilyana sent you, I knew we'd have to take measures to keep her here."

"Are you taking her with you or leaving her here to be blown up when Vargas detonates the house?"

The two of them laughed. The urge to punch both of them in their gaping mouths was almost too much.

"He's not blowing up the house," Adriana told her. "Just the tunnels beneath it."

That would have been useful information to have five minutes ago, before Story was released.

"I don't really like the kid," Shasis confided. "But I know what happens to girls who go back to their pimps."

Killian couldn't stop her eyebrow from raising. Was what they told her true? Killian believed she had something of a radar for people who were sexual predators. None of her instincts told her this information was wrong. In fact, it all made a twisted kind of sense. She never thought she'd take the word of Dirty T over someone else, but she was doing just that.

She was keeping Ilyana's money for her trouble. "What will happen to her if you take her?"

"She'll be looked after, far away from her mother. She can stay with me, or she can stay with Dylan and Miguel if she wants." Shasis shrugged. "What will happen to her if you take her, Che-che?"

Killian met her unflinching dark gaze. "You know, you could have told me this days ago and I'd be home right now, oblivious to any of this."

"I don't believe that, and neither do you."

Killian didn't reply.

Adriana leaned closer. "It might interest you to know that the FBI agent my husband had prisoner escaped."

For a second, Killian was confused. She had told them about Maryl. "Joe?"

Adriana nodded. "They think he had help, but all of my husband's men have been accounted for."

That would explain the increased activity. With Joe gone, Vargas lost some of his bargaining power.

"How much longer before you make your escape?" she asked.

Adriana shrugged, averting her gaze. "I'm not sure."

Killian made a scoffing noise at her poor attempt at subterfuge. "I don't care what you do. I just want to get the fuck away from all of you."

Neither one of them looked the least bit offended. "You could always come with us as well," Adriana suggested, drawing a surprised looked from Shasis.

"Thanks, but no, thanks."

She went back to her spot against the wall, sat down, and closed her eyes for what felt like a moment. When she opened them again, it was because raised voices forced her to, and she knew she'd slept, because her mind was foggy with it.

"What the fuck, Vargas?" Magnus demanded, his face flushed with anger.

Groggily, Killian glanced around. The women who had been in the corner were gone. Where the hell were they? She sat up. A hand came down on her leg. It was Shasis. She put her finger to her lips, indicating she should remain silent. Not far from her sat a very stoned Lyria, who could barely keep her eyes open.

"Lower your voice, Ford," Vargas said smoothly. The two of them stood in the center of the hall. "Losing your temper won't change things."

"We had an agreement."

"And now we don't. Being associated with you has become a liability. We're done." He started to walk away. "Adriana, come."

His wife moved to join them just as Magnus reached out and grabbed Vargas by the arm. "You wetback son of a bitch."

It happened so fast. One moment Magnus was standing there, red-faced and raving, and the next, there was an explosion of sound and he fell to his back on the tiles, blood staining the front of his white linen shirt.

Screams echoed from one of the side rooms. Killian could only assume they belonged to the female hostages. Adriana had frozen in place, dots of fresh blood speckling her face and white tunic. She looked as astounded as Killian felt.

"Fuck me," Shasis whispered. Then she ran to her business partner's side. "Deacon?"

His eyes were wide open as he stared up at her. It was a gut shot—the kind that took a while to kill someone. Vargas could have shot him in the head, but he chose not to. He probably wanted Magnus to think about how he could have handled the situation differently.

"That's one loose end dealt with," Vargas said. Then he turned to Killian, leveling the pistol at her head. "Now let's take care of you."

SIXTEEN

Killian's friends were gifted liars. Their sheer skill amazed Maryl.

The boyfriend was good, but it was the woman who really caught her attention. If she hadn't seen it with her own eyes, and knew the woman was involved in the same line of work—whatever that was—as Killian, she would honestly believe the woman was an innocent bystander and nothing more. She spoke and behaved exactly like someone who had just been through a traumatic event and was slightly in shock. She was a totally different person than the one Maryl had met.

And she wasn't surprised when the time came for the woman to be taken to the hospital to be checked out that it was Dash who was suddenly there to take her. He had gotten Dylan and Miguel to the hospital—with a Bureau escort—and returned almost immediately.

When Story emerged from the gated lane, hands up, squinting against the bright lights, he'd been right there to check her for any apparent injuries. The two of them hadn't even let on that they knew each other, and yet they had to.

This was the part where both of them disappeared, Maryl

realized. As soon as they were in that ambulance, they were lost as far as the Bureau was concerned. She should probably stop them, but she couldn't bring herself to do it. They might not exactly be law-abiding citizens, but they hadn't done anything wrong, as far as she could tell. In fact, they'd done nothing but help her out.

She walked over to the ambulance, wondering yet again how Dash had managed to get his hands on it.

"You're going to take this witness to the hospital?" she asked.

Dash nodded. "That's what I've been told to do."

Maryl turned her attention to the woman. "Is our friend okay in there?"

The woman nodded. "I'm fairly confident they sent me out so she'd be left alone. When the guards brought me out they were talking about a man in the basement who got away. I assume that was yours?"

Maryl nodded. "I'm surprised they discussed it in front of you."

"They think I'm a rich white woman who wouldn't know Spanish if it bit her on the ass." This was said with a slight smile. "I'm glad your partner got out."

"Me too." She cast a glance at Dash, but his attention was on Story.

"There's a lot of movement going on in there. I think they're starting to mobilize. They're definitely getting ready for something."

"We figured the offer to release another hostage was a diversion, especially when Vargas demanded a helicopter. Thanks to

Killian, we know all about the airstrip and the tunnels beneath the house."

"I'm supposed to warn you that some of the men in there were talking about explosives."

Dash stiffened. "What?" Maryl knew that look. She'd worn it herself when she thought there was a chance Joe was still alive. She'd been prepared to storm the house and rescue him herself.

Story put her hand on his arm. "They're not going to blow it up while they're still in it." Then, looking at Maryl: "You and I both know she'll find a way out."

Maryl didn't think that last part was meant just for her. "What about the hostages?"

"I have a feeling they don't really care about them." Story stretched her neck. "The prevailing theory is that Vargas is looking to improve his reputation by doing as much damage as possible before fleeing back to South America."

"Right. Shit." They had to get in there, and get in there fast.

"Thank you for what you did for Joe," she said to Dash, offering him her hand. He hesitated only a second before accepting the gesture. His fingers were strangely rough for a man so classically handsome.

"You'll look out for Killian?" he asked.

She nodded. "I will." She owed both of them that.

"Nice meeting you, Agent Rogers." There was just the slightest emphasis on her last name. Maryl knew better than to assume it was nothing. It was a reminder that he knew who she was and that he would expect her to be accountable for any harm that came to Killian.

"Likewise," she replied, releasing him. "I hope to never see either of you again."

Leaving them, Maryl jogged over to where Thomason stood, dimly aware that behind her the ambulance was already leaving the scene.

"Ma'am, we have a problem." She explained what she'd been told.

"We have to mobilize," Thomason said. Then, into her radio, she advised those listening that there could be a bomb on the premises and they needed to proceed accordingly.

As her boss spoke, Maryl turned her face toward the large house up the hill. How had this operation gotten so out of hand? It should have been simple—almost routine. She'd been involved in more intricate and elaborate jobs that had gone off without incident, but this one had been a clusterfuck since almost day one.

Damn self-help groups.

A shot rang out. It came from the direction of the house. Jaw dropping, Maryl turned toward her boss, who returned her glance with equal alarm.

"Shot fired," voice squawked over the radio. "It came from inside the house."

One of the hostages? Maryl wondered. Or one of the bad guys?

Or Killian?

Then another voice: "We've got movement. Looks like they're bringing out supplies."

"Get into position," Thomason barked as the agents around

her sprang into action. The next thing Maryl knew, she had her weapon and a gas mask in hand as she ran with the others toward vehicles in order to storm the house.

The assault on Incarnyx had begun.

Killian was getting tired of men just wagging their guns in her face like they expected her to go down on them. She met Vargas's gaze and held it.

"Rafa," his wife said in a gentle tone. "Put the gun down. Our *guests* are already upset."

He ignored her, his attention still focused on Killian. "It's your fault we are here. If you had just left Rank Cirello alone, none of this would be happening."

"If Rank Cirello had just left me alone, he'd still be alive," Killian replied calmly. "You want to blame someone, blame him."

"But he is already dead, and I can't kill him. I can kill you."

She shrugged. "Not going to fix your problem, but knock yourself out." She was in full shutdown mode. She loved it. Everything was so clear and simple when her emotions were out of the picture.

One of Vargas's men entered the room from the great hall. "¡Ellos vienen!" Company was coming. Killian could only assume it was the FBI. She could kiss Maryl for her exquisite timing.

Vargas began barking orders in Spanish. Killian didn't understand the words, but she understood the gist. Whatever his plans were, they were being put into action now.

He said something to Rosario. Killian caught enough to know he wanted Rosario to take "the women" somewhere.

"Come with us," Adriana pleaded, grabbing at his hand.

Vargas gently touched her face. "I will meet you shortly and we'll leave this place together." He strode from the room.

"Come on," Shasis said to Killian, gesturing for her to get up. "We got to *go*."

"What about the hostages?" Killian asked, standing.

"The feds will find them," Shasis explained. "Slow them down a bit."

Killian wasn't so sure that was an effective plan, but whatever. Adriana assisted Lyria to her feet and held on to the younger woman. When Rosario motioned for them to follow her, Killian fell into line behind Shasis. They left the gym and continued toward the door that led to the underground tunnel she'd discovered earlier.

Some of Vargas's men stationed themselves in the hall, while others jogged to other locations. They were all heavily armed. It was going to be a bloodbath. Killian hoped Maryl would be okay.

Down they went to the cellar below the house and the tunnel beyond. There were men down here, too, moving crates and boxes. Drugs? Money? Weapons? There was no way to tell. One thing that was visible, however, were the strategically placed blocks of C-4. Shit, they really were going to blow the tunnels.

They made their way over the rough floor toward the heavy door she'd assumed was the way out on her earlier excursion. Rosario had to kick something out of her way to open it. Killian blinked when she realized what it was.

Mina lay on the floor, dead. It was obvious she'd been there for some time. There was a small hole in the middle of her forehead and dirt covered her face and clothes as she rolled to the side.

"I was wondering where she was," she remarked out loud.

Adriana tossed her a triumphant smile over her shoulder. "She forgot her place."

Okay, then. Killian nodded. "If you don't kill 'em, how are they going to learn?"

But Adriana wasn't listening to her; she was speaking to Rosario in rapid Spanish.

Shasis grabbed Killian's arm. "Listen," she whispered close to her ear. "I think Vargas wants this big bull dyke to take you out. I heard him say something."

"Why are you warning me?" Killian asked.

"Because I like you and I don't like Vargas." Then she released Killian's arm and fell back into line as they continued on.

Killian's attention went to Rosario. She was as big as—bigger than—most men. She had to be at least six foot two and in the area of two hundred–plus pounds. She was all well-trained muscle and had weapons to back her up. She didn't appear to be wearing any armor, so at least there was that.

They walked for what felt like maybe a quarter of a mile, give or take. The tunnel began to grade upward once again before giving way to a ladder that led to a trapdoor.

Rosario stopped abruptly, her fingers going to the device in her right ear. "Sí," she said in response to whatever had been asked of her. "Sí. Voy a hacerlo ahora."

Killian didn't miss the side-eye the *sicaria* cast in her direction. This was it. Shit.

Adriana put her hand on the woman's arm. It wasn't an authoritative gesture, but something more intimate. Killian's eyes narrowed as Adriana spoke in a hushed tone.

Rosario climbed the ladder and pushed open the heavy door. Then she helped Lyria climb up before dropping back to the ground. Adriana went up next, followed by Shasis, who stopped and glanced back at Killian from halfway up. She opened her mouth to say something, but Adriana called out to her. Killian waved her on. Nothing to see here. Besides, this wasn't a complete surprise.

"Let me guess," she said to Rosario. "This is the part where you try to kill me."

The larger woman didn't look happy at the prospect. "Yes. I am sorry."

Killian shrugged. "I guess there's no talking you out of it?"

"I can't refuse my employer."

"Or your lover," she added. When the larger woman sighed, Killian swore silently. Fucking Adriana had double-crossed her. At least Shasis had tried to warn her.

She sighed and pushed up her sleeves. "At least give me a fair fight?"

Rosario removed her holster and tossed it a few feet away—farther away from Killian. "I respect you enough to give you that."

Killian shifted her feet into a fighting stance and raised her fists. "Let's get this over with, then."

The *sicaria* came at her. Killian swung her leg out in a high kick that caught the woman under the chin, then pivoted into a roundhouse that sent her flying backward against the dirt wall.

Rosario didn't even flinch. She came at Killian low, grabbing her around the waist and lifting her off her feet. Then she dropped, slamming Killian into the ground. The air was sucked from Killian's lungs. She tried to roll but the other woman still had her, holding her with one hand while she drove her fist into Killian's kidneys, not once but twice. She jumped to her feet, delivering a solid kick to Killian's gut. She barely had time to tighten her stomach muscles. Jesus Christ, it hurt.

Killian grabbed that muscular leg and tried to pull Rosario off-balance, only to be seized by the roots of her hair. Gritting her teeth, she struck out blindly, her fist catching the other woman between the legs. It wasn't as effective as a ball punch, but it still fucking hurt. Then she swept her leg out, knocking the other woman to the ground. Gasping for breath, she grappled with her, getting her legs locked around her and her arm around Rosario's neck, squeezing as hard as she could.

Rosario rolled her, slamming her back against the wall before driving her elbow back into her ribs. Killian cried out as something cracked. She brought her fist down in a hammer punch on the woman's neck as hard as she could, then again to the side of her head.

Rolling away, Rosario came up in a crouch. Killian barely managed to dive out of the way when she pounced. Killian rolled up into a somersault that took her to her feet and away from her opponent. She didn't take time to think; she simply attacked with a flurry of kicks to the stomach and chest that made the other woman curl up like an armadillo. When Rosario grabbed for her leg, she just managed to jump out of reach, almost falling when her foot skidded on a loose rock.

On her feet again, Rosario came at her with a wide swing that Killian easily dodged. It was followed by a left hook that caught her in the jaw, snapping her head back. Lights danced before her eyes, but she shook them off. Another blow struck her hard in the sternum, doubling her over.

Breathing hurt. At least one of her ribs was cracked.

An arm snaked around her neck as the other woman got behind her. Killian clawed at her forearm, trying to release the pressure as she gasped for breath. She struck out and back with her left fist, but Rosario quickly evaded the shot.

Killian shifted her feet. It was just enough to get the leverage she needed. Seizing Rosario's forearm with both her hands, she twisted and arched her body, tossing the larger woman over her shoulder to the ground. Quickly, she went down with her, bracing her knee on her opponent's chest to pivot and wrap her leg around behind her neck. Killian twisted so that she was now the one on the ground, Rosario on her knees above her with Killian's legs locked around her neck. She squeezed.

Rosario grabbed her by the throat, pressing down with her body weight as she choked her. Killian rolled back onto her shoulders, pushing up with her hips to force the woman back. She punched Rosario in the face, feeling her nose crunch beneath her knuckles. Blood dripped onto Killian's cheek, trickling toward her eye. Blackness swamped the edges of her brain as she fought for breath. She felt Rosario's body shift as she let Killian's legs bear the brunt of her weight. Her free fist drove into Killian's already battered ribs once, twice. Killian roared in agony as the already splintered bone cracked further.

Killian pulled back her leg, releasing the hold on Rosario's neck. She kicked her in the chest, then again in the face, knocking her back onto the ground.

Panting, Killian rolled to her side. She had to get up. Rosario was already climbing to her feet, blood streaming from her nose and mouth. Grunting, Killian pushed herself up on arms that trembled. She pushed the pain to the back of her mind. She had to focus on winning. On surviving.

Rosario charged her. She barely managed to dive out of the way of a kick to the head. The momentum rolled her to her feet. When she faced her opponent again, she saw the knife in the other woman's hand.

"We agreed no weapons."

"That was before I realized you might actually beat me. I have my orders."

Killian pressed a hand to her ribs. "That's not very honorable."

"I never said I was." She charged again.

Killian missed the swing of the dagger and caught Rosario in the back of the neck with another hammer punch, then a kick to the kidneys. The larger woman whipped around and smashed her fist into Killian's jaw so hard, sparks burst behind her eyes.

The blade swiped her side. It wasn't a deep cut, but it was enough that she sucked in a quick and agonizing breath. She kicked out her leg, catching the other woman in the gut. Rosario came back with a series of punches that gave her little time to recover. She followed up with some strikes of her own. Head, face, stomach—anything she could hit. Their movements were slowing, each of them exhausting the other. But neither of them stopped. The blade tore into her right hip.

Killian staggered to her knees.

The dagger came down hard and fast into her left shoulder.

Killian screamed and lurched upward, delivering a crushing blow to Rosario's midsection. It wasn't enough. A kick to the head knocked Killian onto her face in the dirt.

She struggled to take a breath. If Rosario didn't have any honor, then fuck it, she didn't, either. Who cared about honor when death hovered over your shoulder? She reached into her pocket and slipped her fingers into the ring of the blade Dash had left for her. She pulled off the sheath with her other hand and shoved it in her other pocket before rolling onto her back.

Rosario bent down, grabbed her by the front of the shirt, and lifted her upper body off the ground. Killian felt like a rag doll, just hanging there. Blood ran down the back of her throat. Everything hurt. Something inside her was broken, bleeding. She didn't feel right and it wasn't just because she'd been beaten up. She'd been beaten up before. This... this felt like dying.

"I'm sorry," Rosario said, bloody saliva dripping from her lips. Both of them had battered each other beyond their limits.

"So am I," Killian replied. Digging in her heels, she pushed hard, driving the energy into her punch. She drove the blade into the bigger woman's neck at just the right angle to sever her carotid. Dark eyes widened in shock. She let go of Killian's shirt. Killian slammed back to the ground.

The blade came with her.

Blood sprayed from Rosario's neck. She tried to staunch it with her hands. Killian could only watch, head spinning, as she dropped to her knees. She didn't even flinch as a spray of warm blood splashed across her face. Their gazes locked as Rosario toppled sideways to the ground. Killian, choking on blood, stared into the other woman's eyes as Rosario bled to death. She knew the precise second the *sicaria* was gone.

Fumbling for purchase, Killian's foot slipped out from under her as she tried to stand. She was bleeding from her shoulder, side, and hip, and the searing pain in her ribs told her they were no longer cracked but indeed broken. Something inside her felt wrong, like it had been detached, or punctured. What was weird was that it didn't really hurt; it just felt... not right.

But she couldn't stay down there. If this was how she went out—and it was *not* how she intended to go out—she'd do it aboveground, not in the dirt.

She pivoted forward on one knee, grabbing the edge of a crate. Splinters lodged in her palm from the rough wood, but the pain didn't even register. Gritting her teeth, she got her forearm up onto the lid and her right foot underneath her, then pushed with all her strength.

A wave of dizziness washed over her as she made it to her feet. She leaned into the crate to keep from falling. Then she staggered toward the ladder, pausing only to grab Rosario's gun from the dirt.

Time to find Adriana.

At the bottom of the ladder, she linked one arm through

a rung and paused to catch her breath. She coughed and her entire body seized. Blood dribbled from her lips as her head swam. One of her knees gave out, but she managed to get it underneath her again, clenching her jaw as her arms strained to hold her up. The blade in her shoulder was excruciating, but she didn't have the strength to pull it out.

The ladder was maybe seven or eight feet up. Normally an easy climb, but at that moment it could have just as easily been Mount Everest. She could only pull herself up with one arm, and that was the one holding the gun. She was pretty sure several of the knuckles on her right hand were busted, and her left knee was definitely all fucked-up. She braced her elbow on the rungs and used that to propel herself upward. At least her right leg seemed to be working okay. One arm and one leg, that was how she climbed.

The hatch opened up into a small garden. Killian frowned. This wasn't an airstrip at all.

"Jesus Christ," she heard someone say. She looked up from where she knelt on the grass. Shasis—two of her—came toward her, slightly crouched and frowning.

"Killian, are you okay?"

She would have laughed if she had the strength. "Help me up, T."

Shasis removed her jacket first and handed it to Adriana; then she offered Killian her arms for support, pulling her gently to her feet. The gun fell from her numb fingers.

"Girl, you're fucked-up," Shasis commented, shaking her head.

"Yeah, I know." She limped away from the hatch, taking in the scene around her. "Where the fuck are we?"

"A property in the next neighborhood," Shasis explained. "Vargas rented it under a shell company months ago. The airfield was a decoy for the feds. The crates are empty, the men working there hired from a nearby town."

And she'd fallen for it. Shit. Not far away, a silver SUV sat waiting, a driver behind the wheel.

Behind them, nearly a quarter of a mile away, a series of explosions shuddered through the night. Killian jerked at the noise, her body screaming in protest. She grabbed at Shasis to remain upright. Smoke filled the air above the Incarnyx house.

Not just the tunnels, then.

Had everyone gotten out? Jesus, she hoped so.

She met Shasis's gaze. "She told Rosario to kill me, didn't she?" Her voice was a hoarse whisper.

Shasis nodded. "I'm sorry."

A noise from behind made both of them turn.

In a plume of smoke, Vargas rose from the hatch, coughing and hacking but otherwise unharmed. He was also alone.

Blood dripped into Killian's eyes as she watched him. She tried to wipe it away but only succeeded in smearing it all over her face.

"*You*," he said with a sneer. The smoke rising behind him made him look like a Latino Lucifer. "You killed my Rosario. My favorite daughter."

Daughter? Oh, hell.

Adriana made a clicking sound with her tongue. "Your bastard is your favorite?"

"I love all of our children, *querida*, but most of them are soft. Rosario was the only one who was like me." Then he turned those black eyes to Killian. "I will finish you myself, like I should have. I will avenge my child."

"Shut the fuck up and do it," Killian challenged, blood and spit spraying from her lips.

Vargas raised his gun, pointing it in her face once more. Killian closed her eyes. Death would almost be a relief...

There was the sound of a shot and then something warm, wet, and sharp struck Killian's face. When she opened her eyes, she saw what it was.

It was pieces of Rafael Vargas's head.

His body lay a few feet away, facedown, the left half of his skull blasted apart. Behind him stood Adriana, a sawed-off shotgun in her hands. Where the sweet fucking hell had she gotten that?

Even Shasis looked astounded by what had just happened. Obviously, the murder of Rafael Vargas had not been something they'd planned.

"A man who doesn't respect his God-given children doesn't deserve the woman who gave birth to them," Adriana pontificated over the corpse. Then she kicked her husband's lifeless body. "Rosario was better in bed than you ever were, *bicho*."

Killian could only stare at her. Her brain felt like it was shutting down. She waited for the shotgun to swing her way.

But it didn't. In fact, Adriana didn't pay her any attention at all. As she walked toward the SUV, Shasis went after her. Killian couldn't hear their conversation over the ringing in her ears.

Adriana put the shotgun in the back of the SUV and said something to the driver, who started the engine before handing her something through the window. She then gave whatever it was to Shasis, who walked back to where Killian swayed on her feet.

It was a file folder. "Here. I think you might want this. You're always welcome wherever I am, Killian Delaney."

Killian took the file with bloody fingers, her legs wavering beneath her. She couldn't speak—all her strength was in remaining upright.

Adriana and Shasis got into the back seat of the SUV without another word. They were just going to leave her there—not that she would have expected anything else. As places to die went, it wasn't that bad. Though she really didn't care for the idea of her corpse being found next to Vargas's.

She managed to stay upright until the taillights faded from sight. Then Killian fell. Her knees hit the ground hard, jarring the breath from her lungs. She pitched forward, falling onto her face in the grass, the folder pinned beneath her.

Her vision blurred, tinted red. Lights flashed in the dark, so bright and red. Had they come back for her? Or was it some of Vargas's men? She hoped they finished her off quickly. She didn't want to linger like Magnus. She tried to close her eyes but couldn't. A dark shape moved in front of the light, blocking it.

"Kill?"

She almost sobbed. Dash. She tried to say his name.

"Don't speak, baby. I got you. You're going to be okay."

He was full of shit, but whatever. It was nice of him to say it. In her mind, she sighed when he picked her up. In reality, it came out a low moan of pain.

"Hang on, Killy," said another voice. It was Story. They'd come for her. They always came for her. Her friends. Her family.

She slumped against Dash's shoulder. It *was* going to be okay—she knew it. She wasn't going to die next to Rafael Vargas. Megan and Shannon wouldn't have to hear that and wonder if she'd been in league with the bastard. No matter what happened, she was good now. She was home.

And then the world went black.

SEVENTEEN

Consciousness fluttered around the edges of Killian's mind. It was like trying to crawl out from beneath a pile of warm, fluffy blankets. Where was she? Why did her mouth taste like metal and dirt? And why did it feel like a large child was sitting on her chest?

She forced her eyelids open, blinking against the daylight that streamed inside. She was in a bed with railings and there was an IV line in her arm. The hospital, right. Of course that's where she was.

How the hell had she gotten there?

Megan and Shannon sat just a few feet away. Megan stared out the window while Shannon tapped away on her phone.

"Hey," Killian said, her voice not much more than a croak.

Both of them jumped up. Megan, her big sister by seven years, reached her first. Shannon hung back as though nervous. Afraid. The last time the kid had seen her beaten nearly half this bad had been the night Rank Cirello finally met his maker. It had to bring back some scary memories for her.

"You don't have to be here, kiddo," she said to the girl. "It's okay if you want to wait outside."

"Don't talk stupid," the girl said. She was so beautiful, some-times it hurt Killian to look at her. Her dark curly hair hung past her shoulders and her eyes shone bright blue against her dark skin. She looked like her father.

She looked guilty, but Killian couldn't imagine why.

"How bad is it?" she asked her sister.

"Pretty bad," Megan replied. "Remember that fight against Torres? You won, but your spleen—"

"I remember. That bad, huh? Shit." That had been for a title and Marcie Torres had been fighting to win. Killian had looked like hell for weeks afterward. But she had won.

"Where's Dash?" she asked, licking her lips. They were dry and split.

Her sister offered her the glass of water by her bed. She took a sip. Christ, she hated paper straws, but the water was so good.

"He went to get some food for us," Megan explained.

Tentatively, she shifted on the bed. Everything hurt. "Any-thing broken?"

"Two ribs and your liver was lacerated. Your left knee is messed up. Your kidneys are pretty bruised and your dia-phragm was knocked out of place, apparently. Um, you've got some muscle damage and torn ligaments and a concussion. I can't remember what else they said."

"There was something about a chest contusion," Shannon offered.

A lacerated liver. She'd never had that happen before. That would explain the feeling she had that something wasn't right inside.

"I don't feel that bad," Killian muttered.

"You're on enough painkillers to take down an elephant," Megan informed her. "You're going to be in rough shape for a while. Seriously, Killy, maybe you should rethink this security job of yours."

Killian didn't say anything. She just took her sister's hand in hers and squeezed it. They talked for a bit before Dash returned with food. It was good to see him. And Megan had to be right about the drugs because the back of Killian's eyes prickled with hot tears. She rarely ever cried, but being impaired usually helped it happen.

The three of them ate lunch together as Killian dozed, then Megan and Shannon had to leave. Megan and Dash talked outside the room for a bit—obviously about Killian—while Shannon said goodbye.

"I was so scared," the girl told her. "When Dash called, I thought you were dead."

"I'm not that easy to get rid of," Killian joked. "I'm like a cockroach."

Shannon frowned, averted her gaze. It was the face she made when she was trying not to cry. Or was debating whether or not to tell the truth.

"Aunt Killy, I—"

"Come on, baby girl," Megan said from the door. "Let Auntie rest."

"Okay, Mom." Shannon turned back to Killian, bent down, and gave her a quick kiss on the cheek. "Get better soon. And...I'm sorry."

Yep, it was definitely the drugs, she thought, as a lump the size of her fist threatened to choke her. "I will," she rasped. "I promise." It wasn't until her niece was gone that she wondered what she had been sorry for. Maybe all the trouble she'd given her before Killian got involved with Incarnyx?

When they were gone, Dash came in and sat with her. Killian wanted to ask him about so many things, but she was too tired. It would wait. If there was anything he thought she should know, he'd tell her.

She was just dozing off, her hand wrapped around his, when there was a soft knock at her door. Killian's eyes flew open.

"I'm sorry," Maryl said. "Were you sleeping?"

"Almost," she replied. "Another couple of minutes and I'd be pissed instead of surprised. Come on in." The sight of the agent probably should have made her uneasy, but she supposed she owed this calm to the drugs as well.

Maryl came in with a vase full of gorgeous lilies that she set on the bedside table. "I don't know if you like flowers or not, but these made me think of you."

"That's sweet. Thanks."

"So...you look like shit."

Killian chuckled. It hurt but whatever. "Flatterer. You look great, but only because I saved your fucking ass."

Maryl laughed as well. "You did. I owe you for that."

"You don't owe me anything."

"I do. That folder you gave me is going to make sure the right people get charged with the right crimes."

The folder. "It was a gift from Adriana Vargas. An apology for trying to kill me, I guess. What was in it?"

"A lot," Maryl replied. "Mostly details of Ilyana Woodward's involvement with Deacon Ford. Joe and I are going to pay her a little visit later today."

"How's he doing?"

"Good. Healing—thanks to Dash." Maryl gave him a bright smile.

Dash looked uncomfortable with the attention. "Sure," he said.

Maryl turned back to Killian. "Ford started singing as soon as he remembered Vargas tried to kill him. I have no doubt Woodward will give up everything she has on him as well. If I have my way, they'll both go away for a long time."

"What about the girls?"

"Her daughters have given evidence against her as well. Lyria sent a statement via her lawyer and Dylan spoke to me in person two days ago."

"How long have I been here?" Killian asked Dash.

"Three days."

"Shit."

"Yeah," he agreed. "Try being the one who wasn't stoned or unconscious."

"I have," she reminded him with a smile.

"I need to get back to work," Maryl announced. "But maybe I could come back later? Visit a little?"

Killian's smile faded slightly. "Should I be worried?"

"Not if I have any say in it. And I do."

"What about Rosario?" She couldn't help herself. She had to ask.

Maryl met her gaze earnestly. "We figure she was killed by a cartel member who escaped, since the weapon was nowhere to be found."

Killian held her gaze for a moment. "That's a sound theory."

"I think so. Okay, you get some rest. I'll see you later."

Killian's gaze followed her out of the room. "That went better than I thought it would."

"She was right. They had nothing on you."

"They could have. It's not a secret that Shasis and I were locked up together. I'm not supposed to associate with old connections as a term of parole."

"I think you're looking for something to worry about."

"I am worried. This is one more thing the parole board could use against me."

"You need to get some rest," Dash told her. "The parole board will be whatever it is. Worst-case scenario, we get you a good lawyer to fight it and you maybe go back in for a couple of months. Best-case scenario, it turns out to be nothing."

He was right. There was nothing she could do about it at the moment.

"Stay with me?"

He pulled the chair closer so he could sit beside the bed. When he was settled, he reached out and took her hand in his. "I'll be here when you wake up."

"Promise?"

"Always."

She closed her eyes then, knowing he'd watch over her while she slept. He'd keep anyone from sneaking up on her.

Hopefully the drugs would keep her from dreaming, because now that she'd thought of Rosario, she couldn't stop thinking about her.

And how it had felt to kill her.

Maryl pulled up to the large, stately house shortly after ten in the morning. Joe, still recovering from his injuries, had insisted on coming with her, even though he was technically on leave. Thomason had okayed it, since there were other agents with them. All Maryl had to do was make the arrest. All Joe had to do was watch.

He had to use a cane, and his movements were slow and stiff, but his doctors expected him to make a full recovery. He'd be back on the job in a few weeks, but for now, he kept a respectful distance behind Maryl and the others as they walked up to the front door and rang the bell.

When the housekeeper opened the door, Maryl flashed her badge. The woman pressed a hand to her mouth as she stepped back to allow them inside. Then she guided them through the house out onto a sunny terrace where two women sat drinking iced tea.

"Ilyana Woodward," Maryl said.

The pale blonde turned to look at them. "Yes?"

She showed her credentials again. "Agent Maryl Rogers, Federal Bureau of Investigation. You're under arrest."

The agents moved in to take her into custody.

"What?" Woodward cried, looking around incredulously. "On what charges?"

"Yes," her companion—a gorgeous black woman—added, rising to her feet. "What charges?"

"Racketeering and human trafficking, to start," Maryl replied.

"This is ridiculous," Woodward said hotly. "I've done nothing of the sort." There was a tremor to her, though, and that was all Maryl needed to know she could break her eventually.

"Your daughters say differently."

Woodward's companion blinked. "What?"

"In addition to evidence compiled against you, we have statements from both of your daughters detailing the years of abuse they suffered with you, and how you prostituted both of them from a young age."

Woodward gaped like a fish out of water. "Lies!"

"Several of the men they named have supported their claims, and then we also have evidence of your involvement with Deacon Ford, aka Magnus, and his organization Incarnyx."

"Magnus is dead."

"Reports of his death have been greatly exaggerated," she quipped. "I assure you Mr. Ford is quite alive, and more than willing to share the contents of his fortunately fireproof safe with us." The woman didn't need to know where the documents against her had actually come from.

Maryl turned to the companion. "You might want to call a lawyer, I think."

But the woman was looking at Ilyana. "Is any of this true?"

"No!" Woodward cried. "Of course not! Obviously this Deacon Ford turned my daughters against me!"

Maryl rolled her eyes. "Take her," she said. And she walked

away so she didn't have to listen to Woodward proclaim her innocence any longer. Behind her, she could hear the other woman
already making a call. Let them hire the best lawyer in the world;
they had so much evidence against Woodward, there was no way
she was going to get out of it. Neither was Ford. Oh, the two of
them would no doubt try to throw each other under the prover-
bial bus, but no matter what kind of deals they made, both of
them would be going away for a good amount of years—enough
that Joe's and Killian's injuries wouldn't be in vain.

If only Adriana Vargas hadn't blown her husband's head
apart, she could have had a trifecta. Now Adriana was back in
South America with not only Shasis, but Lyria Woodward as
well. Dylan and Miguel would soon join them, their testimony
against Ford and Woodward buying them freedom. It wasn't
as though the Bureau had anything concrete against the young
couple, and the information they had to offer was worth more.
They gave evidence against the Desiertos they had in custody,
and since Vargas's drugs and weapons had gone up in flames
with the house, it was all they had.

Someday, Dylan and Miguel might be a cartel power couple,
but for now...well, they were just caught in the unfortunate
circumstances of their families.

Rumor had it that Adriana had taken over her husband's
business. Of course, there was no way to substantiate that
rumor, and no way to know if that's what she'd planned all
along. To be perfectly honest, Maryl didn't care. So long as
the woman never returned to the United States, she didn't care
what Adriana got up to.

Joe walked outside with her. "Feel better?" he asked.

Maryl nodded. "I hate to admit it, but yeah. I feel good."

"Glad to hear it. I need to sit the fuck down."

She got him back into the SUV just as the other agents brought out Woodward. In her flowy palazzo pants and tunic, she looked like she was on a film set, but there was real fear in her expression and it revealed the ugliness beneath her beauty. The media likened her to a swan with her long neck and graceful movements, but she wasn't a swan; she was a vulture, preying on those weaker than her.

What kind of woman sold her own children for her personal gain?

And on the opposite side of that coin, what sort of woman risked her life to save daughters who weren't her own? No, she hadn't forgotten Killian's involvement in all of this. She couldn't.

Maryl watched as they loaded Woodward into the other car. Her girlfriend stood on the steps of the house, talking on the phone. Maryl made a mental note to ask Killian about her when she visited her later that day. No charges were going to be brought against her, and as far as the world was concerned, Killian had been injured in the explosion while making sure there was no one left inside the mansion. She'd been nothing more than an innocent bystander in the wrong place at the wrong time, and Maryl wouldn't have survived without her help. It was mostly true. And really? No one at the Bureau was interested in going after an ex-con who had already served her time for almost killing a scumbag.

Once the car carrying Woodward was en route, Maryl pulled out onto the road and turned in the opposite direction.

"Where are we going?" Joe asked.

"I'm taking you home," she informed him. "You've had enough excitement for one day."

The fact that he didn't argue was proof of just how much rest he still needed. "Are you going to see Killian today?"

"I am."

"Will you ask her to thank her friend for me? And tell her I said thanks for all she did to help you."

She smiled at him. "Sure. I figure I'll let her know the engagement is off, too."

He laughed and winced at the same time. "Ow."

At the house, she helped him inside and got him situated on the sofa while his girlfriend, Sarah, made coffee. She really ought to get back to the office, or go see Killian, but she couldn't make herself walk back out the door just yet. She just wanted to sit with her partner and watch him breathe for a bit. She just wanted to appreciate the fact that he was alive. Ilyana Woodward was in custody and so was Deacon Ford. Rafael Vargas was dead, and right now, the world was a better place—at least for a few minutes.

That was worth taking the time to savor.

The parole meeting came quicker than Killian wanted. She'd managed not to think about it too much while recovering in the hospital—even though Donna had been kind enough to check in on her—but now it was time to face the music.

Part of her had hoped the whole thing would just disappear, but then Donna had called a couple of days ago, asking if she felt up to coming in so they could talk.

A parole officer asking you to come by and talk was like a proctologist asking you to relax.

"Do you want me to come in?" Dash asked when he pulled up outside the doors. He was driving her car—which thankfully hadn't been harmed in the blast at the Incarnyx site—since she wasn't quite up to driving herself. He'd even driven upstate to collect it, along with Story.

"No, I'm good. I'll call if there's a problem."

"I'll pick you up when you're done."

Yeah, if they didn't immediately cart her back to York, sure. The idea of going back in left a sour taste in her mouth, but regret, like shame, was a largely useless emotion. Once a decision is made, you stand by it, no matter what happens after that.

Inside the office, the waiting room was actually busier than she'd seen it in some time. Did more people get paroled in the summer? She sat in one of the chairs beside the magazines and picked one that was relatively current to flip through while she waited, butterflies flapping in her stomach.

She waited almost a full half hour. She'd never had to wait that long before. Donna was always pretty punctual. Maybe it didn't mean anything, but every second spent in that chair made it harder to believe she was going to walk out of there a free woman.

Finally, she walked into Donna's office. Her parole officer stood to shake her hand.

"My lord, girl," Donna began. "You look like you hurt from the top of your head to the tips of your toes."

"It's better than it was," Killian told her, "and looks worse than it is." Bruising always stopped hurting long before it actually faded, and for some reason everyone seemed to find the green-yellow stage more wince-worthy than the red-purple.

"Well, I'm glad to hear that. Other than that, how's everything going?"

"It's good. Did you change your hair?"

"Do you like it?" She turned her head from side to side, tossing the highlighted waves.

"I do." Slowly, Killian lowered herself into the chair in front of the desk. "So, enough of that. Did the board meet?"

For a second, Donna looked surprised by the question. "Have you been worrying about that all this time?"

"Well, yeah." Who the hell wouldn't?

"The parole board has given up its investigation."

Killian blinked. "Why?"

"An agent, Maryl Rogers, told them how you recently assisted her in the case against Ilyana Woodward."

Killian blinked. "She did?"

Donna arched a brow. "You seem surprised. Is it not true?"

"No, it is. I just...I just didn't think she knew anything about the parole stuff."

Shrugging, Donna smiled. "I guess she did. I don't want to know how you got involved or why. I'm just glad she spoke on your behalf. But even if she hadn't, I think we could have made it go away regardless."

"Yeah. Me too." She thought for a moment. "Donna, what was the problem in the first place?"

"You don't know?"

Killian shook her head.

"Oh dear." Folding her hands on the top of her desk, Donna leaned forward. "Your niece called the board. She told them she was afraid you were doing something you shouldn't."

"Shannon?" It was like a kick to the chest.

"She called back a few days later and said she'd been wrong. Of course, we had to look into the matter regardless. They didn't find anything, by the way, and then Agent Rogers got involved and everyone assumed that's what your niece had been referring to."

Killian shook her head. She and Shannon were going to have a talk about this. A loud, one-sided talk that set some boundaries, made some threats, and basically tore a strip off the little brat's hide. She could have seriously fucked things up.

Donna's lips curved slightly. "I hope I'm not overstepping, but I have a sixteen-year-old daughter too. I know how difficult these years can be. Sometimes they do the most hateful things because they want to know we love them."

Killian stared at her. "Shannon's not my daughter."

"Yeah. I know." But there was something in her tone that said she did know—that she knew everything.

"Donna—"

The other woman slapped her palms against the top of her desk. "Two more months and you are officially off my watch. You think you can stay off the board's radar for that long?"

"Yeah. Sure." Since she was still recovering from what Rosario had done to her, that shouldn't be difficult.

Rosario. Two nights ago she'd woken up in a sweat with the woman's face burned into her brain. Sometimes when she closed her eyes, all she could see was Rosario's dead gaze, or worse, all she could see was herself, driving that blade into Rosario's neck.

Dash said it was normal to have flashbacks after killing someone. It was trauma, he said. Thoughts of what she'd done to Cirello had never affected her this way, but then, she didn't regret doing what she'd done to him. She regretted killing Rosario, who had only been doing her job.

Fucking regret. Useless emotion. Eventually she'd remember that, because there was no bringing Rosario back.

"All right, then." Donna smiled at her. "I'm glad you're okay, Killian. I was pretty worried about you when I found out what happened."

"Thanks. I don't really remember much of it. The doctors don't seem to think that's weird, though." Actually, it was the perfect excuse to avoid talking about it. Perfect.

"Maybe that's for the best," the other woman allowed. "So, I'll see you back here next month, then?"

"Not in two weeks?"

"Oh no. I think we can wean it down again." Another smile. "I'm proud of you, Killian. You've really turned things around for yourself."

She'd been beaten within an inch of her life and her parole officer thought she'd changed her life. That was just surreal. But, like everyone else, Donna had bought the story that she'd been injured in the blast because it had come from an FBI agent. And an FBI agent would never lie, would she? The thought might drip sarcasm, but the truth was she was damn thankful Maryl was such a good liar.

"Thanks, Donna. A month from today, then. Same time?"

Donna confirmed the appointment and then Killian rose stiffly from her chair. She was ten times better than she'd been when she left the hospital, but she still had a long way to go. Despite what her sister said, she didn't remember it taking this long to recover from the fight with Torres. But, then, that had been twelve years ago, when her regenerative powers were at their prime.

"Oh, and, Killian?" Donna's voice stopped her at the door.

Killian turned. "Yeah?"

"Tell Maxine you deserve some vacation time."

The bottom of Killian's stomach fell. Donna knew Maxine? Maxine, her boss? How much did Donna truly know about her and what she did? "Yeah. Sure." She couldn't limp away fast enough.

She called Dash and told him she was ready. He picked her up outside the office and took her out to lunch to celebrate. Later that afternoon, she thought about calling Shannon, but she didn't. Instead, she called Maxine and told her she was taking some more time off—and that Dash was, too. Then they packed a couple of suitcases and tossed them in the trunk of his Corvette. Then they dropped Hank and his bowl, bed, and toys off at Megan's. Shannon could start her penance by shoveling dog shit for a few days.

"We'll figure out the rest of your apology when I get back," she told the girl, handing her the leash.

Shannon started to cry. Killian wanted to give her a hug, but she didn't. That was Megan's job, not hers. As much as it hurt her, Shannon wasn't the only one who needed boundaries. So Killian just patted her niece's shoulder and left the house. She climbed into the passenger seat of the 'Vette with a sigh.

She couldn't wait to get away. Couldn't wait for it to be just her and Dash, having fun like normal people. No drug lords or vengeful ex-cons. No one in need of saving—or of killing.

She was healing physically, but she needed to heal mentally and emotionally. And she needed to learn some ways to protect herself from her job. From herself. She'd taken Ilyana at her word because she was a mother, and to Killian that meant doing whatever was necessary to protect your children. Real mothers didn't do the things Ilyana had done to her daughters.

Would Raven install someone to protect her lover in prison? Killian didn't care. She hadn't spoken to Raven since Ilyana's arrest. If her former cellmate wanted to hate her for turning Ilyana in, she was welcome to it. Killian wasn't going to lose any sleep over that. The woman was a monster and she deserved whatever terrible things prison did to her.

"All set?" Dash asked as she buckled her seat belt. She had to maneuver it so it didn't pull against her still-tender ribs.

"So set," she replied, leaning back against the seat. "Have you decided where we're going?"

"North," he said, putting the Corvette in gear. "I've rented us a quiet little cottage on the ocean in a yet-to-be-disclosed location. I can tell you this—it's pretty damn remote. It's just going to be you and me and the seagulls."

Killian smiled as she covered his hand with her own. Maybe once they were there she'd tell him how much he truly meant to her. No regrets. "I can't wait."

ACKNOWLEDGMENTS

I just want to take a few lines to thank some very important people. First of all, thank you to my husband, Steve, for his support and encouragement. Thanks to my agent, the amazing Deidre Knight, for always being in my corner. Thank you to Lisa Marie Pompilio for giving Killian such kick-ass covers, and last, but certainly not least, thank you to my editor, Bradley. You are fabulous, and you know just how to get a fire under me without me lighting myself ablaze. Thank you so very, very much for being such a delight to work with.

MEET THE AUTHOR

Photo Credit: Kathryn Smith

As a child, KATE KESSLER seemed to have a knack for finding trouble, and for it finding her. A former delinquent, Kate now prefers to write about trouble rather than cause it and spends her days writing about why people do the things they do. She lives in New England with her husband.

if you enjoyed
CALL OF VULTURES

look out for

IT TAKES ONE
An Audrey Harte Novel

by

Kate Kessler

"Deliciously twisted.... Kate Kessler's positively riveting It Takes One *boasts a knockout concept and a thoroughly unique and exciting protagonist, a savvy criminal psychologist with murderous skeletons in her own closet." —Sara Blaedel, #1 internationally bestselling author*

Criminal psychologist Audrey Harte is returning home after seven years.

Less than twenty-four hours later, her best friend is murdered.

Now Audrey is both the prime suspect and the only person who can solve the case....

It Takes One *is the opening to a thriller series where a criminal psychologist uses her own dark past to help law enforcement catch dangerous killers.*

CHAPTER ONE

"Would you kill for someone you love?"

Audrey Harte went still under the hot studio lights. Sweat licked her hairline with an icy, oily tongue. "Excuse me?"

Miranda Mason, host of *When Kids Kill*, didn't seem to notice Audrey's discomfort. The attractive blonde—whose heavy makeup was starting to cake in the lines around her eyes—leaned forward over her thin legs, which were so tightly crossed she could have wound her foot around the opposite calf. She wore pantyhose. Who wore pantyhose anymore? Especially in Los Angeles in late June? "It's something most of us have said we'd do, isn't it?"

"Sure," Audrey replied, the word forcing its way out of her dry mouth. "I think we as humans like to believe that we're capable of almost anything to protect our loved ones." Did she sound defensive? She felt defensive.

A practiced smile tilted the blonde's sharply defined red lips. "Only most of us are never faced with the decision."

"No." That chilly damp crept down Audrey's neck. *Don't squirm.* "Most of us are not."

Miranda wore her "I'm a serious journalist, damn it" expression. The crew called it her Oprah face. "But David Solomon was. He made his decision with terrible violence that left two boys dead and one severely wounded."

It was almost as though the world, which had gone slightly askew, suddenly clicked into place. They were talking about a case—a rather famous and recent one that occurred in L.A. County. Her mentor, Angeline, had testified for the defense.

It's not always about you, she reminded herself. "David Solomon believed his boyfriend's life was in danger, as well as his own. The boys had been victims of constant, and often extreme, bullying at school. We know that Adam Sanchez had suffered broken ribs and a broken nose, and David himself had to be hospitalized after a similar attack."

Miranda frowned compassionately—as much as anyone with a brow paralyzed by botulism could. "Did the school take any sort of action against the students bullying the boys?"

Audrey shook her head. She was on the edge of her groove now. Talking about the kids—especially the ones driven to protect themselves when no one else would—was the one place she felt totally confident.

"A teacher suggested that the attacks would end if the boys refrained from provoking the bullies with their homosexuality." *Asshole.* "The principal stated that there would hardly be any students left in the school if she suspended everyone who picked on someone else." *Cow.*

"Why didn't the boys leave the school?"

Why did people always ask those questions? Why didn't they run? Why didn't they tell someone? Why didn't they just curl into a ball and die?

"These boys had been raised to believe that you didn't run away from your problems. You faced them. You fought."

"David Solomon did more than fight."

Audrey stiffened at the vaguely patronizing, coy tone that seemed synonymous with all tabloid television. She hadn't signed on to do the show just to sit there and let some Barbara Walters wannabe mock what these kids had been through.

Maybe she should thank Miranda for reminding her of why she'd dedicated so much of her life to earning the "doctor" in front of her name.

"David Solomon felt he had been let down by his school, his community, and the law." Audrey kept her tone carefully neutral. "He believed he was the only one who would protect himself and Adam." What she didn't add was that David Solomon had been right. No one else in their community had stood up for them.

Miranda's expression turned pained. She was about to deliver a line steeped in gravitas. "And now two boys are dead and David Solomon has been sentenced to twenty years in prison."

"A sentence he says is worth it, knowing Adam is safe." David Solomon wasn't going to serve the full twenty. He'd be out before that, provided someone didn't turn around and kill him in prison.

Miranda shot her an arch look for trying to steal the last word, and then turned to the camera and began spouting her usual dramatic babble that she used in every show about senseless tragedies, good kids gone bad, and lives irreparably altered.

This was the tenth episode of the second season of *When Kids Kill*. Audrey was the resident criminal psychologist—only because she was friends with the producer's sister and owed her a couple of favors. Big favors. Normally, Audrey avoided the spotlight, but the extra money from the show paid her credit card bills. And it upped her professional profile, which helped sell her boss's books and seminars.

She'd studied criminal psychology with the intention of helping kids. In between research and writing papers, she'd started assisting her mentor with work on criminal cases, which led to more research and more papers, and a fair amount of time talking to kids who, more often than not, didn't want her help. She never gave up, which was odd, because she considered herself a champion giver-upper.

Thirty minutes later, the interview was over. Miranda had had to do some extra takes when she felt her questions "lacked the proper gravity," which Audrey took to mean drama. Audrey dragged her heels getting out of the chair. It was already late morning and she had to get going.

"Don't you have a flight to catch?" Grant, the producer, asked. He was a couple of years older than her, with long hipster sideburns and rockabilly hair. His sister, Carrie, was Audrey's best friend.

Only friend.

"Yeah," she replied, pulling the black elastic from her wrist and wrapping it around her hair. She wrestled the hairspray-stiff strands into submission. "I'm going home for a few days."

His brow lifted. "You don't seem too happy about it."

She slipped her purse over her shoulder with a shrug. "Family."

Grant chuckled. "Say no more. Thanks for working around the schedule. Carrie's been harping on me to be more social. Dinner when you get back?"

"Sounds good." There was no more use in stalling. If she missed her flight, she'd only have to book another. There wasn't any getting out of the trip. Audrey gathered up her luggage and wheeled the suitcase toward the exit.

"See you later, Miranda," she said as she passed the older woman, who was looking at herself in the mirror of a compact, tissuing some of the heavy makeup off her face. Audrey would take hers off at the airport. She hated falling asleep on planes and waking up with raccoon eyes.

"See ya, Audrey. Oh, hey"—she peered around the compact—"you never answered my question."

Audrey frowned. "I'm pretty sure I answered them all."

Miranda smiled, blue eyes twinkling. "Would you kill for someone you love?"

"Of course not." Huh. That came out smoother than it should have.

Miranda looked contemplative, but then, too much plastic surgery could do that. "I'd like to think I would, but I doubt I could."

"Hopefully you'll never have to find out. Have a good day, Miranda."

The woman replied, but Audrey didn't quite make out the words—she was too busy thinking about that question.

No, she wouldn't kill for someone she loved.

Not again.

It was an eight-and-a-half-hour flight from L.A. to Bangor, with a stopover in Philly. It was an additional two hours and change from Bangor International to Audrey's hometown of Edgeport, on the southeast shore of Maine. She was still fifteen minutes away, driving as fast as she dared on the barren and dark 1A, when her cell phone rang.

It was her mother.

Audrey adjusted her earpiece before answering. She preferred to have both hands on the wheel in case wildlife decided to leap in front of her rented Mini Cooper. It was dark as hell this far out in the middle of nowhere; the streetlights did little more than punch pinpricks in the night, which made it next to impossible to spot wildlife before you were practically on top of it. The little car would not survive an encounter with a moose, and neither would she.

"Hey, Mum. I'll be there by midnight."

"I need you to pick up your father."

Something hard dropped in Audrey's gut, sending a sour taste up her throat that coated her tongue. Could this day become any more of a cosmic bitch-slap? First the show, then she ended up sitting next to a guy who spent the entire flight talking or snoring—to the point that she contemplated rupturing her own eardrums—and now this. The cherry on top. "You're fucking kidding me."

"Audrey!"

She sucked a hard breath through her nose and held it for a second. *Let it go.* "Sorry."

"I can't do it, I have the kids." That was an excuse and they both knew it, though Audrey wouldn't dare call her mother on it. In the course of Audrey's knowledge of her father's love affair with alcohol, never once had she heard of, nor witnessed, Anne Hart leaving the house to bring her husband home.

"Where's Jessica?"

"She and Greg are away. They won't be home until tomorrow." Silence followed as Audrey stewed and her mother waited—probably with a long-suffering, pained expression on her face. Christ, she wasn't even home yet and already everything revolved around her father. She glared at the road through the windshield. She'd take that collision with a moose now.

"Please, babe?"

Her mother knew exactly what to say—and how to say it. And they both knew that as much as Audrey would love to leave her father wherever he was, she'd never forgive herself if he decided to get behind the wheel and hurt someone. She didn't care if he wrapped himself around a tree. She *didn't*. But she couldn't refuse her mother.

Audrey sighed—no stranger to long-suffering herself. "Where is he?"

"Gracie's."

It used to be a takeout and pool hall when she was a kid, but her brother, David, told her it had been turned into a tavern a few years ago. Their father probably single-handedly kept it in business.

"I'll get him, but if he pukes in my rental, you're cleaning it up."

"Of course, dear." Translation: "Not a chance."

Audrey swore as she hung up, yanking the buds out of her ears by the cord. Her mother knew this kind of shit was part of the reason she never came home, but she didn't seem to care. After all these years, Anne Harte still put her drunken husband first. What did it matter anymore if people saw him passed out, or if he got into a fight? Everyone knew what he was. Her mother was the only one who pretended it was still a secret, and everyone let her. Classic.

Rationally, she understood the psychology behind her parents' marriage. What pissed her off was that she couldn't change it. Edgeport was like a time capsule in the twilight zone—nothing in it ever changed, even if it gave the appearance of having been altered in some way. When she crossed that invisible town line, would she revert to being that same angry young woman who couldn't wait to escape?

"I already have," she muttered, then sighed. Between Audrey and her husband, Anne Harte had made a lot of excuses in the course of her life.

Although seven years had passed since she was last home, Audrey drove the nearly desolate road on autopilot. If she closed her eyes she could keep the car between the lines from memory. Each bump and curve was imprinted somewhere she could never erase, the narrow, patched lanes—scarred from decades of abusive frost—and faded yellow lines as ingrained as her own face. The small towns along that stretch bled into one another with little more notice than a weathered sign with a hazardous lean to it. Long stretches of trees gave way to the odd residence, then slowly, the houses became more clustered together, though even the nearest neighbors could host at least two or three rusted-out old cars, or a collapsing barn, between them. Very few of the homes had lights on inside, even though it was Friday night and there were cars parked outside.

You can tell how old a town is by how close its oldest buildings are to the main road, and Ryme—the town west of Edgeport—had places that were separated from the asphalt by only a narrow gravel shoulder, and maybe a shallow ditch. Edgeport was the same. Only the main road was paved, though several dirt roads snaked off into the woods, or out toward the bay. Her grandmother on her mother's side had grown up on Ridge Road. There wasn't much back there anymore—a few hunting camps, some wild blueberries, and an old cemetery that looked like something out of a Stephen King movie. When *Pet Sematary* came out there'd been all kinds of rumors that he'd actually used the one back "the Ridge" for inspiration, though Audrey was fairly certain King had never set foot in her mud puddle of a town in his entire life.

She turned up the radio for the remainder of the trip, forcing herself to sing along to eighties power ballads in an attempt to lighten her mood. Dealing with her father was never easy, and she hadn't seen him since that last trip home, years earlier. God only knew how it was going to go down. He might get belligerent.

Or she might. If they both did there was going to be a party.

Gracie's was located almost exactly at the halfway point on the main road through town. It used to be an ugly-ass building—an old house with awkward additions constructed by people devoid of a sense of form or beauty. The new owner had put some work into the old girl, and now it looked like Audrey imagined a roadhouse ought to look. Raw wooden beams formed the veranda where a half dozen people stood smoking, drinks in hand. Liquor signs in various shades of neon hung along the front, winking lazily.

She had to park out back because the rest of the gravel lot was full. She hadn't seen this kind of crowd gathered in Edgeport since Gracie Tripp's funeral. Gracie and her husband, Mathias, had owned this place—and other businesses in town—for as long as Audrey could remember. Gracie had been a hard woman—the sort who would hit you with a tire iron if necessary, and then sew your stitches and make you a sandwich. She and Mathias dealt with some shady people on occasion, and you could always tell the stupid ones because they were the ones who thought Mathias was the one in charge.

Or stupider still, that Mathias was the one to be afraid of.

Audrey hadn't feared Gracie, but she'd respected her. Loved her, even. If not for that woman, Audrey's life might have turned out very differently.

She opened the car door and stepped out into the summer night, shivering as the ocean-cooled air brushed against her skin. Late June in Maine was a fair bit cooler than in Los Angeles. It was actually refreshing. Tilting her head back, she took a moment there on the gravel, as music drifted out the open back door of the tavern, and drew a deep breath.

Beer. Deep-fryer fat. Grass. Salt water. God, she'd *missed* that smell. The taste of air so pure it made her head swim with every breath.

Something released inside her, like an old latch finally giving way. Edgeport was the place where practically everything awful in her life had taken place, and yet it was home. An invisible anchor, old and rusted from time and neglect, tethered her to this place. The ground felt truly solid beneath her feet. And even though she'd rather give a blow job to a leper than walk through that front door, she didn't hesitate. Her stride was strong and quick, gravel crunching beneath the wedges of her heels.

The people on the veranda barely glanced at her as she walked up the steps. She thought she heard someone whisper her name, but she ignored it. There would be a lot of whispers over the next week, and acknowledging them could be considered a sign of weakness—or rudeness—depending on who did the whispering.

She pushed the door open and crossed the threshold. No turning back now. Inside, a country song played at a volume that discouraged talking but invited drinking and caterwauling along. There were four women on the dance floor, drunkenly swaying their hips while they hoisted their beer bottles into the air. Most of the tables were full and there was a small crowd gathered at the bar. Whoever owned this place had to be making a killing. Why hadn't someone thought of putting a bar in Edgeport before this? Drinking in these parts was like the tide coming in—inevitable.

Audrey turned away from the dancing and laughter. If her father was drunk enough that someone needed to fetch him, then he was going to be in a corner somewhere. She didn't doubt that he'd provided quite a bit of entertainment for Gracie's patrons a couple of hours before. He thrived on attention, the narcissistic bastard. How many songs had he shouted and slurred his way through? How raw was the skin of his knuckles?

She found him slumped in a chair in the back corner, denim-clad legs splayed out in front of him, a scarf of toilet paper—

unused—draped over his shoulders and wrapped around his neck like a feather boa. He reeked of rum but luckily not of piss. He'd better keep it that way too. She'd toss him out on the side of the fucking road if his bladder let loose in her rental.

John "Rusty" Harte wasn't a terribly big man, but he was solid and strong. He had a thick head of gray hair that used to be auburn and mismatched eyes that he'd passed on to only one of his children—Audrey. Thankfully she'd gotten her mother's dark hair and looks.

Audrey approached her father without fear or trepidation. Her lip itched to curve into a sneer, but she caught the inside of it in her teeth instead. Give nothing away—that was a lesson she learned from her mother and from Gracie. Show nothing but strength; anything else could be used against you.

She stretched out her foot and gave his a nudge with the toe of her shoe. He rocked in the chair but didn't stir. Great, he was out cold. That never ended well.

She reached out to shake his shoulder when someone came up on her left side. "Dree?"

Audrey froze. Only one person ever called her that—because she never allowed anyone else to do so since.

She bit her lip hard. The pain cut through the panic that gripped at her chest as years of memories, both good and terrible, rushed up from the place where she'd buried them.

Not deep enough.

She turned. Standing before her was Maggie Jones—McGann now—grinning like the damn Joker. She looked truly happy to see Audrey—almost as happy as she had the night the two of them had killed Clint.

Maggie's father.